Mrs. Alice Ward Bailey

Mark Heffron

A novel

Mrs. Alice Ward Bailey

Mark Heffron
A novel

ISBN/EAN: 9783337027292

Printed in Europe, USA, Canada, Australia, Japan

Cover: Foto ©Andreas Hilbeck / pixelio.de

More available books at **www.hansebooks.com**

MARK HEFFRON

A Novel

BY

ALICE WARD BAILEY

NEW YORK

HARPER & BROTHERS PUBLISHERS

1896

MARK HEFFRON

I

THE day was hot and dusty, as only a dry July day can be ; half a dozen wilted women and a whimpering baby occupied the car. Mark Heffron glanced hastily around and retreated to the smoker, where he remained until all the passengers who meant to go to bed had done so. The return was also an escape ; once in his berth he wondered why he had lingered so long among heavy jokes and twice-told tales. The car was cool and quiet. The odor of hemlock and pine, of wintergreen and sassafras, came in at the window, telling they had left the prairie and were now in the woods. It was a cloudy night, lit by an unseen moon ; through its mysterious atmosphere glided the tall forest trees.

Mark arranged the pillows under his head and prepared to enjoy the night. "I suppose it is getting back into the old groove which makes me feel as I do," he mused. "I've hunted the world over for thoughts which come with this experience as easily as the lullaby with the cradle."

Ten years before he had travelled the same road when the moon was hidden as now, there had been the same picture of gliding trees, and out of the mingled scents which came to him then he missed not one. Mark believed in the value of those ten years, but to-night he loosed his hold upon them and was again freshly graduated from college, going up to Beau Lieu Summer University to teach Greek. The fancy pleased him, although it changed the man to a boy and took away what he had worked hard to win; for it gave in return the grasp and vision of youth, its buoyant faith and all-embracing charity. To wake and watch with these he found more refreshing than sleep.

The dawn came unexpectedly soon—a red glow, against which naked tree-trunks stripped by fires stood up like masts. The morning-star shone silverly, and a little wood-thrush answered in a note that caught its gleam. The forests grew less dense and clearings appeared; then came, here and there, mean board houses, from which issued slovenly men and children, who stared at the train with dull, sleepy eyes.

The solitary settlements became towns with regular streets and avenues of young trees—such towns as figure in the papers as bargains in real estate. The towns in turn yielded to "resorts" with pretentious hotels and picturesque cottages. They were nearing Beau Lieu.

Ah, there it was! the tiers of cottages among

the hills—how they had increased in number!—
the towers of the college buildings overlooking
the bay, the big wooden tent of the auditorium,
the little railway station, and the Reverend William Billings himself, looking not a day older than
when he told Mark his services would not be required another year.

"I owe him one for that," said Mark to himself,
"but I'll wait until I can pay the interest. He
has a nice girl with him — that's natural, too.
Hullo, Zeb, can't you shake hands with an old
friend? You've forgotten me."

"Zeb" squinted his small, twinkling eyes.
"No, I ain't," he declared; "I carried your baggage last summer."

"That's a lie!" cried Mark. "I haven't been
here for ten years, and then I carried my own bag."

"It's Mark Heffron!" exclaimed the disconcerted drayman. "There goes my job!"

"No, I'll let you have it this time. Can you
put me up at the Beau Lieu House?"

Zeb shook his head. "All full a week ago.
Everything's full. Never was such a crowd at
Bu Lu."

Mark smiled at the familiar name. "So Bu
Lu is booming, is it?"

"You bet. P'r'aps Mr. Billings can tell you
some place. Hi, Mr. Billings!"

The President of the Beau Lieu University and
Summer Assembly turned at the call. He was
large and fair, with unsteady, light eyes, and a

long gray beard, which he stroked with a shapely hand.

"Here's Mr. Mark Heffron come back," said Zeb, by way of introduction. "An' he hain't got nowhere to stop at. I thought p'r'aps you'd know some place."

"Ah, Mr. Heffron," responded the president, touching Mark's hand gingerly, "we're pretty full, but I think they would take you in at the Hubbard cottage. You might try them, Haskins. I hear you've been quite a traveller since we last saw you, Mr. Heffron. If our lecture list—"

"No, no," interrupted Mark. "I merely ran around here on my way North to see how you were getting on. You have a large school this year?"

"Eighteen hundred and twenty-one," replied the president, accurately. "Nine registered this morning; two from Louisville, one of them the young lady I was addressing. Yes, the school increases. Pleased to see you at our cottage. Good-morning."

"Good-morning," rejoined Mark, briefly, and hastened after Zeb, who had caught six trunks and a brace of canvas bags in the interim.

"You wanter make terms with the Widder Hubbard," he counselled, as they clattered up the stony road. "Folks think because Bu Lu advertises rooms from two to four dollars that they're goin' to get in for two. Widder Hubbard's all right, but you don't wanter take things for granted and then kick afterwards."

"Certainly not," agreed Mark. "Here you go! Never mind the change."

"Thank you, sir. Any time, Mr. Heffron, that you wanter move or go away, here's my card." Mark received it quizzically. This bit of professional formality was certainly new to Beau Lieu.

The Widow Hubbard "took in" the stranger with alacrity, and escorted him to a tiny chamber under the eaves. Mark walked to the window and looked out; it framed the splendid azure of the bay. "I'll take it," he said, promptly ; then, remembering Zeb's caution, "How much is it ?"

The widow cleared her throat. "I'd really ought to have four and a half," she said, hesitatingly; "but Mr. Haskins says you uster belong to the Assembly. I'll let *you* have it for four."

Mark drew a handful of silver from his pocket. "I'll take it for a week," he said ; "but," pointing to a thin square of cotton hanging dejectedly from a decorated rack, "I want plenty of water and towels, and I want the privilege of doing what I please in this room."

The widow stared and retreated. "Ye-es, sir," she faltered. "You can do as you're mindter, and I'll send up the water and towels."

Soon Master Charlie Hubbard came stumbling up the stairs, spilling water all the way from a tin pail upon two skimpy towels ; but before he reached the attic room the iconoclastic hand of

the new lodger had swept together the gay pictures and gayer paper flowers which nestled in
every niche, and had bestowed them under the
bed, setting a woollen puppy, bristling with pins,
to guard them.

II

At noon the high, worn terraces about the Beau Lieu House presented the appearance of a large and highly colored ant-hill. Swarms of men, women, and children in bright summer dress went in and out of the big white building. It was exciting and more or less irritating to press through the crowd to the dining-room door, where the deaf proprietor held a chain across the entrance until the meal-ticket was safe in his hand.

"Like cattle waiting for the bars to be let down," murmured the girl whom Mark Heffron called "nice," and who Mr. Billings had said was from Louisville. The elderly woman upon her arm put up a delicate hand in remonstrance.

"It is," pursued the girl; "I feel degraded."

"We can go home," suggested her companion, meekly.

"No, indeed," said the girl, quickly. "I didn't mean to complain, auntie, but it makes me cross to have you wait for the second or third table and then find everything 'out.'"

"Don't mind me," urged the other, in the soft, many-vowelled speech of the old South. "Really,

I get on very well; the waitress is considerate. Look, Eloise, there is a chance."

Haughtily tossing her head, Eloise presented herself before the chain.

"I dunno," said the hotel-keeper, vaguely; "I'll ask Marthy. Marthy, is there any room for these folks?"

Martha passed them in review. "Do they live in the house?"

Eloise responded in the negative.

"Then they'll have to wait; we have to 'tend to our own folks first."

The warm blood mounted into the cheeks of the girl outside the chain. "Come," she ejaculated, drawing her aunt from the door. "Didn't I say so? Cattle! they herd at their meals and at their lessons. They have so much to say about 'culture'; they don't know what it means."

"Eloise!" implored her companion ; "those gentlemen will hear you."

"Gentlemen!" rejoined the girl, scornfully, as the loud laugh of one filled the air. He was a short, clumsy man, with a bald head and a bare face responding with many a line to his merriment. The young man beside him looked annoyed.

"I hear the Episcopalians have been letting you preach in their house this summer," said the bald-headed man.

The other assented. "It hasn't been consecrated yet," he added.

"That explains it," replied the elder, with a derisive roar. "I'll bet they didn't let you inside the chancel?"

"N-no," answered the young man ; "but the pulpit's outside."

"I told you so!" shouted the bald-headed man, hearing only what he chose.

It was auntie's turn to look disgusted, but before she could escape conversation shifted to another theme.

"Did you hear Dr. Greenough?"

"No, I was busy ; what did he speak on?"

"Church Unity ; it was good, too ; said he'd sign all the creeds, but he wouldn't do away with the hedges. Said he'd cut them low enough so that people could shake hands over them, but he'd keep them there."

"How about one Body, of which we are all members?" put in a new voice.

"Oh, well, no one expects that. You can't find any one principle that they'll unite on."

"How about the principle of truth?" suggested the voice.

"How do you know when you've got the truth? Here are all these different denominations claiming they've got it."

"Truth," said the voice, deliberately, "satisfies the demands of reason."

"That isn't enough," cried the bald-headed man. "You've got to have authority and revelation as well as reason."

"So you accept the divorce between reason and authority ?" asked the voice, sarcastically.

"Nothing of the sort, nothing of the sort. But look at your Age of Reason; what was it? Anarchy, upheaval, ruin !" The speaker threw his hand back with such violence that he knocked a stray baby endwise. The baby howled, a woman darted to the rescue, the bald-headed man was profuse in apologies, and what had promised to be an interesting discussion was precipitately brought to a close.

Only Eloise, drawn near by the pressure of the throng, heard the low words, "The Age of Reason was the Age of Feeling, nothing more;" while a feminine voice buzzed behind her, "He's an infidel, that dark man; John says so."

Then a wave of complacent faces surged outward from the dining-room, meeting the wave of discontented ones which surged in. Eloise and her aunt found themselves under the protection of the "infidel," whose long arm was more than once outstretched in their behalf. Within the dining-room they were not separated, but, following Marthy in single file, were directed to adjoining seats. Eloise sat beside the stranger, whom she regarded curiously. Sitting, he towered above her; standing, his eyes had been almost on a level with her own. With his massive head, bulky torso, and long, sinewy arms, he should have been a giant in stature. His face, too, was a surprise; the winning tenderness of his smile had given place to a keen, restless glance like that of an untamed animal; his beardless lips, proud and just when he had spoken, had settled into lines of sensuality and cynicism. Eloise shrank from him into the atmosphere of chaperonage which "auntie" conscientiously diffused. If he noticed this, he made no sign. After obtaining fresh napkins for the two women, and emptying the contents of the cream - pitcher into their tumblers of skimmed milk, he fell into a reverie from which his dinner only partially aroused him.

While they were dallying with their dessert he left them, bowing abruptly, and they saw him pass the window, walking rapidly in the direction of the bay. "A peculiar person," murmured auntie; "but he was most attentive, Eloise."

Her niece made no reply. She was watching the stranger pick up a romping urchin and swing him lightly to a broad shoulder. Another and another came about, all finding a place to cling and be carried on. Thus, hung as thick with children as a barbaric maid with ornaments, he disappeared. Then she turned to her aunt.

"He is the only interesting person here. Come, dear, I must take you home and go and see to my pictures."

"Shall I not help you?"

"No, indeed. You are going to lie in the hammock until I come back."

"But—"

"A very nice Epworth League boy is to hang

the pictures. Mr. Billings sent him around this morning to see about it. Good-bye. Go to sleep —I'll be back at five."

There was no one at Langley Hall when Eloise reached it, save a solitary woman who rocked and read on the piazza; but the doors were open, so she went directly to the large room in which she was to deliver her lectures on Dutch and German Art. It had been appropriated already by the representatives of the W. X. Y. Z. Por· traits of estimable women prominent in the association, wreathed with garlands, filled the place, together with banners great and small, and mottoes of startling size and significance. Eloise stood in the centre of the room and regarded them scornfully. "If Mr. Billings thinks I am going to rally around those standards he is very much mistaken," she said to herself. "I wish that Epworth League boy would come."

As if summoned by her desire, the object of it appeared in the doorway.

"What did Mr. Billings say we could do?" inquired Eloise, when he had brought in his stepladder and tools.

"He said we might do as we pleased," returned the boy.

"Then," said the young rebel, in the mood which fired on Sumter, "take down those banners."

Down they came, "Mother, Home, and Heaven" losing three cotton-wool letters, and "Woman's

Cause the World's Cause" dropping a gilded tassel. Eloise wrapped them up unceremoniously and tossed them into a closet under the hall stairs.

"We'll put the Old Flemish Masters up there," she said, gayly; "that lovely Van Eyck in the middle and this dear Quentin Matsys over there. Here's a good place for the 'Christ Bearers.' We'll put a Van Dyck over this woman; you needn't take her down."

"How about this one?" inquired the boy, indicating another with his hammer.

"Down with her!" cried the girl, exultantly. "I can breathe better already. Here's 'The Jolly Man' to hang in her place."

So they went on with Rembrandts and Hobbemas, Kaulbachs and Pluckhorsts, hiding what they did not remove, transforming the stronghold of the W. X. Y. Z. into a throne-room where Art was queen. At least, that was what Eloise thought; some one else thought differently. Routed out of her rocking-chair by the hammering and the talk, the woman on the piazza had drawn gradually nearer to the scene of the disturbance. For full thirty seconds she stood, horror-struck by what she saw. Then she took to her heels as if the Old Flemish Masters and the gentle Düsseldorf School had been so many emissaries of the Pit.

"Where is Mr. Billings? Has any one seen Mr. Billings?" she gasped, running against a large man who turned a corner in time to present himself as an obstacle to her flight.

"You'll find him over there, madam," said the obstacle, lifting his hat and pointing to a platform under the trees, where the Reverend Billings was putting up posters. Without the ceremony of a thank you, she hurried on, and soon returned followed by the President of the Assembly.

"Might as well see what's up," said the obstacle, falling into line. "Aha, it's the Louisville girl."

Unconscious of the stir which she had created, Eloise stepped back to view the result of her afternoon's work.

"Isn't it lovely?" she said to the Epworth boy; but the Epworth boy was looking towards the doorway, where stood the party of the second part.

"Ahem, Miss Gordon," began Mr. Billings.

"Upon my word," interposed a sonorous voice, "this is the finest collection of foreign photographs I ever saw. Mr. Billings, you and Beau Lieu are to be congratulated."

"It is a—a private collection," responded Mr. Billings. "Miss Gordon, let me present Mr. Heffron," and Eloise recognized her companion at dinner. "Mrs. Harwood, Miss Gordon—Mr. Heffron." Mrs. Harwood bowed distantly. What were fine collections compared with the tremendous issues with which she and her companions dealt? She turned her back on a cherub complacently viewing his own chubby proportions, and encountered—"Eve Before the Fall!" In desperation, she looked straight at the President of the Assembly and nowhere else.

"Mr. Billings, we have no time to lose if we are going to change things around before to-night," she said, hurriedly.

"Yes, yes," agreed Mr. Billings. "Miss Gordon, at the reception to-night the women of the W. X. Y. Z. receive here, and they are naturally desirous to have the decorations which they have put up partly for this reception remain until after the event. So we'll just put these things away until to-morrow, when they can go back again."

Just put these things away! Did he realize that it had taken hours of careful work to arrange the schools of art by themselves and to place together congenial subjects? The eyes of the young lecturer filled with angry tears. "As you please," she said, haughtily. "It is immaterial to me whether or no the pictures appear at all."

"Why don't you put her over in 'Bible Hall?'" asked Mark.

"Do you mean Stacey Hall?"

"We used to call it Bible Hall."

Mr. Billings reflected. "We might do that; suppose we go over and see, Miss Gordon?"

Eloise looked at her advocate. "Will you go, too?" she asked.

"With pleasure," Mark replied, and forthwith assumed charge of the expedition.

In less than an hour "The Night Watch" and "The Jolly Man," Eve and Eros had left Langley Hall, while a band of zealous women were reverently replacing the cotton-wool letters lost from "Mother, Home, and Heaven," and the gilded tassel which belonged to " Woman's Cause."

"This is the first experience I ever had of this kind," said Mrs. Ransom, viciously biting her thread. "I don't know what Beau Lieu is coming to."

"It's my last summer if things keep on," said Mrs. Puffer.

Mrs. Harwood, the Chairman of the Executive Committee of the W. X. Y. Z., said nothing, except by mien and gesture, as she mounted the stepladder, trailing an evergreen wreath. She was not given to words, but could act when occasion demanded. If any of the pupils of the Summer University, young or old, attended the lectures on Dutch and German Art, it would not be her fault.

"This is my first experience," Eloise herself was saying, in reply to Mark's counsel not to mind the Philistines. "I have only talked in parlors and to friends."

"Don't let them bluff you," he urged. "Keep your head up and believe in yourself; then they will believe in you. Where will you have this picture?"

The Epworth boy had gone to a lecture, but her new assistant was worth a whole League of Epworth boys, decided Eloise, thankfully watching her gallery fall into place. It was delightful to have her treasures handled by some one who knew their worth. In an incredibly short time the last nail was driven and Mark was locking the door of the hall behind them. "I am very grateful, Mr. Heffron," she said, earnestly, as they walked home together under the lengthening shadows.

"I expect to get it all back to-morrow when you lecture," said Mark.

"Are you coming?" asked the girl, with a startled glance.

"Of course."

"But you won't like it," she demurred. "It's only the things you find in books."

"You won't shut me out, will you?"

"Oh no."

"Then I'm coming." And he came, not long after the doors were opened and there was still a choice in seats. She spied him early in her talk, but by his friendly smile he told her he was there to help, not to criticise.

He did help, wonderfully, stimulating attention by his own evident interest, leading the applause, warming and enlivening the audience, which was not small in spite of Mrs. Harwood's efforts—perhaps because of them.

As Eloise had said, there were "only the things found in books" in the lecture, but the manner saved the matter from being dull, as it often does ; and it was Mark Heffron who saved the manner, so he congratulated himself.

"Summer, the man and the maid; it is not good for either one to be alone," quoth Mark, hunting under the bed for his tennis-shoes.

The woollen puppy eyed him suspiciously. "It is true, although you may not believe it," said Mark. "What do you know about such things, anyway?"

He ran down the front stairs, whistling merrily, and the Widow Hubbard crept up the back stairs to mourn, for the twentieth time, over her denuded room.

"I've had a good many resorters in my house, first and last," she muttered, "but I never had one like him." She lifted the edge of the bed-quilt to look at the pin-cushion puppy and the paper flowers, and let it fall with a groan. "I told him he might do as he was a mindter, and four dollars ain't bad for two flights up," she said, by way of consolation. "But it's pretty hard, after I've took so much pains to make it pretty and pleasant—there he goes over to play ball with that girl. Awful independent, ain't you, swingin' along!"

The tennis-ground was on a plateau overlooking the bay, the most inviting spot in Beau Lieu. The forest was at its back, and two or three generous beeches at the side extended protection from the sun to those who watched the games, always a fair number, for the tennis-ground lay in the direct route from the hotels to the halls.

There were more spectators than usual this morning, partly because it was too warm to listen to a lecture on Sociology, partly because the game was a good one and the graceful girl in the white gown was ahead.

"Who is she?" Philip More asked his friend, Jo Allen.

"Miss Kentucky, the boys call her. She is from Louisville. Jack," nudging a long-haired youth in front, "what's Miss Kentucky's real name?"

"Gordon," replied the youth, without turning his head.

"Yes, that's it—Gordon. She is lecturing on something or other."

"That can't be Eloise Gordon," murmured Philip. "Do you know her first name?"

"Jack, what is Miss Gordon's first name?"

"Eloise," responded the long-haired youth; "Good one, good play! Gee whizz, she's a dandy!"

Philip More elbowed his way through the crowd until close to the players, who, oblivious of the eyes upon them, sent the light ball to and fro. "It *is* Eloise Gordon. What under the sun is she doing here?"

The game was concluded amid the appreciative shouts of the bystanders. Philip lost no time in pressing forward, cap in hand "Congratulations, Miss Gordon!" he cried. "You have not forgotten me?"

"No, indeed, Mr. More," she replied, another flush added to those of exercise and victory already in her cheeks. "What are you doing here?"

"Geologizing ; and you?"

Eloise grew grave. "I am lecturing upon art," she said, hurriedly. "Mr. Heffron, this is an old friend, Mr. More." The two men shook hands, Mark with a cordiality which Philip did not entirely reciprocate, and the trio walked to the cottage gate, where Mark took his leave.

Of course, Aunt Harriet remembered Philip most pleasantly, and told him so with a confiding glance up at him and a confiding pressure of his hand. Really, it would be a great relief to have this young man, whose antecedents were known to her and who was so deferential in his manner, take the place of that baffling Mr. Heffron, of whom they knew absolutely nothing except what he chose to tell, and who took their mutual relations as a matter of course. She made Philip sit beside her on the sofa, and let him wield her old-fashioned fan, august and clumsy as an eagle's wing, while Eloise went to make some lemonade.

As soon as the door had closed, Philip seized his opportunity. "Do tell me, Miss Larrabee, what it all means."

"Isn't it terrible! Isn't it shocking!" cried Aunt Harriet, flinging out her helpless little right hand, every finger stiff and straight as the rays of a starfish. "Can you conceive of anything more heart-rending?"

"But how did it happen?" pursued Philip, still in the dark.

"Is it possible that you have not heard?" inquired Aunt Harriet, reproachfully.

"I assure you I know absolutely nothing. How could I? I went abroad directly after that winter in Louisville, and have only just returned. I thought I had recovered."

"Poor boy," sighed Aunt Harriet. "Eloise has changed. Mr. More, that girl is a *wonder!*"

Philip made no answer.

"Let me tell you," said Aunt Harriet, excitedly, "what she has done. When her father passed away—is it possible you did not know? Yes; he passed away in the Main Street of Louisville, going to his office, right after breakfast, and a beautiful morning. I never shall forget how he came back and kissed us all around. He was very fond of me." She put her handkerchief to her eyes. Philip maintained a sympathetic silence, and she soon resumed her story. "You never saw such mourning; the whole city felt that it had sustained a personal loss. There was no one more thought of than Max Gordon."

"What became of Mrs. Gordon?" asked Philip.

"My sister never recovered from the shock," replied Miss Larrabee. "I am all that Eloise has left. I stand in place of father and mother."

In spite of himself, Philip looked relieved. He sincerely regretted, for Eloise's sake, the loss of her parents, but he could not fail to realize that his cause might profit by their removal. "Dear Miss Larrabee," he said, softly, taking her little nervous hands in his large magnetic ones, "it is in just that relation that I wish to appeal to you. You know the story of that winter. I want to try again. I didn't know that she was here. I came here only by chance, a happy chance, if it turns out as I hope. Miss Larrabee, may I count on your permission, your assistance?" And Aunt Harriet, seeing in the honest young face before her the promise of deliverance from vulgar boarding-houses and still more vulgar duns, from anxiety and economy, and from that dreadful Mr. Heffron, responded, fervently, "You may, Mr. More, you may!"

At that moment the door opened, and Eloise and Mark appeared in comradish proximity, Eloise with the glasses, Mark with the pitcher, and both laughing heartily over something Mark had said; for Eloise had found the sugar-bowl empty, and, slipping out to replenish it, had encountered Mark at the grocery and brought him home with her, introducing him quietly through the back door, where she had made her exit; and Mark had been so helpful and so droll that the lemonade-making had nearly put out of their heads the existence of the two in the parlor settling the fates of all concerned.

Philip bit his lip with a frown, and Aunt Harriet manifested by a certain frigid little manner, retained along with her India shawl and cameo brooch from the luxuries of other days, that she considered the presence of her niece's companion no less than an intrusion.

Then it was that the devil entered into Mark; he would have said it was his Irish temper. He dared Miss Larrabee and mocked at Philip; he seated himself at the piano and sang "Green grow the rashes, O," making mischievous eyes at Eloise as he declared, in a rich baritone, "The sweetest hours I ever spent were spent among the lasses, O;" he filled the tiny parlor with dash and sparkle and life, until Philip nestled, red and angry, on his seat, and Aunt Harriet tapped her narrow foot upon the wooden floor, while Eloise fluttered like a fascinated dove before the serpents in those brilliant dark eyes.

She followed Mark to the piazza when he left, and gave him her hand in farewell. He waved his again and again until he disappeared among the trees. His mouth had settled into the lines which repelled the girl on the day of their first meeting, but if she saw she did not care. The strange new stirring in her blood was all she knew or wished to know. She rebelled from returning to that tame, colorless pair sitting on the sofa in the parlor. Glancing hastily about her, she stepped noiselessly from the piazza to the turf-muffled ground and ran down to the shore.

Mark had climbed stormily up the hill, growling below his breath, " *Check*, you young jackanapes ! I'll teach you not to cry *Gardez* to me."

He came again the next day, and the next ; he came every day, sometimes twice and even three times. Aunt Harriet fretted and Philip fumed, but they might as well have interfered with wind or flame ; they only hurt themselves.

IV

Three weeks had passed of the Beau Lieu University and Summer Assembly. It was very warm, for Beau Lieu does not always adhere to the "cool, bracing weather" advertised in the prospectus. The lake was a dull, opaque gray, and stagnant as a mill-pond. The opposite shore had withdrawn into the haze, so that water, earth, and air seemed to unite in one vague substance which was neither of the three. Aunt Harriet lay, exhausted, on the sofa, looking so worn and white that a pang of remorse softened the obdurate heart of her niece. "Pull yourself together, auntie," she cried, "and we'll go around the bay."

Aunt Harriet brightened visibly.

"That would be very nice," she responded, humbly. "But are you sure you want to go, Eloise?"

"Of course. Where is the air-pillow? And your vinaigrette? You had better take a light shawl. Come along."

They found the pier filled with people waiting for the boat; women, babies, and small children, the summer girl and the summer boy, the idler

with the novel under one arm and a pug-dog
under the other, the student recreating the outer
man while the inner man solved a problem. The
air was thick and stifling. All of the children
and most of the women munched pop-corn with a
desperate earnestness suggesting a charm in the
dry morsel against the weariness of delay. The
hot, buttery smell of Beau Lieu's sole dissipation
met the fastidious nostrils of the young Ken-
tuckian, and they quivered disdainfully. No one
cared. No one on the pier knew her or the bundle of dignity and remonstrance leaning on her
arm. Women who breathed of onions as well as
pop-corn doubled them up and talked over them
about dinners and dressmaking and Mary Jane's
last tooth.

At last the *Paragon* came up slowly, and they
went aboard. Then came more crowding and
confusion. Finally, every one was settled and
they steamed down the bay, the canvas awning
flapping merrily above their heads, the water rip-
pling coolly against the sides of the boat. The
haze lifted and took them in. The beautiful
green water was all around them. A hush fell
upon the company, broken by some pious soul
who felt the divine peace and loveliness, and for
whom, piety and melancholy being synonymous,
there was no vent save a lugubrious hymn. There
were a few feeble attempts on the part of the
other passengers to follow the tune ; then the
song died away. The women began again with

dinners and dressmaking and neighborhood tales. The summer boys flirted with the summer girls. Feeble jokes were cracked and empty laughter resounded, and the ubiquitous pop-corn boy set up his stove on the lower deck, whence the rustle and snap of his commodity were plainly to be heard.

The boat stopped at Roaring Brook, and half a dozen individuals went ashore, among them Eloise and her aunt. They seated themselves on a mossy log and conscientiously watched the brook which, in default of roaring, as it was booked to do, purred like a kitten among the stones. Eloise looked and felt unutterably bored. Aunt Harriet made wild attempts to be entertaining, attempts which failed dismally, and were followed by a chilling silence. Eloise waited for the last boat, and was patiently attentive until she landed her companion at the cottage door. Two squares of paper showed white against the green of an arbor-vitæ; one was Philip's card, bound to a branch by a long grass blade, the other was impaled upon a twig, and bore Mark Heffron's scrawl.

The cottage occupied by Eloise and her aunt was one of the row which nestled, like dove-cotes, among the trees on the shore. There was a slender fence about the yard, and a pathway of painted blocks led to the door. Long piazzas encircled the house, and a balcony ran out into the shrubbery, a rustic affair, with uneven floors and a low lattice of twisted limbs. On this balcony Eloise sat, while the sun, like a great drop of glowing wine, dripped down the murky sky. She could see, through the trees, the light dresses of the women below her, and could hear the crisp tread of the men who accompanied them. No one was alone save herself. She had snubbed Aunt Harriet into retiring early, and now she wished her back, if only to fill the empty seat opposite. The heavy air was full of forebodings; even the trees waved tragically.

The footsteps sounded less frequently on the pathway and finally ceased. It was growing late. She crept up to her chamber, and flung herself, face downward, on the bed.

How long she lay there she could not tell, but all at once she was wide awake and listening. Did some one call her? No, there was not a sound. Her heart beat violently.

What strange power drew her to the window, down the stairs, into the warm night air which blew softly towards the lake, out upon the rough floor of the balcony?

"Don't be frightened," said a low voice, and Mark Heffron took her cold hands in his. "How did you know I was here?" he asked, laughing. "Don't be frightened," for she shook from head to foot.

"I don't know—I awoke—I thought I heard some one call me—did you call?"

"Not aloud." He laughed again. "I did not expect to succeed so well. Sit down, child."

Mechanically she obeyed him. He continued talking and she listened without hearing, unaware of place or time or personality save his, towards which great coiling chains, thrown by some unseen force, drew her ever closer.

She stood up before him, panting. He bent out of the shadows to look upon her yielding face.

"Go to bed, child," he said, coldly. "It was too bad to disturb you."

In an instant he had dropped from the balcony and was walking rapidly away. The girl remained where he had left her, feeling the jar, the shock, the disappointment, the helplessness of one who miscalculates the way and steps off into space.

Gradually came the consciousness that she had been played upon, befooled, betrayed. The hot blood surged into her cheeks. Her head sang like a vibrating wire. Blindly she groped her way along the hall and up the stairs. Through the open door of Aunt Harriet's room she could hear the sleeper's peaceful breath. An impulse came to enter and arouse this woman who loved her, and find some defence, however feeble, against the vague terrors which assailed ; but she dismissed it and went on alone.

V

Before Eloise had reached her own room a wind arose, swift and searching; it bent the branches of the trees and the long, reed-like grass upon the shore; it rocked the low shrubs and rattled the dead leaves of a transplanted elm. Then came the rain and beat out sweet odors, so that the tiny square about the cottage grew as fragant as a garden. Lightning and thunder followed, piercing and purifying the heavy air.

When morning dawned the girl who watched for it by the window uttered a low cry of delight. The dull white bay had been smitten into color, gray-green by the shore, deepening through amethyst to purple as it met the purple mountains. Every boat-house stood up straight and clean against the sky. The black line of the wharf accentuated the dazzle of the foam.

The scene increased in beauty as the day advanced. The wind became a gale, driving before it the great white breakers. The sun came out from the clouds, and intensified the brilliance of shifting water and glancing foam. The figures of the men and women on the beach cut the air like silhouettes. All the neighborhood were there.

Aunt Harriet and Eloise followed, and later Philip joined them.

"I am so glad you have come!" cried Eloise, and turned to him almost appealingly.

"Were you afraid of the storm?" He felt big and manly as he put the question.

"I am glad it is over and that you are here," she answered, evasively.

Philip was puzzled, but he did not mean to let that stand in the way. He had been patient and he had been a gentleman. He was filled with the courage of those who have nothing to regret. Equally magnanimous was Aunt Harriet's self-control; by not so much as the quiver of an eyelash did she recognize the change. No one mentioned Mark; all three would have been glad to forget him.

Mark would have been glad to forget himself. It was with this intention that he went the rounds of the college buildings, which were filled with enthusiastic crowds. The season was at its height, and all the institutions, educational and otherwise, which had their headquarters at Beau Lieu, were in full swing—assemblies and circles of every description, leagues and associations without number, including the Hay-Fever Association. Mark's spirits began to rise as he looked about him.

He strolled leisurely along under the trees. Every one else was in a hurry; even the big bell ringing in a wooden frame on the campus tipped up excitedly, this way and that, as if it could not get the sound out half fast enough. In one direction went a squad of college boys, flannel clad and lightly shod, making up their "conditions" with as little discomfort to themselves as possible; in another a group of pretty girls with banjo-boxes set out for Music Hall; in all directions, in an unbroken procession, old and young, bent and straight, with the country color still in their cheeks and with solemn, sallow faces, dull and gay but invariably anxious, went those overworked and unappreciated members of the body politic—the teachers of the public schools. They were not carrying banjos or reading the *Anabasis;* neither were they enjoying the Field and Forest Club or the School of Art; but wherever the knottiest problems were being discussed, or the display of learning was most tremendous, there they were to be found, leaning over their writing - tablets with the absorbed attention of those who compress a complete course of instruction into four short weeks. Mark followed them from hall to hall, hoping that their seriousness might cure his own.

They led him to the Auditorium, where the bald-headed man with whom he had come into argumentative contact upon the day of his arrival was lecturing upon the "Contentions of Peter and Paul." The great wooden curtains on both sides of the building were rolled up as high as they could go. The open archways revealed glimpses of the forest and of the wind-swept bay. Upon this peaceful background a man soon appeared, narrow shouldered, angular, clad in faded jeans, his slouched hat drawn down to meet a grizzled beard, which flowed from temple to chin and over his hollow chest. He seated himself on a bench outside the building, crossed his sharp knees and long, limp hands, and listened, satisfaction proclaimed in every line. As points of doctrine came up, one by one, to be dealt with, summarily and according to orthodox methods, he expressed a still keener relish, wagging his rough head and swinging to and fro the foot which was free.

Mark left the amphitheatre and walked around where the old farmer sat. "How did you enjoy it?" he inquired, as applause greeted the close of the address and the audience arose to go.

"*First rate! first rate!*" was the answer, delivered with an emphasis which left no room for doubt of its sincerity. "Tell you what," he continued, as they walked on together, "seemed like old times. This here," and he swung his hand comprehensively about him, "used to be all Methodist; now it's Baptist, Congregationalist, Presbyterian, even Gymnastic." His voice was vibrant with contempt.

Mark's eyes twinkled. "You don't say so!" he rejoined, sympathetically.

"Yes, *sir,*" continued the old man. "There's a woman down there, in that buildin' yonder, who says that Gymnastic is her religion, an' she's got all the gals in the neighborhood a-balancin' on one toe an' flingin' up their arms an' the Lord knows what all. Might do for the dancin' dervishes, but it ain't *my* religion."

"How did you learn of these—"

"These goin's-on?"

Mark assented with a nod.

"My gal Cynthy's one on 'em, an' she's had so much to say about this *new life*—you'd a thought she'd been to a revival—that I went and peeked in the winder. There was a hull room full on 'em, my Cynthy among the rest, goin' through the *durndest* pufformances, a-swingin' their arms an' a-tip-toin' back'ards an' for'ards. I told Cynthy she'd got to quit, but, Land, she's so obstinate! Her mother right over!"

"Is her mother alive?"

"You bet she is, an' backs up the gal ; says it's what's goin' on all over everywhere, only I ain't heard about it. You just come along with me an' I'll show ye. You wouldn't s'pose sech things would be tolerated."

He led the way, and Mark followed, filled with curiosity. The cottage was the smallest of the college buildings, and hidden from the pathway by a wall of dense cedars. Between this wall and the cottage the old man began to wriggle his way. Mark caught him by the arm. "Hold on there ; what are you going to do?" he demanded.

"Show you where you can peek in."

"Not much; you don't catch me," replied Mark, sternly.

"They won't ketch ye," returned the veteran Paul Pry, mistaking his meaning. "It's dark as a pocket behind them cedars."

"Don't care if it is. They are coming now; you had better get away from there." The patter of feet and the hum of voices confirmed his words. Presently forty or fifty women and girls trouped out of the cottage, putting into application the instruction they had received, chins up, chests out, backs and legs stiff and straight.

Mark and the old farmer stepped aside to let them pass.

"The backbone is a spiral; you must pull it up like this!" cried a plump, brown-eyed girl, elongating her chubby person.

"That's the 'military line,'" called another girl out of the crowd in the rear. "That isn't the 'artistic life-line.' The 'artistic life-line' goes like this." She ran forward to illustrate. The old farmer slunk into the bushes.

"Cynthy, no doubt," decided Mark. "But who is this?"

Between two tall young girls, like a queen between gendarmes, advanced a small, graceful woman, exquisitely dressed, a drawing-room flower. What was she doing at Beau Lieu? To his surprise she came towards him with a smile of recognition, her hand outstretched in greeting.

"I am so glad to meet you, Mr. Heffron," she said, in tones as perfect as her figure and poise. "You do not remember me—Marguerite Duvray? It is not strange; I should not have known you —Mr. Billings pointed you out to me."

Mark vowed he was charmed and delighted; it was a fortunate chance which brought him to Beau Lieu—threshing, meanwhile, his chaff of memories for one grain of recollection. Who the deuce is—was—Marguerite Duvray?

The gendarmes fell behind, and he walked on with the fascinating stranger, artfully leading her to speak of herself, trying to find her in Boston, New York, Philadelphia — even in London and Paris.

She brought him back to Beau Lieu with a bird-like nod of her pretty head. "Here is my cottage. I am at home, usually, in the afternoon at four. *Au revoir!*"

No sooner had she left him than Mark took a bee-line for the Billings Cottage. "If old Billings can straighten this thing out for me, he has got to do it," he said to himself.

Mrs. Billings was on the piazza, rocking deliberately to and fro; her idle hands were folded in her lap, her attitude was that of one who has no interest in anything. She looked up languidly as Mark mounted the steps and gave him a feeble good-morning. No; Mr. Billings was not at home, and she did not know where he was. There were people after him all the time.

"Mr. Billings is a very busy man, I suppose," vouchsafed Mark, seating himself on one of the splint-bottomed chairs which adorned the piazza.

"Busy!" cried Mrs. Billings, with more warmth than she had shown; "he's killing himself just as fast as he can!"

"I hope it is not as bad as that," returned the visitor. "He looks pretty well nourished."

"Oh, he eats well," granted his pessimistic spouse, "and he sleeps pretty well; but *I* don't see anything of him from morning till night."

"Oho!" thought Mark, "that's where the shoe pinches. You have some good teachers," he continued aloud, in a wily endeavor to lead her around to the subject in which he was interested.

"That don't do me any good," she responded, dismally. "I never go anywhere. Mr. Billings is always too busy to take me, and there is no pleasure in going alone."

"There seem to be more women than there used to be," pursued the investigator.

"Altogether too many," said Mrs. Billings, shortly. "They are fussing all the time about something; they don't give Mr. Billings a minute's peace. There are a lot more trying to get in; a woman with three daughters who has taken the Hunt Cottage wants to teach china-painting, and her daughters want to read and pose. They are kind of pretty, but they know it too well."

"Who is teaching Elocution?" inquired Mark, bearing around on another tack.

"Milton Jones, that man with the long nose. He don't call it Elocution; he calls it Oratory and Expression. A lot of ministers are taking of him. Mademoiselle Duvray has some scholars in what she calls Voice Posing, whatever that may be."

At last !

"Who is Mademoiselle Duvray," he inquired, carelessly.

"That little woman with sort of reddish hair, that steps around so spry; there's lots of get-up to her. They say she's been all over the world picking up ideas for these gymnastics; they ain't gymnastics quite, either, though they go through a lot of motions."

"Delsarte ?" suggested Mark.

"She don't like to have it called that, either; it's a system of her own; the women are crazy over it. I must say they do improve after she gets hold of them; they get so's they stand up and act as if they were somebody."

"Where does Mademoiselle Duvray come from ?" pursued Mark.

"I don't know," was the disappointing reply. "She's new to me; I never heard of her before that I know of. Queer Mr. Billings don't come. It's most dinner-time."

"I won't wait for him," said Mark, rising at the hint so delicately conveyed. "I did not have any particular business. He asked me to call."

"You needn't hurry," said Mrs. Billings, adopting the formula of hospitality. "Come again."

VI

So Mark left the Billings Cottage no wiser than he came, and subsequent efforts during the day failed to bring the information which he sought. But, as he was falling off to sleep at night, a wan little face framing two great eager eyes appeared before him. Marguerite Duvray, of course; the young French girl who studied Greek with him ten years ago, and upon whom he used to try his theories! The big, loutish boys who made up the remainder of the class had been after Greek, enough Greek to enable them to pass their examinations; she had been after ideas. But what particular hypothesis had she laid hold of and carried away to be an "inspiration," and all the rest of it? He had been full of theories in those days, and as plausible in the explication of each one as if he never expected to have another. "Yes, that is Marguerite," said Mark. "Now, what in the name of Aristotle did I say to her?"

Punctually at four on the following afternoon he presented himself at Mademoiselle Duvray's cottage, armed with a bunch of scarlet poppies and the *Daily Resorter*. She received them with an air of embarrassment; they were so foreign to her idea of him that they put completely out of her head the questions she had meant to ask.

"There seems nothing else indigenous to the soil," he said, by way of apology. "Considerable 'local color' about these."

He fitted himself into a willow chair, which bent beneath him, and continued, banteringly, "If ever there was an educational orgie it is this Assembly. There isn't an ology or an ism under the sun which cannot be found here on tap, and you can carouse in any one of them for two dollars and a half. No wonder inebriety is universal when it comes so cheap. Do you know the learned individual who teaches Literature?"

"Only by sight."

"I have been to hear her exposition of Romeo. 'Shakespeare wrote everything with an ethical purpose. If Romeo had gone to Papa Capulet, like a little man, and asked for Juliet, he would have saved himself and her lots of trouble. The prince would have become his backer.'"

"You are testing my credulity," cried Marguerite, "the lecturer never said such things."

"Words to that effect. I stood up to make a few remarks, but when I looked around on the audience I hadn't the heart. They liked their kind of a Romeo so much better than they would mine."

"Mr. Billings says the object of the school is not so much information as stimulation," she returned, laughing, in spite of herself.

"I know what Mr. Billings thinks of the school," said Mark significantly, "and I know what Mrs. Billings thinks. She is only waiting for the Reverend William to go to pieces, and if there is anything in telepathy she'll fetch him."

Marguerite laughed again, a little uneasily this time. "The scientific department is well represented," she said, tentatively.

"The representation is unlimited," he replied. "Billings must have gone out with a drag-net and brought in everything he could find. Tell me, how did you happen to come?" Again that insincere tone which hurt her like an ache.

"It was a whim, an impulse," she said, hastily, feeling naked and exposed before his curious gaze. Not for worlds could she confide to him her desire to help others as she had herself been helped at this school of Beau Lieu, nor could he, in his hope of her favor, confess that he had forgotten what he said to her ten years ago.

"What was I studying then?" he asked himself, as, after an hour of aimless talk, he left the cottage and walked into the woods alone. "What did I believe, or think that I believed or pretended that I believed?" He tried to revive the mood of that time by calling up its images and associations, and setting himself in their midst. "There was something on the train that night coming here; what was it?" he asked. But the thoughts of that night had faded like other formless shades, like the thoughts of ten years ago. "Go on and be—eternally blessed !" he cried, when they ignored his urgent invitation to reappear. "I don't care. There are plenty more of you. But I should like to see my invention if I have lost the patent; it makes a woman charming. Here is one of those circles fate draws so prettily, bringing a man back to beg for what he threw away. Does Marguerite realize that I threw it away, and that I am trying to find it again ?"

Marguerite realized very little just then but her own bewilderment. After supper, as was her charitable wont, she met the waitresses, Susan Gray and a company of maidens from Cologne College, on hand for intellectual crumbs from the Beau Lieu tables. They were all thin, pale, and self-abnegatory ; Mark had dubbed them Saint Ursula and the Eleven Thousand Virgins. This and every other mocking thing which he had said came between the teacher and her pupils as they stood up before her, looking gaunt and grim in the lamplight.

The girls felt the difference between this lesson and the last. "She's getting tired," explained Susan on the way home. "Every one gets tired here, though it did seem as if nothing could use her up."

That was what all her friends said, "Mademoiselle Duvray is getting tired."

"I'm not anything of the sort," she exclaimed, when her cousin and companion, Mrs. Burnham, took up the common cry.

A few minutes later she asked abruptly, "Fannie, what do you think of Mr. Heffron?"

Mrs. Burnham deliberated. "He is extremely clever," she said. "But he makes me feel as if my gown did not fit, and that is a very bad sign in a man."

The nineteenth session of the Beau Lieu University and Summer Assembly was drawing to a close. The various leagues and circles had each had their "day." There had been parades and processions, a brass-band had been up from Willitonquit, and there had been excursions from all over the state. People were beginning to leave. Zeb Hastings was to be met at any hour of the day or night looking for baggage. He invariably presented Mark a card, which Mark invariably received.

At last, one morning, an avalanche of wagons went past the Hubbard Cottage, and a torrent of pedestrians followed. As Mark climbed the terrace he met Susan Gray and her company coming down. "It's all over," she called, cheerily. "Most everybody's getting out to-day."

"Have you had a profitable summer?" inquired Mark.

"Tolerably so: but that isn't what we came for," returned Susan, virtuously. "We came to learn something, and there can't anybody come to Beau Lieu without learning something." Having voiced the sentiment of the place, Susan and her maidens swept down the hill to the station.

A clatter of chairs and a cloud of dust greeted Mark at the cottage where Marguerite Duvray had surrounded herself with an atmosphere of tranquillity.

"Yes, sir," said the woman who wielded the broom, "Miss Duvray and her folks left last night—they went sudden at the last. No, sir, they didn't leave no word," and she resumed her sweeping.

Surprised and chagrined, he turned and walked away. Marguerite had told him, the day before, that she meant to remain another month, and she had seemed to encourage his own idea of remaining also. He went to the post-office for a possible note of explanation ; there was nothing there, except a growl from New York asking what he was doing and when he would be through. "Through to-night; leave at ten," he telegraphed, then returned to the Hubbard Cottage, packed his trunk and paid his bill.

There were still several hours before train-time. He set out to walk them off, taking the path along the shore. It was quite deserted.

The sun went down in rose and the moon came up in amber. The bay was full of light. Slowly it faded, and clouds covered the sky.

Hurriedly he retraced his steps, but the rain was upon him, big, pelting drops, which ceased as soon as he had reached a sheltering tree. The moon came out again, brighter than before, and showed him where he was. On that bench by the shore he had often sat ; the gate of that slender fence had often clicked for him ; up that pathway of painted blocks he had walked many a time. There were pools of water between the blocks and in the hollows of the uneven floor of the rustic balcony, to which he climbed as once before.

The moon streaked with silver the crooked lattice, and placed a small bright image of herself in the broadest pool. Drawn by this *ignis fatuus*, a white moth darted down and plunged into the cold water, fluttering piteously. Mark lifted the tiny creature out and watched it fly away.

VII

The pastor of the First Church of Wesley, in the State of Kansas, sat in his study with a new text before him. Suddenly the door-bell was pulled with a vehemence which sent its tinkling peal reverberating long through the house. Whoever was there had forgotten or did not know how easily it responded to the lightest touch.

The Reverend Jerome Crosby pushed back his chair from the study-table and himself answered the summons, expecting to find a stranger. Lucretia Harwood stood on the door-step, her round face alight with the importance of her errand.

"How do you do? Come in, come in!" cried the reverend gentleman with extraordinary civility, considering how deep he had been in his sermonizing.

Lucretia hurried him through the hall to his study, beginning before she had seated herself, "Mr. Crosby, I shall die if I don't go to the World's Fair. I must go, I shall go, and that's all there is to it."

She extricated herself from the conditional mood and from her bonnet strings in the same breath, and continued: "I've thought about it day and night, and there's no use talking. I can't pay my own expenses, but I can work, and I'm not afraid to. They want matrons in all the State Buildings, and I'm going to apply for the position in our own."

"Are you acquainted with any influential person from Kansas?" inquired Mr. Crosby, becoming interested.

"Only yourself," replied Lucretia, artlessly, "and that's what I'm here for. I want you to write a letter to the authorities, saying I'm honest and capable, and I'll take it up to Chicago myself."

"What if the position is already filled?" he asked.

"Then I'll do something else," she replied, firmly. "There ought to be enough for a sensible, able-bodied woman to do. I'm going to see that Fair if it is the last thing I do. You can't imagine what those buildings are to me. I know them as if I'd built them, I've watched them so close in the newspapers. You ought to see my scrap-book."

"I should like to, very much," said Mr. Crosby, politely.

Lucretia had started to her feet in her excitement and tied her bonnet strings, but remembering the incompleteness of her mission she untied them and sat down again.

"Where do you propose to stop in Chicago?" inquired Mr. Crosby. "You know it is a pretty big city, and not any too honest." He shook his head dubiously, as if a vision of the modern Babel rose before him.

"That's all settled," returned Lucretia promptly. "Daniel has a cousin's wife coming on to Chicago from the East to take in the World's Fair people. Of course now in March and April she won't be full, and I can get a room reasonable for a few days. I've written to her, and she's sent back word to come on."

"And what you want of me is a letter." He drew towards him a large sheet of paper, and seized the quill pen, which he used for sentimental reasons, standing it on its point and causing it to splutter as it moved across the page.

Lucretia watched him narrowly while he covered one side and began on the other. "I don't believe they'll read all that," she interposed.

"Just as well to have it," replied the minister, shortly, determined that his first and perhaps only communication to the officials of the Great Exhibit should not be scrimped. He carefully read over the composition, punctuated, folded it, and placed it in a large envelope, where it assumed the proportions of a public document.

Lucretia received it with a sigh which might indicate gratitude or concern, and moved towards the door, followed by her dignified sponsor. "Will Daniel go too?" he asked.

"He wants to; I don't know whether to let him or not."

"You had better. Chicago is no kind of a place for a woman to go around alone in."

"I'll see about it," she deliberated. "Good-bye, and I thank you from the bottom of my heart, Mr. Crosby !"

"*Good*-bye, Lucretia ; God bless you !"

For once Daniel Harwood manifested a dogged determination to "see about" his own case, and feminine enterprise embarked under masculine auspices. It was Daniel who bought the tickets and Daniel who looked up accommodations ; when the train from Kansas drew under the smoky arches of the Chicago station and the passengers surged out upon the platform, the hopeful candidate for a position in the Kansas Building hung, with womanly reliance, on the arm of a big brown figure unmistakably Daniel's.

It was the last of March, but very cold. Winter lingered in the steely depths of the lake and in the shadow of the bleak, high buildings. "I shall freeze to death," chattered Lucretia, withdrawing into her cloak and slipping her stiff fingers up her sleeves.

"It *is* quite a change," assented Daniel, rubbing his nose.

The wind followed them, caught at Lucretia's skirts and the tails of Daniel's coat, drove them, choking and blinded with dust, to the corner, and there beat upon them with the malice of a fiend, while they waited for a south-bound car.

"Want to find some place?" queried a police-man built on the scale of the Auditorium.

"We're going to Jackson Park," said Daniel importantly.

"The other corner," directed the policeman, pointing thither. "Cars don't stop here. There's a car now. Tell them to let you off at Fifty-ninth Street."

A cable car came thundering towards them. In his great open cage, the gripman, fur-clad, leaned on his brake like the conventional stuffed bear on his pole.

The pilgrims scrambled aboard the rear car and stood clinging to the straps; for Easter was near, and shopping women overflowed the seats. Every jar threw them against one another and into the laps of their neighbors, but they held on bravely, peering out of the windows for glimpses of the city, and hailing signs of the approaching drama to be enacted at Jackson Park; swaying columns and mouldings bearing on perishable staff the imperishable lines of Corinth and Ionia, straggling groups of men and women from the Midway Plaisance, in gay tunics and picturesque hats, striding along with the unencumbered gait lost to civilization.

"They can't hold 'em in," commented a scrub-by-looking individual, pointing with his thumb at the strays, "Wild as a pack o' deer. 'Fraid as death of the cable, so they hoof it down and back. Be'n out to see the Esquimaux?" he inquired of

Daniel, who shook his head. "Great sport ; but it's all rot, their lyin' down on the ice, and that sort of thing. Told me they never suffered so much from the cold in their lives as they do here, the air is so damp. They'll get it hot enough this summer," and he grinned at the thought. "I heard they was goin' on a strike to leave off their furs. The manager won't hear to it; says that's what makes them inter*esting*. Be'n out to the grounds, ma'am ?" he inquired of Lucretia, who backed away from his easy familiarity, murmuring an unintelligible response. In her retreat she felt herself caught and held by a pair of deep black eyes. They belonged to a large, handsome man who stood near, twisting a pair of gray mustaches, thrusting out his full red lips and turning his head restlessly to and fro. Lucretia noted with awe the curious gold medal suspended from a brooch under his chin. The studies of the past year told her it was an " order," and that he was one for whom his own work had gained distinction in science or art. So absorbed was she in watching him, as he wrote in his note-book and scowled and whispered to himself, that Fifty-ninth Street faded utterly from her mind, and it was Daniel who bestirred himself and stopped the car.

Some time elapsed before they could cross the street, debarred as they were by a procession of huge drays, bristling with chair and table legs or piled high with mattresses, destined for the hotels which had sprung up, like mushrooms, in the vicinity of the park.

Suddenly Lucretia revived and looked about her. "This ain't Fifty-ninth Street!" she exclaimed. "We'll have to walk back. Come on, Daniel!"

She plunged into the crowd. Daniel followed leisurely. He will never forget that hurrying figure, how it appeared and disappeared, how it led him to the corner, made a mad rush before a car, gesticulating wildly, then suddenly went down out of sight. Two men had jumped from the car and helped her to her feet when he reached the spot. They were wiping the dirt from her face and examining her with professional solicitude.

"For pity's sake!" she ejaculated; and then, "My soul alive!"

"A fracture here," said the elder of the two doctors, touching her right wrist, from which the hand drooped dismally. "A Colles fracture—see? She's all right except that." His companion nodded. "Get a splint as quick as you can," ordered the elder. "Go into that drug-store over there and ask for a piece of board a foot and a half long. I'll bring her right over. Now, if you will take my arm, madam. Do you feel able to walk?"

"Oh, my, yes," replied Lucretia, but came to a sudden halt. "There's something the matter with my—limb," she said, apologetically.

"Let me see," said the surgeon gently; "take a swallow of this," and he pulled a tiny flask from his pocket.

With indescribable dignity she drew herself up before him. "Sir," she said, stonily, "you are addressing the President of the Wesley Branch of the W. C. T. U."

There was a heterodox smile in the surgeon's eyes as he begged her pardon and returned the flask to his pocket, but Lucretia did not see it. She allowed him to assist her to the curbstone, and submitted to an examination of the injured member. By this time the younger man had returned, accompanied by a tall, graceful girl, whom he introduced as "My cousin, Miss Gordon;" adding, "the drug-store is in Miss Gordon's hotel, the Lake View. I don't mean that she owns it; she boards there. Don't you think we can carry the lady across the street?"

"The lady" looked up from the curbstone.

"Perhaps Miss Gordon—" she began, hesitatingly.

"I shall be glad to render you any assistance in my power, Mrs. Harwood," said Eloise, quickly.

Her cousin glanced in surprise from one to the other.

"I met Mrs. Harwood at Beau Lieu two years ago," explained Eloise. "If you and Dr. Humphrey can make a 'chair,' this way, with your hands, it will be easy to carry her. This gentleman," indicating Daniel, "can take charge of the injured foot."

So, with the doctors stooping over her, and Daniel clinging to the foot as he backed before them, while Eloise hurried ahead to open the door, Mrs. Harwood made her solemn entry.

The room to which Eloise conducted them was on the top floor, the tenth, a large, airy apartment, thickly hung with sketches in black-and-white and color. As they entered, a door was softly pushed together by some one in an adjoining room. Another door, through which came glimpses of a canopied bed, with a gay silk dressing-gown thrown across the foot, was hurriedly closed by Eloise, who cleared the way to a broad couch by the window.

"I'm making an awful lot of trouble!" exclaimed the injured woman. Her face looked drawn and white among the bright pillows.

"It is a pleasure," responded Eloise, wondering, nevertheless, if Mrs. Harwood recognized Eros and still resented Eve, smiling as complacently down on her as when they disputed her possession of Langley Hall. If Mrs. Harwood saw the obnoxious figures she gave no sign. Patiently she endured the manipulations of the surgeon and without complaint listened to his verdict: "It will be six weeks before you can use this hand. I have put on a permanent bandage which can remain three weeks. The ankle is only wrenched a little and will be all right to-morrow. The hand, of course, you cannot use."

"That settles it," said Lucretia, grimly. "Daniel, we'll go back to Kansas to-night."

But they did not. They took a room across the hall from Eloise and Aunt Harriet, in whose manner native courtesy struggled with memories of that unfortunate encounter at Beau Lieu.

Courtesy prevailed, however, and, as Mrs. Harwood told the neighbors on her return home, her "own sister couldn't have been kinder or more attentive."

Ready to depart, her well hand on Daniel's shoulder, the lame one in a sling, she stood uttering her farewells when a sudden thought occurred to Eloise.

"You haven't seen the Fair buildings yet!" she cried. "Come into the studio. I have a glass." She led her companion across the hall, and drew up the curtain as high as it would go. "There!" she exclaimed, triumphantly, putting the glass into Lucretia's hand, which trembled as she lifted it.

Below her lay the soft yellows, reds, and grays of many houses, tipped with chimneys and turrets, and separated here and there by narrow parks, where gayly clad children fluttered like early butterflies.

The fog had lifted, and on the left the lake blossomed into violet under the influence of the spring sunshine.

But what was this, what vision as of an unearthly city, uplifted into the mellow southern sky? It was indeed the city of her longing, the

City of Delight, the home of art, beauty, and aspiration, the dream of artist, architect, and poet, of mechanic and musician, of statesman and socialist.

Above the débris of enormous preparation and of enormous disuse, out of sheath and scaffolding, beyond the grasp of avarice and the machination of fraud, unmarred by loss of life or thwarting of hope, radiant as Aphrodite from the foam of her ocean birth, rose the White City.

Lucretia gazed with parted lips ; in spite of the unreality of its exquisite beauty, the picture was so familiar in every line.

There climbed the dome of the Administration Building; the sunlight flashed upon the figures at its base. There stretched the broad back of the Temple of Manufactures. There were the stately colonnades of the Art Gallery. She knew every one. She recognized the low roof of the Fisheries and the glass globe which topped Horticultural Hall.

"The others are there, somewhere, I suppose," she murmured, laying down the glass, which suddenly blurred.

"You ought to drive out there before you leave," said Aunt Harriet, gently.

"No, I must go right home," said Mrs. Harwood, her eyes filling. In her heart she vaguely felt that she had somehow been granted all the joy of the coveted summer in one swift glance, and that if she tried to gain more it would be less.

"Perhaps you can return," suggested Aunt Harriet.

"Bimeby," supplemented Daniel. They thought she was mourning her lost opportunity. Only Eloise, from a point of view not unlike that of her singular guest, understood her fully.

"How queer it all is!" she mused, re-entering the studio, after seeing Lucretia and Daniel carefully packed into the hansom which was to convey them to the station.

"What, dear?" inquired Aunt Harriet, mildly.

"The—the divine machine," laughed Eloise, mirthlessly. "It sometimes seems as if the Engineer had set it running and could not stop it."

She prepared to continue her work, but her brushes refused to obey her—nearly a year since she had vowed to forget Beau Lieu, and here it was thrust again upon her!

She took out Philip's last letter and read it resolutely. Faith and faithfulness were in every line. "And that is what I want," she assured herself, but herself knew better.

VIII

"Some one's taken my apern," chanted William Pleasant. It was early morning, and the only occupants of the dining-room were the boys in their trim jackets and the head-waiter stalking to and fro. "Some man has taken my apern," repeated Pleasant, "and I'm goin' to talk about his people. I see a gray goose flyin' over. His father's a thief and his mother's a thief—"

"Here's your apern," cried Caleb, thrusting it towards him, "I only borrowed it."

"You call it borrowin', but it don't come back. At my home Out West—"

"Out West!" interrupted Caleb, scornfully. "Don't have men black as you Out West. West Virginny, you mean. Some little place, a feller ridin' thoo could see every house lookin' over his shoulder."

"Where you live," rejoined Pleasant, contemptuously, "the engine get thoo the town befo' it stop whistlin'!"

"Attention, boys!" called the head-waiter, and the combatants fell into line ready to respond when the roll was called.

The dining-room of the Lake View Hotel is

one of the most attractive in Chicago, light and lofty, with many windows in the walls and stained glass in the roof. It was especially inviting that morning with the sunshine upon the tables and upon the trim figures of the waiters standing, each in his place, motionless and dumb, while the great doors swung open with impressive deliberation. Gradually the room filled. Pleasant watched anxiously : a number of men in business suits flourishing the morning paper; two or three women in their hats—if his "folks" did not appear soon he might be sent to another table; Mrs. Shipman and her daughter—the head-waiter was looking his way. Pleasant glanced out of a neighboring window until the head-waiter looked at some one else—the Colocynths, the Thompsons—ah, there they were at last! He pulled out Miss Gordon's chair with a flourish, and shoved Miss Larrabee's tenderly into place, threw down their napkins as one throws a bouquet to a prima donna, and with his elbow high in air filled their waiting glasses.

It is a source of incalculable satisfaction to an artist to have the details of his work recognized and appreciated. Pleasant was an artist ; no other waiter at the Lake View read, as did he, chops, steak, or soft-boiled egg in a patron's face, and had the order half ready before the word was given; no other waiter gauged the ripeness of the fruit to the very point of perfection, and calculated the exact moment at which to offer the finger-bowl ; no other waiter knew instinctively when it would be presumption to offer cakes and syrup, and when toast, nut brown and smoking hot, offered an irresistible appeal to a jaded stomach.

On the other hand, only Pleasant's "folks" could give to these delicate attentions their full value. Peter Glenn, who sat at the same table with his wife and two children, would stupidly repeat his order when Pleasant had it two-thirds ready, and was as blind as a bat to the arrangement of the napkins. So, although Peter was prodigal with his quarters and Eloise was forced to be sparing with hers, it was Eloise who was served like a princess while Peter was forced to be content with what was appropriate to a well-to-do American gentleman boarding at a first-rate American hotel. Moreover, there was a genuine princess in the Lake View at the same time, to say nothing of a marquis and two or three counts, who would have been glad to pay good Columbian dollars for such service. Proximity to Jackson Park and to the Illinois Central had rendered the Lake View very popular, World's Fair year, especially with World's Fair officials, who made the place gay with uniforms and decorations. Mrs. Shipman said "the atmosphere of the house was really European," and Mrs. Shipman ought to know; she had been "across" three times with her husband, who travelled for the Liebensteins (Shirt and Hose).

Mrs. Shipman said some other things which also carried weight, unfortunately for the Colocynths, with whom she had been "intimate" the winter before. Mrs. Colocynth told Aunt Harriet all about it, as they rocked a duet in the rotunda after breakfast, and Aunt Harriet came up-stairs and told her niece. It seemed that Mrs. Shipman had "made a great deal" of Corinne Colocynth, aged nine, and had given Corinne's mother several "remnants" for the child, declaring that she herself should never wear in Chicago the dresses to which they belonged. Since the quarrel, however, Mrs. Shipman had taken a malicious delight in wearing those very dresses, and Corinne was forced to return to her old clothes or appear to have been "left over" from Mrs. Shipman. Moreover, Mrs. Shipman had said that the French artist who had been doing a portrait of Corinne was only a fresco-painter. Mrs. Colocynth wished that she had known Miss Gordon did portraits. Aunt Harriet had a great deal of sympathy for Mrs. Colocynth. "And you are as white as that paper," exclaimed Eloise, pointing to the sheet upon her easel. "Why do you stay down there with those people? They always give you a headache."

"You know why I do it," cried Aunt Harriet, reproachfully. Eloise made no reply. Since their advent at the Lake View, a year and a half ago, Miss Larrabee had assumed a new and most inappropriate rôle. From being a silent partner of the modest firm, looking after the mending and offering sympathy and counsel when these were needed, she had become conspicuously active, meddling with the bills and, worse yet, attempting with transparent diplomacy to "drum up trade" for her niece. Not that trade came by drumming; the shrewd Northern women whom she undertook to beguile into buying pictures took her hyperboles for what they were worth, and when she told of the orders "flowing in" made no effort to swell the stream.

There is nothing more pathetic than the attempt to be sharp on the part of those who were born honest. Eloise, however, felt the humiliation too sorely to recognize the pathos. "There isn't one of those women who would put ten dollars into a sketch," she said, hotly.

"The princess might," suggested Aunt Harriet, with meekness.

Eloise laughed outright. "The woman with the souvenir spoons?" she inquired, mischievously.

Aunt Harriet looked puzzled.

"Italia and Græcia and Columbia," explained Eloise, humorously. "The babies named for the places they were born in."

It was Aunt Harriet's turn to look annoyed. "Eloise," she said, sorrowfully, "the change in your attitude towards life and—and things grieves me beyond measure." She went into her own room, and there was silence in the studio while Eloise painted industriously.

What Aunt Harriet had said of her was true. She had changed; but it was necessary, she told herself. The change should have come earlier, and here her hand trembled and gave the Great

God Hermes a most ungodly leer. She laid down her brush and waited till her hand should grow steady.   Her mind returned to Philip, for it was Philip whom her aunt meant under the vague allusions.   Philip was the thorn in her side, the cloud in her sky, the gravel in her porridge—all the sharper, the heavier, the more grinding because his name was not mentioned.   When Aunt Harriet paraded the darn in her stocking and last year's rose on her bonnet, when she sacrificed her own dignity and that of her niece in vain attempts to gather custom, when she pined for a little brightness in her monotonous life, she was reminding her rebellious niece that "things might be different."

If Eloise had been less kind to Philip before they left Beau Lieu neither he nor Aunt Harriet would have been so persistent; but they had planted a vigorous hope then and there, and they guarded it jealously, waiting for a return of the gentleness and dependence which had been its sunshine and dew.   They decided to let the girl have her way, to let her struggle with the world until she had enough of it.

Eloise seemed only to toughen with the struggle. She lectured and taught and painted better than ever before. She grew taller and more upright and more defiant, carrying herself like a young Diana, and, like her, hating any one who came too near.   Once she had been taken off her guard, once she had been lured out of her defences; she shut her teeth and clinched her hands whenever she thought of it, and of the limp, helpless creature she had become at that time. It was a wonder that she had not surrendered to Philip's tenderness then, or in the year which followed. She went over it dreamily: her first glimpse of Chicago; that ride up Cottage Grove Avenue in the cable-car; the heat, the dirt, the smells; the flaring advertisements of whiskies to make one drunk and of seltzers to make one sober; of dissipations to take out the color in one's cheeks and cosmetics to put it on again; the sentimental Indians before the tobacconists; the bilious bears and mangy buffaloes before the furriers; and the people—oh, the people! They were much as they are in every large city when Money and Leisure have left town, and the long spoon of August has been stirring and bringing the dregs to the surface ; but to the tired traveller there had never been, never could be, anything so horrible. Then, through the filth and the noise and the hopeless vulgarity, she had found her way to the group of white buildings in Jackson Park. And that was Chicago, too !

She had learned afterwards that these were not all; that in Chicago, as well as elsewhere, there are representatives of every class ; but the first impression lingered and influenced the development which Aunt Harriet called "the change in her attitude." It was less a change than a differentiation, a separation of her subtler, more artistic part from the part of her which met and mastered her financial problems, dealt hardly with Philip, shook off Aunt Harriet, and snubbed the uninteresting women in the house. She thought she had solved the riddle of existence; she had only avoided it. But this avoidance served to steady her hand now, as it had done many times before; she took up her brushes and restored his dignity to the Great God Hermes.

The first of May brought changes. Rents went up with a spring, and a general upheaval ensued. The usual unhappy spectacle of moving day was rendered more melancholy this year by the fact that in nearly every instance tenants were driven out to make room for World's Fair people.

Everywhere the waving flags of the processions met the top-heavy drays, into which had gone, as into the ark, a specimen of what was to be saved. Before the rising tide of dukes and duchesses, lords and ladies, ambassadors and exhibitors, this flotsam and jetsam drifted into the corners, while mayor and alderman, committee and delegates pressed gayly forward, bowing and rubbing their hands. After all, it was not Royalty or Progress whose approach they hailed, but another, graver divinity, the Pluto of our modern faith—Business. It was the triumph of Business, who is the god of the multitude; so all were submissive, even those who were sacrificed. After the upheaval had subsided, the poorest and most remote took heart again and joined in the general effort to "make a dollar," renting rooms and selling meals, all that they could spare—and more, as the death-rates for that year testify.

The Lake View was no exception to the rule. The old guests were turned out or crowded together to make room for the new ones. Eloise and Aunt Harriet gave up their bedrooms and slept in the studio, one on the couch and the other in a folding-bed which simulated a writing-desk. Eloise had an exhibit of miniatures at the Fair; this gave her a pass, and she spent much of her time at Jackson Park preparing a course of lectures to be delivered at Beau Lieu in July, for the summer university was to follow the example of the magazines and have a World's Fair "number."

IX

Three men were smoking their evening cigars in a cozy library in South Chicago: an old man, evidently the host, and two young men, his guests. It was a pleasant room, rendered more pleasant to-night by contrast with the dull drizzle without and with the chill which came up from the lake, although it was May. There were books on shelves which ran almost from floor to ceiling, leaving space only for windows and doors and for a huge portrait of Emerson set like a jewel in a shrine among the volumes; there were books on the broad inlaid table which held nothing else except a lamp with a porcelain shade ; and there were books in the corners piled high in happy confusion.

The face of the old man reflected the refinement and scholarship amid which he sat, but his dark eyes looked out appealingly under their white brows, and one suspected a sensitive tremulousness of the lips hidden by the close white beard. His frame, too, although large, was loosely put together, and had a helpless look as if the owner had never learned to utilize its strength.

Quite otherwise appeared the man who sat opposite him, alive in every part, covering every object at which he gazed, seeming larger than he actually was for the vitality which emanated from him like an atmosphere. The third member of the party was younger, smaller, slighter, with golden hair and beard and laughing gray eyes.

The two young men were telling a story, each interrupting the other, somewhat as follows:

"I was coaching Joe in Greek at the time, and had promised his mother to keep him out of mischief."

"Danger, Mark," corrected the other.

"That was the only mischief she feared, poor soul! One night there was to be a cane-rush between Freshmen and Sophomores, and she came to me and begged me to keep him in."

"A lot you did! I'd have gone if I had chosen."

"Be quiet, Joe. My gentle Freshman was so submissive that I gave him a long rope after that, and he did as he pleased. At last, one cold winter night, he surprised me with an invitation to go down to South Boston to see a prize-fight."

"You should have seen his face, uncle," broke in the young man, laughing.

"Well," continued Mark, "I remembered something I had read about the sanguinary appetites of refined women, and—"

"Come off!" interrupted Jo.

"—and being interested in psychological investigations I concluded that I would go and see the effect of this terrible scene upon my charge."

"Symonds, too—don't forget Pious John Symonds. He went along for psychological purposes, too. He was studying for the ministry, uncle."

"Our Freshman appeared promptly," continued the story-teller, "wrapped from neck to heels in a long ulster, and with his cap pulled down to meet his collar. I thought nothing of that, the night was cold. But he certainly manifested an astonishing familiarity with South Boston and with the toughs who filled the hall into which he led us—the worst crowd I ever saw."

"Nonsense!"

"Our young friend took us to a conspicuous position near the ring, and then slid off, leaving us to listen to the comments going on around us. A new star, an amateur—The Melrose Bantam—was going to try conclusions with a wiry old sinner who had already appeared, scowling defiance on all sides. By-and-by the Bantam came out to meet him—you could have knocked me over with a feather; it was my gentle, golden-haired cherub! I was dreaming out a plan to carry home the pieces and tell his mother there had been a wreck on the train as we came from Mission Sunday-school when I suddenly awoke to a realization of the fact that the cherub had won the purse by the most scientific dodging that South Boston ever saw."

"And the way he shot me into my ulster and patted me on the back, and scolded me and patted me some more—" cried the hero.

"And never let him out of my sight again until he was safely graduated," concluded Mark.

"But then he cut sticks for a beastly hole up in the Northwest, and I never got sight of him again all summer," complained Joe. "What's more, he dug back there again two years ago and has never been the same since. Sits up all night reading ghastly books on hypnotism and Black Art, and I don't know what it's all about."

Mark smiled. "Don't try to talk about it then, Joey," he said, patronizingly. "Have a light, Mr. Norton?"

The old man received the proffered courtesy, and devoted himself in silence to his cigar for some minutes. At last he said, slowly, "I've often wondered how much truth there is in all that—what they call hypnotism."

"Ask Mark," replied his nephew; "he can tell you. He's a regular wizard." Mark looked as if he did not hear.

Mr. Norton leaned forward in his chair and regarded him earnestly. "Do you think there is really anything in it?" he asked.

"I was with Charcot one day when he brought up a blue swelling on a woman's wrist and dispelled it in fifteen minutes," said Mark, "and I know a physician, a reliable man, who saw the red cross which Backman put on his servant-girl's arm every Friday for three months."

"Meanwhile this investigator was supposed to be doing business for the firm," put in Joey.

"Did the firm suffer?" inquired Mark.

"Can't say that it did, but—"

"*How* do you explain it, Mark?" exploded Mr. Norton. "How *do* you explain it?"

Mark drew in a long breath and sent it out again laden with azure smoke. "There is only one explanation possible," he said, quietly. "It is to be found in the subjection of the body to the mind, and the submission of one mind to another."

"But that seems so—horrible!" cried Mr. Norton, bringing his hand down on the table with a force which made the lamp-shade rattle. "Such a terrible power to put into the hands of one person over another."

"It is a responsibility," said Mark, gravely. "But you must remember that we are discussing a universal law, not a particular endowment. The very susceptibility of that poor woman to Charcot's influence was the indication that she shared with the operator the power of suggestion. Her submission was the other half of his control."

"That doesn't help me any," returned Mr. Norton, disconsolately. "The fact that one person is made to receive an impression and another is made to give it is just what I deplore."

"But see here," returned Mark, with a luminous smile, "What if you determine beforehand what sort of an impression you shall receive?"

"Can you do that?"

"Assuredly."

"Do you mean to say that I can fortify myself, that I can get myself ready before the operator takes hold of me, and that he cannot hurt me, cannot give me any idea which I have decided not to receive?"

"Precisely; an auto-suggestion is more powerful than any suggestion from another."

"Then susceptibility—"

"Is one's own weapon, after all," finished Mark, "which doesn't let out the operator—he is still accountable."

There was another pause, during which Joey routed a huge tiger-cat out of his nest in a corner, and pretended to make passes over him, a performance at which Dan blinked benevolently.

"Mark," continued the elder man, at length, "I believe that auto-suggestion of yours would explain a great many things, a great many phenomena of science and religion which have puzzled and bewildered us all our lives."

"Undoubtedly," returned Mark, with emphasis. "It is by auto-suggestion that the pilgrim to Loudres is healed. It is by the same law that faces take on characteristic lines according to the occupation of their owners. As Paracelsus says, 'The mind is the master, the imagination is the tool, the body is the plastic material.'"

"If you've begun on Paracelsus I'm going to bed," cried young Norton, putting down the cat, which stretched and yawned and walked solemnly back to the cushions in the corner.

"All right, Joey," replied Mark, "I'll be up presently."

"No you won't," replied Joey sceptically. "I know you. But I can't help myself. Good-night!"

After he had left the room, his uncle walked restlessly up and down, evidently stirred by some deep emotion. Finally he stopped in front of Mark and said, softly, "Mark, I want to tell you something. When I was a boy of sixteen I had what they called then a change of heart. I *experienced religion*, as they used to say. There was a new heaven and a new earth for me. I was in love and charity with all men. It was natural to be good; it was unnatural not to be good. By-and-by—" the old man sighed and shook his head. "By-and-by I got over it and became pretty much like every one else, hard and cold and selfish—and unhappy. But, Mark, I'd give all I possess to feel as I did when I had that change of heart. Do you suppose that was auto-suggestion?"

Mark looked up quickly, but it was some time before he spoke. His voice was very gentle as he said, "I suppose it was."

"Then," inquired the old man, eagerly, "Why can't I do it again? I've tried. I've read good books and been to church; but I can't get hold of it. *I can't get hold of it.*

Mark rose and laid his long right arm across the old man's shoulder. "Do you know why? Because you didn't believe half of what you read ; you believed almost nothing of what you heard."

A faint smile broke over the other's face. "I guess that is about so," he replied. "But, Mark, you can't believe to order."

"No, you can't, but you can have it out with yourself and know where you stand."

"And then?"

"Then when you are sure of something, act as if you were sure. That is what you did when you 'experienced religion.'"

"I don't quite understand."

"Perhaps I can explain by telling you my own experience. When I was in college twelve years ago (sit down, it's a long story), all this Modern Philosophy, as we call it now, was looked upon as possible but not proven. I wanted to believe it, and so I did, after a fashion. I swore by Spinoza and defended Berkeley ; I dipped into Buddhism and tried to be a Yogi ; in short, I played all sorts of tricks with myself, and then, on graduation, went up to the Beau Lieu summer school to teach Greek. Among my scholars was a young French girl, a delicate, determined little creature, who swallowed everything I said ; and I said a great deal. The queer part of it was she set to work to apply what I preached, and when I came back ten years later, having lost all my beautiful theories, she was a living example of what could be done with them. Like Una, she 'made sunshine in the shady place.' Everywhere she carried brightness and courage and a new hope. I went back to New York possessed with a determination to hunt up my old note-books and see what I could do in the way of Idealism." Mark stopped and broke into a laugh. "Of all the moonshine!" he continued, "I might as well try to live on cobwebs strung with dew. But *I knew it was there*. Fortunately I fell in with some scientific men and had an opportunity to watch their experiments. There I had the actual proof that thought can control and can be controlled. I began to see the inside working of the human engine. But I tell you what, Mr. Norton, I realized as I never had before the awful significance of the soul, its appalling opportunities for self-preservation and self-destruction. How any one can deny Freewill in the face of the unlimited chances a man has to make a mess of it beats me!"

"I don't care anything about that. I don't care anything about the will," broke in the old man, impatiently; "what I want is faith, the faith of my boyhood, the realization of the power outside of ourselves, not of ourselves, which makes for righteousness!"

"Realization?" repeated Mark. "There it is. You want one thing and you are looking for another. You want something tangible, something to satisfy your reason, and you are looking for the intangible sentiment of your boyhood. That is quite a different affair, and you won't get it again if you are anything like the rest of us."

"But the other is so cold, so cold," murmured the old man. "A mere matter of the intellect. There is no heart in it."

"What was your boyish feeling? The intellect was there, only exercising another function. You make as much of the heart as the doctors used to make of the liver. We have learned that both are the healthier for being sometimes ignored."

"And you haven't told me yet what faith is," pursued the old man, querulously.

"'Faith is the fealty of the soul to reason,'" quoted Mark.

"Now, what *do* you mean by that?"

"The adhesion of the soul to its reasonable hypotheses. You must have hypotheses, even in science, but they must be reasonable, or you have superstition instead of faith."

"But you can't govern that by the will," broke in the other impatiently. "How has the will anything to do with faith—that's what I want to know."

"To see the truth is a matter of the will, isn't it? To acknowledge it when seen is a matter of the will. To hold fast to it when acknowledged is a matter of the will, always," returned Mark.

His vehemence warmed for an instant the aged face turned wistfully towards him. Then the light faded, and the chill came back like a veil. "It wouldn't be like the other," sighed the old man. "Your faith is very different from mine, very different. Well, good-night, Mark, good-night."

"Good-night and good-bye," said Mark, holding with a close grasp the hand which was offered him.

"Good-bye?"

"Yes, we must get away early, to-morrow, before you are out of bed or ought to be out of it."

"Can't you wait for breakfast?"

"We shall get breakfast aboard the train."

"Well, well! But you will be back?"

"In September, probably. There is talk of my coming here to establish a branch of the business. Good-bye."

Long after he had heard his host climb the stairs, Mark sat thinking, in his own room, of what had been said.

"The snake is wise," he mused. "It sloughs its old skin; the bird moults and the bear sheds its fur; but a man will hug an old opinion to the exclusion of all new ones. That will not I!" and he went complacently to bed, not realizing that facility in the exercise of a virtue proclaims the ease with which it may become a vice.

X

THE idea of the Columbian Celebration developed much as the strawberry grows—by offshoots from a central purpose. There was the vigorous architectural plant at Jackson Park, there was the clump of congresses at the new Art Institute, and there were innumerable "runners" setting out from these and coming up into tufts of investigation and argument all over the city.

One of these may be designated the Hindoo tuft. It struck root in favorable soil. Philosophies and cults more or less incomprehensible had harrowed the spot for several years. A number of women and some men had openly avowed their intention of living on a higher plane than that which satisfied their neighbors. To this end, they had studied "abstraction" and "projected thought" until their heads swam ; but they needed a guide, a leader. The climate, the surroundings, and a certain practical bent induced by the open-eyed, hard-fisted struggle of their fathers rendered it extremely difficult for them to *relax*. The Hindoo, Haridass Goculdass, not only told them how it was done, but did it, and did nothing else, wrapping himself with meditation as with a garment, sublimely unconscious of material needs. He had learned by experience how easy it was to find some one to manage that part for him. In this instance, the Ross girls were the proud and happy ministrants to Goculdass's physical comfort. The Jewetts and the Laphams and plenty of others would have welcomed the opportunity had it come their way, but the Rosses inherited him from their cousins in Boston, who discovered him soon after his arrival in America.

The Rosses leaped into immediate and conspicuous popularity. Carriages with liveried footmen stood before their door all day. Invitations poured in for luncheon, dinner, and breakfast, addressed to the three women and their distinguished guest. Goculdass affected an elegant seclusion, accepted few invitations, and absolutely refused to speak in public. His methods were not those of ordinary lecturers; he issued no tickets, charged no admittance, employed no manager, and was content with voluntary contributions, which Julia Ross received for him. Permitted an unlimited generosity, his patrons paid as much as they pleased for the privilege of hearing how much wiser and holier than the Americans the Hindoos are, together with a great many wonderful and excellent teachings from the Atharva Veda and the Upanishads. It was not for himself that Haridass Goculdass received any return for his priceless lessons, but for the school in which he had been instructed, and which seemed to be as poor in a worldly sense as it was rich in spirituality.

Uncle Oliver Ross remarked upon this state of affairs to his niece Julia when she tried to explain the basis upon which Goculdass operated. "Lots of religion and no money; so they want to swap off," he commented. "That's business-like, I'm sure." His small eyes twinkled significantly.

Julia tossed her head. "Nothing of the sort, Uncle Oliver. Goculdass felt *impelled* to come to us; he felt that we were *ready* for him. He is not begging for his college, but people are so grateful for what he gives that they *insist* upon some return."

"And then they are grateful some more for being allowed to make the return. That's what I call a slick deal."

Julia pouted. "Do you want to come or not? People are perfectly *crazy* for the chance. I've been having telephone messages all the morning just *begging* to be let in."

"I suppose it's a kind of a woman show."

"Dr. Humphrey is coming and Carl Dering."

"Jim Humphrey interested in this thing?"

"Very much interested. And I stopped at the rectory and invited Mr. Sawyer.

"What does he think of it?"

"I don't know," replied Julia. "But he is coming, unless he happens to be called out of town to an old parishioner who is very low. Do come, Uncle Oliver."

"I'll see. I'll see. To-morrow at four?"

" We've said four, but people are so unpunctual, it will probably be five when we begin."

It was somewhat after five when Dr. Humphrey and Carl Dering entered the Rosses' reception-hall, a large room, open to the roof, with winding stairways in the rear leading to the second and third stories. On these stairways and in the galleries between, young girls were sitting, bright as flowers in their spring dresses. The hall below and the parlors opening on either side were reserved for their elders. There were few men among them ; Mr. Savage, alert and critical, Uncle Oliver, with his cynical eyes half shut and an amused look on his face, a half-dozen youngsters from the University, and Professor La Motte, who taught the Ross girls French, his mustaches freshly waxed and his most courtly manner on.

Julia Ross came forward, as Dr. Humphrey and Carl entered, and led them to seats commanding a view of the stairway. "He has not come down yet," she said, softly. "Mrs. Ayre, Miss Ayre, let me present Dr. Humphrey, Dr. Dering."

A blond matron and a still more blond maiden looked up with welcoming smiles, but, before they could speak, a little flutter ran through the assembly, and Julia Ross whispered, " Ah, there he is !"

A massive figure, before which the parterre of bright dresses swayed like blossoms before a breeze, came slowly down the stairs. Goculdass was attired in a red robe girt with a cord of the same color. He was tall and broad-shouldered, with a chest like that of an ox. Bovine, too, were his sleepy, dark eyes, and the calm of his smooth, handsome face suggested the repose of Apis, the representative of Osiris, after a hearty meal. Everything about him betokened comfort and personal ease. The hand on the balustrade-rail, by which he guided his deliberate descent, was brown, but shapely and well kept.

With superb self-possession, he fronted the eyes, reverent and curious, uplifted to him, and with magnificent leisure advanced to the seat prepared like a throne in the centre of the room. Here he paused, an effective instant, before he began to speak, in tones almost childlike in their sweetness and unconcern, and with an accent which went up at the end of the sentences, indescribably airy and charming.

At first his voice was low and passionless, but when he mentioned his people his throat swelled with a note like that of a trumpet, while his heavy lids were lifted to let out a glance of fire.

The Associated Charities would not have liked what he said, neither would the American Board of Foreign Missions, but so subtle was the attack upon Occidental methods that few among those that listened recognized more than an eloquent appeal for a consideration of the philosophies of the Orient.

"I hope it isn't all over Uncle Oliver's head," thought Julia Ross, and wished that Goculdass would say less about the Hindoo's imperviousness to heat and cold ; Uncle Oliver would declare he could get along with an umbrella and an over-coat. And all that eloquent description of the mystic going down to the banks of the Ganges to relinquish his hold on physical life would strike her practical kinsman as what he would call "bosh." To her relief, Goculdass began to quote from the Vedas, arching his beautiful mouth like the roof of a temple, sending the mysterious words ringing through the house.

"You will ask," continued the speaker, resuming his ordinary tone, "Is this practical? What can we get out of it for our life? But what is your life? It is an opportunity for the animal to become a god. What is more practical than a faith that will assist man to do this, to recognize himself as divine?

"There is a story of a maiden who discovered the outline of herself in a muddy pool. She saw it again afterwards, more distinctly, in running water. Again she saw her image more plainly reflected in polished metal. At last she saw herself in a mirror. So it is with man. He must come to know himself. It is not possible all at once. We have various religions for the different degrees of man's comprehension. All are good in their way, but they only prepare for another development. The *Devas*, the Bright Ones, of one period become the devils of another.

"We are continually outgrowing our beliefs,

because we are continually developing into something higher. It is nonsense to say that religion came from heaven. Religion is the outgrowth of human consciousness. It is from within. Man looks out and up at first, but finally returns to himself. He has been praying to himself, all the time. He discovers that the god is within, not outside nor above. Then he says, 'I am He! I am He!'"

The most delightful feature of all right-minded courtship is the assurance of the beloved by the lover that she is more than human. The maturer women present had experienced this; the younger women had at least imagined it; but none of them had been told that she was divine, and by one who seemed to have no doubt of the truth of what he said. It was incense in their nostrils and meat-and-drink offerings in their mouths. They tasted for the moment the joys of Olympus, which are but human joys, after all.

Again he paused and began to chant in that strange, sweet monotone which thrilled the sensitive women before him like a draught of wine. Then back again to his rambling discourse: "My old master used to say, 'On a sultry summer evening we sit and fan ourselves. By-and-by a breeze comes along and we throw away the fan. So books and churches and sects and denominations serve to help us until we come to the *personal realization* of God. Then away they go!"

Julia Ross glanced uneasily towards Mr. Sawyer, but that exponent of transitory institutions gave no sign of discomposure.

"If you are Aryans, you are the renegades, not I," pursued Haridass Goculdass authoritatively. "Christianity was forced on the Anglo-Saxons at the point of the sword. Charlemagne was converted by his wife, and set out to convert the world. On the banks of the Rhine it was, 'Heads off with those who resist! Dump the rest in the water! They come up baptized Christians!'" Professor La Motte, the old cynic, was smiling broadly. The university boys were evidently impressed.

"I can't help it if they're not all pleased," said Julia to herself; but her thoughts wandered during the remainder of the "talk," and were only recalled by the sudden consciousness that Haridass Goculdass's musical voice had ceased, and her sister Maud was saying softly, "These meetings never seem complete without the Sanscrit benediction."

Then every one stood, while Goculdass repeated the ancient words and translated them: "Peace on earth! Peace in the creatures of the earth! Peace in man! Peace in heaven! Peace in the Lord!"

"Wasn't it lovely?" inquired Miss Ayer of Carl Dering, as every one turned to his or her neighbor to seek or express an opinion.

"It was all very interesting," replied Carl, "the audience as well as the speaker."

"How sympathetic they were!" cried the girl. "I think Goculdass must have felt their sympathy; he was so frank, so outspoken—did you notice, mamma?"

Mrs. Ayer turned with tears in her eyes. "It was wonderful," she murmured. "I could follow such a leader to the end of the world."

Her emotion disturbed Carl; he attempted to divert her by a change of theme. "I think, Mrs. Ayer," he began, cheerfully, "that I know a relative of yours, Dick Ayre; I met him at the Athletic Club. He is a big, broad-shouldered fellow, plays a capital game of tennis."

"He is my son," replied Mrs. Ayre, gravely. "He is still living for the physical. I hope he may get some light as he goes along."

Carl looked and felt uncomfortable. He seemed somehow to be sitting in judgment on Dick Ayre in the latter's absence and against his own will. He wondered what could have become of Humphrey, and finally spied him across the room talking with a small, graceful woman, who seemed very much interested in what he had to say.

"Do you know Mademoiselle Duvray?" asked Miss Ayre, whose eyes had followed his.

"Is that she with Dr. Humphrey? No, I have not had the pleasure."

"It would be a pleasure," returned Miss Ayre, warmly. "She is the dearest woman in the world."

"Have you known her long?"

"I have studied with her all winter. You should hear her talk about these things!"

"A sort of Hypatia?"

"Hypatia was—*crude* beside her."

Once started on the subject of Mademoiselle Duvray, Miss Ayre forgot time, place, everything but the subject in hand. Her mother moved away. People were leaving. Dr. Humphrey had started to cross the room, but was stopped half-way by Uncle Oliver, who was spoiling for a fight. Haridass Goculdass had been surrounded by a bevy of women who beset him with all sorts of questions. Had he ever seen a Mahatma? Could he levitate? What was the knob for, on an Indian bracelet which its owner bought at the Fair? Goculdass seemed to be aware that the questions were merely excuses for an interview, and answered them carelessly; the godlike calm which had distinguished his entrance again settled down upon him, rendering him impervious even to the admiration of his disciples.

"What do you think of him?" asked Carl, as he and Humphrey left the Rosses' door.

"I'd like to secrete some of his passive energy," laughed Humphrey, "to tide me over that tracheotomy case to-morrow."

"How do you suppose he does it?"

"Born so, and then concentrated what he had. I've been listening to some entertaining stories about him."

"What did she say about him?" asked Carl.

"Oh, all sorts of things," replied the other, throwing off the inquisitive youngster with an assumption of indifference.

Sensitive Carl shut up like a mimosa, and asked no more questions.

XI

MADEMOISELLE DUVRAY'S studio was in the business portion of the city, convenient for the women who dropped in before or after their shopping, but her "home," as she called it, was in the most fashionable hotel of the most fashionable quarter. She had been in Chicago only two years, and had already established herself as a power there. Her advent had been timely; she came in with the preparations for the Fair, and owed her success, in a large measure, to her familiarity with the foreign words and ways which then became prominent. As Americans, there is little of importance which we do not know; as cosmopolitans, we are uncertain on some points which have not been brought to our notice — the use of titles is one. We have a mere handful of our own, and are in the habit of throwing them carelessly about, hitting a farmer with "Squire" and a trader with "Colonel," and making our political leaders "Honorable" in spite of themselves. The accurate European aim which never sends a missile of this sort at the wrong head has not been practised here; so, when a woman appeared as skilful with these significant syllables as a juggler with his balls, never letting one go astray, she found a profession ready-made for her. Just then she needed encouragement. The visit to Beau Lieu had been an impulsive one, born of a desire to seek out the spot where from a dreaming girl she had become a woman with a purpose. It was a part of Marguerite's philosophy to respect such desires. Disappointing as the experience had been, she still insisted that it was to teach her something—self-reliance, if no more. If one is bound to believe, there are no obstacles, there is nothing which cannot be explained in accordance with one's belief.

The principal danger with those who are on the lookout for lessons to learn, is that they are inclined to learn too much. There was an unlimited opportunity for Marguerite to learn self-reliance, and she learned it, unlimitedly.

Her pupils and friends learned the obverse of the lesson, depending utterly and entirely upon their teacher and guide. This was not always best for them; but she was so sympathetic, so strong, so full of resource, holding fast to her Idealism with one hand while with the other she accumulated worldly wisdom as fast as the need came, that her belief in herself and theirs in her were not to be wondered at. She had expected something quite different, a " post in some high, lonely tower," a period of seclusion, a solitary preparation for the work which she had to do ; she planned it all out the night she left Beau Lieu, lying wide-awake among the pillows, while her cousin and companion, Mrs. Burnham, plunged gayly into slumber on the hither side of a snore.

Hardly had she reached Chicago, however, before she found herself a committee of the committees, a minister of the ministers, an authority in matters of decorum and etiquette. If she met her fate half-way, it was only in deference to the self-reliance she meant to learn.

The mission was a pleasant one, and led to others of a more serious character. From social problems, she passed to the review of family skeletons and the examination of family sores, and as many of the former were of papier-maché, and many of the latter but skin-deep, she found few instances beyond the reach of her philosophy.

She sat by the bow-window the day after Haridass Goculdass's lecture, pondering what she had heard. Much that he had said was familiar to her, but she had never carried the idea of self-development so far. It was an exhilarating thought that in herself she could find the ultimate truth, the unlimited power. "I am He! I am He! I am He!" The exultant words throbbed through her brain, and her sympathetic pulses answered like an echo. So absorbed was she in her reverie that a rap at the door brought a positive shock. A note and a card were handed her. She broke the seal of the first and read hurriedly, a smile playing about her lips. "Wait!" she said to the boy, and, turning to her davenport, wrote a few words on a card, hastily enclosing it in an envelope and addressing it. "See that this goes *immediately!*" she ordered. The boy lingered.

"The other?" he asked, respectfully.

"Oh, yes, tell the young lady she may come up."

Louise Ayre was not slow in making her appearance. She came in flushed and elated.

"Your eyes are as blue as the sky, my dear," said Marguerite, holding out both hands.

Louise received them timidly. She stood greatly in awe of the small woman before her; but the importance of her errand gave her confidence.

"I have something to tell you," she began.

"I am sure of that," cried Marguerite, with her delicious little laugh. She led the girl to a seat on the sofa and released her hands with a gentle pressure, herself assuming an attentive attitude.

"I have just had a long talk with Dr. Dering," pursued Louise, "about 'advanced thought' and all those things. Of course, I could give him only a *hint* of what you give us, and he is just *wild* to see you. He says he has felt for *a long time* the limitations of his profession, and he *feels sure* that the question of mental thera—thera—"

"Therapeutics," finished Marguerite, encouragingly.

"Mental therapeutics is the *coming question.*"

Louise paused and drew a long breath.

"I would do anything," said Marguerite, earnestly, "to get a doctor out of his profession. It is missionary work. I would not tell every one, but I will tell you ; you have no idea how many doctors are thinking of those things. When your card was brought to me, a note came with it from a prominent physician whom you know, asking for an interview."

Louise drew another long breath, and the two women gazed at each other, fixedly, as Clotho and Lachesis might gaze over the thread they manipulated.

"Will you see Dr. Dering?" inquired Louise, at length.

"Of course," replied Marguerite. "Bring him to me."

"He is down-stairs now," exclaimed Louise, springing to her feet. "He came over with me."

"Bring him right up. Stay, I will ring for a boy."

"Perhaps I had better go down and speak to him."

"Very well."

Louise flew down the long corridor, caught the elevator on a downward trip, and in an incredibly short time found Carl sitting tranquilly in the reception-room, laughing over the latest number of *Life*. He glanced up with the smile still overspreading his boyish face. "There are some awfully good things in *Life*," he said, holding out the paper. "Look at this." But Louise put it aside as a mother puts aside her child's playthings on Sunday morning.

"By-and-by," she said, firmly. "Mademoiselle Duvray will see you now."

"Now?" repeated Carl, blushing.

"Yes, now. It is very kind of her, she is so full of engagements, but we are lucky enough to catch her at a moment when there is no one here. Come."

Carl went wonderingly down the hall, in the wake of Louise's tall figure. While they waited at the elevator, Louise leaned towards him confidentially. "I don't know as I ought to tell you," she whispered, "but it may encourage you to know that you are not the only physician who is looking into these things. There is another, of *high standing in Chicago*, coming to see her this afternoon."

Carl straightened himself and assumed his professional bearing, dignified yet affable. Louise glanced approvingly at him; he seemed several years older than the boy whom she had caught laughing over the pictures in *Life*.

Why are the young so ashamed of youth, and the old so proud of any vestige of it, retained in spite of themselves? There was an air of precocity about Marguerite herself, as she stood in her doorway awaiting them, but the Sphinx of Egypt, with the riddle of the centuries hidden away under her cap, was not more wise and inscrutable. She received Carl in a manner befitting the importance he had hoped to grow to in a decade or so, and encouraged him, as none ever had before, to utter his opinions freely; indeed, the flattering attention she gave him, and the gracious nod with which she responded at every pause, led him to put forth other opinions of whose existence he had not dreamed. He discovered that he had been searching blindly all his life for these inspiring truths, that he had been filled with vague cravings which nothing would satisfy, that the opportunities for usefulness in his profession seemed poor and meagre. Mademoiselle Duvray, on her part, assured him that he had come to the right place, she could put him in touch with those who would recognize his worth.

"You have a great future before you," she said, earnestly. "We need men like you, men of intellect and education, men who are practical as well as thoughtful."

The trio sat hushed and silent after these words, feeling the importance of the moment; then Mademoiselle Duvray rose and said in the tone with which she dismissed her classes, "I am sorry to send you away, but I have an engagement. You will come again?" The invitation was made a request. Carl promised and went blindly down the hall after Louise, his head buzzing with the swarm of new ideas which had been let loose there.

"Well," ejaculated Louise, turning from ringing the elevator bell, "isn't she lovely?"

"Yes, she is," granted Carl.

"I never saw her so cordial to any one as she is to you," continued the girl.

The boy smiled complacently.

In the lower hall they caught a glimpse of a man entering the reception-room. "It's Humphrey!" ejaculated Carl. "I didn't know he had a patient here. It must be a new one."

"I don't believe," said Louise, sagely, "that I would say anything to him about this."

"I don't mean to," rejoined Carl, confidentially. Their three hours together had put them on a basis of thorough good-fellowship. They felt as if they had been friends for years.

XII

Tнe intimacy between Carl Dering and Louise Ayer ripened at an astonishing rate. When a young woman is assisting a young man in the development of his soul, she may be permitted many things which might be considered imprudent and forward under other circumstances.

She may write him little notes inviting him to take her walking in order that they may talk without interruption; she may send him books with passages marked for his perusal; she may encourage him to tell her his hopes and ambitions and desires, and she may think of him continually because thought itself is helpful. Mademoiselle Duvray also invited Carl to walk with her, and held long, confidential interviews with him, and helped him by her thought. He seemed lifted in mid-air by these sympathetic spirits whose breadth of pinion offset his own lack of wing-power. The world of foolish boys and girls, of careless men and women, lay far below his feet, and the world of thought spread far before him, inviting him on.

After a while he began to try some of the practices of this thought-world on his patients—he

7

had been taking Dr. Humphrey's overflow for a year—but discovered with some dismay that Physic and Metaphysic do not always make the most harmonious of yoke-fellows. Especially was this true in the case of old Mrs. Tremaine, who bowed down before the Moloch of her maladies and offered whatever was most costly and most dear. When she started on a long description of the symptoms in which Moloch revealed himself, the disciple of another faith made light of these revelations, and sought to divert her from their influence. She turned upon him a look of withering scorn. "Young man," she said, her indignation vibrating in her capstrings and in the feather on her bonnet, "If you don't want to listen to what I have to say, I will find a doctor who *does*."

Carl, being, as it were, but a short distance from shore, put back in a hurry until the tempest was over, and then meekly offered her the biggest and blackest pills he had. When she had departed, still agitated but victorious, he sat down in the office chair and meditated. It had always seemed a part of the business of his profession to sacrifice to Moloch or to any other divinity which it might suit the whims of his clients to set up; the ceremony was really a part of the cure; but in the gospel according to Mademoiselle Duvray such practices were condemned. They were said to bring ruin on those who indulged in them.

Here the door opened softly, and pretty Grace Merriam entered. Her lovely eyes were dim, her cheeks had lost their roundness. "Oh, Dr. Dering," she murmured, sinking into a chair, "I am almost dead. Between the Fair and company and papa's being so blue about business, I am completely exhausted and so discouraged."

The pretty eyes filled with tears.

"I'll try it on her," thought Carl. He took her gently by the hand and began to talk of a picture at the art gallery which he knew she would like, looking fixedly at her and saying mentally, "Peace! Peace!"

Grace began to revive, and withdrew her hand, but the young metaphysician kept steadily on with his soothing words, looking straight into her eyes. Presently the color came to her cheeks. "I—I think I must go," she said, bashfully. "I feel much better, thank you. Perhaps all I needed was to sit here quietly for a few minutes."

Carl accompanied her to the door and watched her down the hall, following her with an absorbed gaze until she waved him farewell and disappeared around a corner; then he returned with a light step. Swinging his arms jubilantly to and fro, he whispered, "By Jove! I'm getting on to it! How that girl changed! The way the color came into her face was simply wonderful!"

He glanced at the office clock; only four, but he was quite sure that no one would be in; he must go and tell Mademoiselle Duvray what he had done. He caught up his cap and rushed excitedly over to The Cynthia. Mademoiselle was at home, and received him as a priestess might receive a neophyte.

"I knew the first time I met you that you were an advanced soul," she said with feeling. "I never saw any one so ready for this line of thought. But now we must not hold you back. You are ready for the next step; you must have regular instruction. I must pass you on to others who can teach you more than I."

Carl tried to recall what he had read of tests and trials by the Four Elements and initiations; but he was "bound to see the thing through," he told himself.

"I am thinking where I shall take you," she mused. "I have a friend in the Enterprise who gives lessons; I will take you to him."

"Now?" inquired Carl.

"Yes, if you are ready."

"Of course," he replied, bravely.

Without another word, she put on her hat and conducted him to the place. It was on the top floor of the building, in a corner overlooking the bay—a large room with three windows. There were bookcases in it, a piano, and a reading-desk, and at one side a pile of folding chairs. A tiny, blond woman, with a white, determined face, met them. Mademoiselle Duvray addressed her as Mrs. Symonds, and inquired for "The Doctor."

"He is busy just now," said Mrs. Symonds, glancing towards a screen which shut off one corner of the room. "Come in here." She disclosed a door behind another screen, and led them through it into a small room arranged like a parlor.

"This is Dr. Dering, of whom I spoke," explained Carl's chaperone. "He has been making remarkable progress by himself. He had an 'instantaneous demonstration' this afternoon, but he feels that he needs guidance. I thought I had better bring him to Dr. Symonds."

Mrs. Symonds sat with her small head on one side like a meditative canary, scrutinizing Carl.

"I see; quite right," she responded. "Dr. Symonds has a patient now, but I can make an engagement for to-morrow. The young man can begin his lessons then." She took up a note-book and turned to the page which bore the date of the following day.

"Come at three to-morrow," she said, conclusively. "That will be your hour for the present."

"Thank you," said Carl, politely. Three o'clock was office hour. He wished that he might see more of the working of this new machine before he relinquished his hold on the old one. He would have given all he had in his pockets for a glance behind the screen, where undoubtedly Dr. Symonds and his patient were even now sitting together. Dr. Symonds's business-like little wife had darted away, and now returned with a small package. "Put this in your pocket," she directed, and Carl obeyed. Then she let them out through another door into the hall with a cheerful, "Good-bye until to-morrow."

"I do not think you will ever regret the step you have taken," said Marguerite, kindly.

The trustfulness with which Carl had followed her would have touched a heart more secure than hers in the righteousness of its methods. "It is magnificent mental training, even if you don't do anything in particular with it," she continued.

Carl became conscious of a feeling of disappointment. Were people as uncertain on this plane of thought as they were on the other? She read his face—it was not a difficult face to read—and quickly changed her manner, calling his attention to the carriage and gait of those they met, and giving him hints how to read the manifestations of the unseen in the seen. At the door of The Cynthia she insisted upon bringing him in with her. "We will have dinner *à deux* in my parlor," she said. "Mrs. Burnham is away for the night."

What a dinner it was, ordered with a prescience of what he would like, served in the daintiest manner possible, and sauced with clever stories and amusing descriptions of places and people! She was wise and witty, grave and tender, by turns. Carl watched and listened and worshipped. The air was full of the incense steaming up from the pure censer of his boyish soul.

At half-past eight she dismissed him, rather suddenly, he thought, and before he left her door a card was brought to her. Ah, well, one could not expect to keep a woman like that to one's self. It was an inestimable favor to have had her so long—four whole blessed hours.

A hand was laid somewhat heavily on his shoulder. "Hullo, Carl!" cried a familiar voice. "What are you doing here?" It was Humphrey.

"What are *you* doing?" demanded the younger man, rendered self-confident by the delicate flattery of Mademoiselle Duvray's attention.

"I don't know as it is anything to you what I am doing," returned Humphrey, flushing.

"I might say the same," retorted Carl, jauntily.

He passed on, uneasy in spite of his bravado. The afternoon had been trying to his nerves; the interviews with Mrs. Tremaine and Grace Merriam, and the talk with Mrs. Symonds, had told upon his endurance. The bewildering sweetness of the tête-à-tête with Mademoiselle Duvray had an effect no less exhausting than it was stimulating.

Underneath all was the uneasy consciousness that he was undertaking something which his chief would disapprove.

But Humphrey had no right to hinder and oppose him in a thing of this sort—it was a personal matter, anyway. To be sure, if he gave up the afternoon office hour, he would have to tell Humphrey. This was a scientific investigation, though, and Humphrey himself was ready to sacrifice anything "in the interests of science." He had said so, many times, and he had said of this same psychical research that "there was something in it." Who knew but that Carl himself might be on the verge of some tremendous discovery? Mademoiselle Duvray was a woman of experience, and she had said that he had a great future before him, that he was peculiarly fitted for just such work as this. He felt the truth of the words. There was something within him which responded to these mysterious influences as to a personal appeal.

He hurried back to the office and turned on the electric light to examine the package which Mrs. Symonds had given him. Four small paper books and half a dozen thin blue circulars slipped out when he untied the bundle. The books were variously named "Faith," "Hope," "Charity," and "The Miracles."

Carl's face fell. "Sermons, as I'm alive," he ejaculated. "It's nothing but some sort of a religious business." Then he took up the circulars. They proclaimed, in no uncertain terms, that Dr. Symonds taught at the rate of fifty dollars a term, and healed at the rate of five dollars a "treatment."

"Fifty dollars, by Jupiter!" exclaimed the disappointed pupil. "If they think I am going to pay fifty dollars for a lot of Sunday-school lessons they are awfully mistaken."

But, when three o'clock of the following afternoon arrived, an irresistible desire pulled him to the Enterprise. "I may as well see what he has to say for himself," he decided.

A tall, slight man, with dark side whiskers, was turning down the passage which led to Dr. Symonds's office when Carl left the elevator.

"It can't be—by Jove, it *is* Humphrey! and he is going to that place. I'll hide in this corner until he comes out."

It was not long before Humphrey appeared with a roll of papers. Carl waited until he had entered the elevator, then advanced briskly.

"He's getting it on the sly without saying a word to me," he thought, with a swelling heart. "I'll show him two can play at that game." He entered Dr. Symonds's office and found him waiting.

XIII

In spite of Carl's resolution to keep his movements from the knowledge of his colleague, he longed to talk things over with him the very next morning. He sat and watched the back of Humphrey's head through the open door of the inner office, wishing that some one would come in and make him turn around ; but no one came in, and Humphrey did not turn around till noon. Then he told Carl abruptly that he himself was going off for the remainder of the day, adding, "You may close the office and go, too, if you choose."

Carl welcomed the opportunity. He was not due at Dr. Symonds's until the next day. Meanwhile, he felt that he must confide in some one. He telephoned to the Lake View for Eloise to accompany him to Jackson Park. It would be better, on the whole, to open his heart to her, and he would be saved from breaking his half-promise to Louise Ayer. But Eloise was almost as difficult to reach as Humphrey himself. She was in a freakish, unreasonable mood, and avoided serious conversation. Then, when he took refuge in his own thoughts, she reproached him for his inattention.

"I don't know what has come over you," she said, petulantly. "You go mooning around as if you had lost your wits. I don't believe you know where you are at this minute."

"We are on a bench under a tree on the Wooded Island," returned Carl, tranquilly.

"And you haven't listened to a word I've been saying," pursued the girl.

"Yes, I have. You were talking about the Congress. You told how Millicent Glenn stood up in a chair and called out, 'I'm not going to clap that woman. I didn't hear a single word she said.'"

"You didn't look as if you were listening," returned Eloise, only half mollified. "I do enjoy talking to a wooden image."

"What do you want me to do?"

"Look interested, if you don't feel so."

"All right, go on; what else did you see at the Congress?"

"Women who want Universal Peace escorted to the platform by policemen; another who wants an inconspicuous dress arrayed in yellow gaiters and a sky-blue tunic; a man who preaches spiritual development looking as if he would enjoy a fifteen-course dinner and an American cigar more than all his theories."

Carl became wide awake at once. "What man do you mean?"

"That Hindoo with an unpronounceable name."

"Haridass Goculdass?"

"Yes; what do you know about him?"

"I heard him speak at the Rosses', the other day, and I tell *you*, Eloise, he's *great!*"

"How is he great?" asked Eloise, with her delicate nose in the air.

"He has more magnetism than any one I ever saw; and he is logical, too. You ought to have heard him lay out us Americans for our scramble after the Almighty Dollar."

"Did he pass the hat, then?" inquired the cynical Eloise.

"No, he didn't; he doesn't even charge admittance to his lectures; he doesn't think of such things. And you ought to have seen his audience! He had those people right in his hand."

"I don't doubt it," replied Eloise, mockingly. "They are always right in somebody's hand."

"I don't know what is the matter with you," retorted her cousin, warmly. "You have changed ever since that summer at Beau Lieu, and you keep growing harder and harder — no, I don't mean that," as she turned a pair of reproachful hazel eyes upon him, "but you're not the girl you used to be."

"I hope not," she answered, positively, adding with sudden gentleness, "I am afraid I haven't much faith; I have only works. Do you suppose works without faith are dead as well as faith without works? Does each need the other to keep it alive?"

"But you are so mistaken about these people," continued Carl, disregarding her confession. "You think they are just silly, fashionable women, but they are not; they are earnest, lovely, sincere—"

"I teach some of them," said Eloise, shortly.

"Yes, and you won't let any of them show her best. I've heard them complain of your reserve, and of how impossible it is to break through it."

"If they did succeed in breaking through it, that would be the last of me," said Eloise, fiercely.

"I wish you could see Mademoiselle Duvray," persisted Carl. "You couldn't help believing in her."

"I know all about Mademoiselle Duvray," replied Eloise, stiffly. "She was at Beau Lieu the first summer I was there."

"Did you ever talk with her?"

"No, I never did. I could if I had chosen."

"Well, then, how could you know about her?"

"It was enough to see the girls dangling after her wherever she went. I hate that sort of woman."

Carl stared, but felt quite sure that Eloise only needed to know the facts in order to be convinced, and, man-like, was ready to present them to her.

"She is immensely popular, abroad as well as here. They say she is entertained by the nobility over there."

"Oh yes; I have heard the whole story many times," returned Eloise, irritably. "She teaches 'court etiquette,' and there is no place in America where there is such a demand for 'court etiquette' as in Chicago. People here are not satisfied with being well-bred men and women ; they must assume the air and gait of lords and ladies, with gorgeous clothes, elegant carriages, and lackeys in livery. Of course Mademoiselle Duvray is 'immensely popular !'"

Carl blushed to the roots of his hair. He hastened to change the subject. "Dr. Humphrey had a letter from Mrs. Harwood the other day," he began, courteously. "She says she is quite well, and is going to make up for not going to the Fair by hearing Miss Gordon lecture at Beau Lieu."

"Really ?"

"Yes, really. Eloise, you are lots prettier when you smile."

"I wonder how she is going to get to Beau Lieu !"

"Going to take boarders."

"That will be just the place for Mrs. Glenn and the children ; they want to go. Oh, I shall be glad to get away !"

"Queer how we can relish getting back into a broil after being out of it," laughed Carl.

"It all depends upon the sequence," returned Eloise, quickly. "After the fire, the frying-pan becomes actually endurable. Carl, I'm cross !"

"No, you're not," cried Carl, chivalrously. "Everything gets to be a bore when you're tired, even the Fair."

Many felt what Carl expressed. The early

glory of the Fair had tarnished, the bugles had a labored sound, and the tired men and women on the coaches played their hilarious parts with an effort. The opening gush of hospitality with which Chicago welcomed her guests had yielded to a fear that "the thing was not going to pay, after all." The dukes and duchesses, and the lords and ladies were leaving, driven before the first hot wave. In their places came Sunday-school children bringing their own luncheon, and farmer-folk, spending as little as possible over and above mere necessities. The action of the great drama certainly lagged. The two cousins wandered dispiritedly about, and started for the hotel while the sun was yet some distance from the horizon. Outside the gates the pretentious brass bands had ceased to play, and in their stead the mechanical piano blossomed into insistent chords and interminable trills on every corner, ripening into an explosive bang which seemed to say, " On time, you see ! We get there, you bet !" It was the very slang of music, the spirit of "hustle" in a sound.

"Let's get out of this !" exclaimed Carl, taking Eloise by the arm. They almost ran until they were beyond reach of the racket, and pulled up in front of the hotel, quite out of breath.

"Come in to dinner, Carl," said Eloise, hospitably.

"Can't do it, thank you," and he turned away. Then she saw the wistful look upon his face.

"Carl!" she called after him. He returned with a smile. "Is there anything the matter—a love affair, or a dun?"

"Neither, thank you." He lifted his hat, still smiling, and then walked away again.

"I am sure there was something," mused Eloise. "What can it be?"

Aunt Harriet was awaiting her impatiently in the studio. "My dear," she said, impressively, following Eloise into her bedroom, "the house is filling with the most extraordinary people. All the nice people are going away. Mrs. Glenn told me this afternoon that she should keep her room hereafter except at meal-time."

"I suppose so," answered Eloise, lifting her face, dripping and rosy, from the wash-bowl.

"Mrs. Shipman says they have put a man at their table who eats with his knife."

"Shocking!" cried Eloise, smoothing her hair before the glass. "Come on, dear."

She found the rotunda gay and noisy with the new guests, to whom the sojourn at the hotel seemed an important part of the visit to the Fair.

Something unusual seemed going on at the other end of the room. Eloise stood on tiptoe to see what it was, then pulled Aunt Harriet by the sleeve, whispering, "Look, look! the Glenn children!" Down the rotunda, between the rows of men, women, and children, who parted to let them pass, marched the young Glenns, nine-year-old

Milton bearing a pole, on which was tacked a placard announcing, "Peep Snow, One Sent," while golden-haired Millicent, confidently following the lead of her older brother, carried proudly the "Show," a cigar-box with a picture inside, and a calico curtain across the front. William Pleasant had arranged it for her. Having made the round of the rotunda, they set up business in the reading-room, planting the standard in the painted tub of a huge palm.

Aunt Harriet hurried to the rescue of respectability. "My dears, my dears," she murmured, warningly, "you must go right up-stairs to your mother."

"Who said so?" asked Milton, not disrespectfully, but for information.

"I say so," replied Aunt Harriet, authoritatively.

"I don't see why," demanded Milton, while Millicent hid behind the palm and awaited developments.

"May I look in?" inquired Eloise, strategically. "Here is my penny. Oh, I have a much prettier picture up-stairs. Come with me and I'll give it to you."

"That will do for to-morrow," replied the showman, promptly, "after they've seen this."

"*Milton Howard Glenn!*" broke in an agitated voice; "you and Millicent go right up to my room!" Poor Mrs. Glenn! she was red with shame and vexation.

"Don't mind," whispered Eloise; "every one will understand."

"Another dream of commercial prosperity gone," put in a friendly voice; it was Philip More's. "I thought I would run up and help you get ready for Beau Lieu," he explained. "How do you do, Mrs. Glenn. Don't punish the youngsters; it is too good a joke." He stood and talked with the three women while the culprits escaped. "He's a brick, that feller," said Milton to his confederate, as they made off with the Show.

"You're right," lisped Millicent. "I'll be his friend jus' as long's I live."

Tᴜᴇ September sun reddened the tops of the trees and the clustering roofs below the window where Mrs. Glenn sat with her sewing. Every now and then Milton or Millicent ran in from the hall where they were playing to ask what time it was.

"I'll let you know in season, so that you can be down there," said their mother. "Come in, Mrs. Shipman," as that lady appeared in the doorway. "Take this chair; it is more comfortable."

"I'd rather sit by the window," replied the visitor, leaning forward to look out and down. "My, but you're high up, here."

"I like to be above the noise," said Mrs. Glenn. "No, Milton; I told you I would let you know when it was time."

Milton collided with Millicent, who was close behind him. "She'll let us know!" he shouted, and away they went.

"Are you expecting company?" inquired Mrs. Shipman.

"Miss Gordon and her aunt return this afternoon," replied Mrs. Glenn. "My children are very fond of Miss Gordon."

Mrs. Shipman's eyes sparkled. "Is Miss Gordon's *fiancé* with them?" she inquired.

"Miss Gordon's *fiancé*?" Mrs. Glenn repeated, warily.

"Mr. More. I hear they're engaged. Of course, we've been expecting it."

"I suppose he is with them," granted Mrs. Glenn.

"I hear he's very wealthy, and has no near relations," buzzed the visitor. "She's mighty lucky. My niece, who was married the other day, got a moneyed man, but there are a thousand, more or less, to hang on him and take it all. Miss Larrabee will be right on tiptoe."

There was a pause, during which both women scanned the street.

"The train's late," vouchsafed Mrs. Shipman. "She may not be here for an hour yet."

"God forbid!" ejaculated Mrs. Glenn within herself, not outwardly. Outwardly she smiled and said, "That is very pretty lace you are crocheting!"

"Isn't it! I got the pattern from Miss Brown. Were you down in the parlor when she was reciting, the other evening? You ought to have been there. I thought I should die. She recited one of those swearing Bret Harte things, and a speech by a drunken orator. They were altogether *too good*. That Englishwoman with the four girls took them out in the midst of the first piece, and then Mrs. Colocynth followed with Corinne. The

Princess and I sat it out, though. The Princess thought it was great fun."

"She seems very happy here," said Mrs. Glenn, with another glance out the window.

"She is. She enjoys everything except the hops. She goes down in all her finery, and not a man asks her to dance. She said to me the other evening, 'I will spik to my Poll (his name is Paul), and he will spik to the landlord, to get me partners. My Poll pays as much as any one. I will not sit here like a what-do-you-say—*wall-flower*.'"

Another pause ensued, broken by Mrs. Glenn, who inquired, "How is Mrs. Johnson—do you know?"

"Better," replied Mrs. Shipman, promptly. "She's trying Mental Science now, and thinks she is getting help. She sleeps and eats, and is going to sit up in a few days. By-the-way, they say that young Dr. Dering, Miss Larrabee's nephew, the one that used to come to dinner Sunday nights, has gone into Mental Science head over heels—did *you* hear anything about it?"

"I heard something," replied Mrs. Glenn, guardedly, "but I don't know how true it is."

"I heard that he tried to put old Mrs. Tremaine to sleep, and the old lady opened on him. They say he practises on all the girls, and each one thought he was in love with her until they got together and compared notes. But that was along back some weeks ago, before he left Dr. Humphrey's office."

"Has he left Dr. Humphrey?" cried Mrs. Glenn, completely off her guard.

"Didn't you know *that?*" exclaimed Mrs. Shipman, triumphantly. "That's old. He and Dr. Humphrey had a tremendous row, and Dr. Humphrey ordered him to leave. They've both of them got quick tempers. Dr. Humphrey's taken in a son of old Dr. Jones in Dering's place. I don't know what Dering's going to do. Perhaps he'll start out as a 'healer' himself. They make a lot of money. I was in a house in this city, Monday, when one thousand dollars walked out to a healer, and my own sister paid four hundred. There they are now. Yes, there's Mr. More. He helps Miss Larrabee out as if she was made of china."

"Run, children, the carriage is here," interrupted Mrs. Glenn, opening the door.

"Oh, mamma!—you—promised—" floated back from the hall. "Quick, elevator, down!"

"Miss Gordon looks well. Being engaged agrees with her," pursued the visitor, enjoying to the full the prospect for which she had come.

"I am *so sorry* about the children," pouted Mrs. Glenn.

"Do you know when they are going to be married?" continued the relentless inquisitor. "I presumed you might have heard. Miss Larrabee's so confidential, you probably will hear all about it."

"He's come! He's come!" sounded jubilantly

from the hall. The door flew open, revealing Philip with Milton and Millicent clinging each to an arm.

"I am afraid they are dreadful bores," apologized their mother. "Mr. More, Mrs. Shipman," and Mrs. Shipman obtained a long-coveted opportunity, described afterwards to her latest intimate friend, "There she had been telling me that it was Miss Gordon the children went to see. She knew all the time it was *Mr. More.* She's deep ; these soft-spoken women always are. Needn't tell me. I caught her good, and she knew it, too ; colored up to the roots of her hair. She's been setting them on — pretending not to know how much money he had!"

Philip lingered but an instant, and then hurried away to dress for dinner. Mrs. Shipman soon made her adieus, and the children came in to have their hands and faces washed.

"Look a-here !" called Milton, putting his hand into his pocket. "An eight-blader, scissors and everything."

"And see this, too, mamma—a little gold heart on a chain," added Millicent.

"He said I was his best friend once," said Milton.

"Now, Miltic, he said I was, too."

"That was because you asked him."

"Well, he said I was, anyway."

"And he said next year we should go up to Beau Lieu, and stay just as long as you'd let us."

"And he said we'd have another boat to beat that one that went to pieces the day him and me was out."

"I'd say *he and I were out*," corrected his mother.

"He and I was out," repeated Milton, hurriedly. "That's why I'm his best friend, isn't it, mamma, because we was out in that storm together. Millicent wasn't out in the storm."

"But I was down on the rocks with Miss Gordon, and she held on to my hand just as tight. She'd have been awful lonesome if I hadn't been there, she said so, 'cause Miss Larrabee was asleep up at the cottage."

"Well, you can be Miss Gordon's best friend and I'll be Mr. More's."

"I'm Mr. More's, too," wailed Millicent, "ain't I, mamma?"

"Hush! children; stop your quarrelling this instant, or I won't let you take these roses to Miss Gordon."

"Well, anyway, Mrs. Harwood said us children made the match between Miss Gordon and Mr. More," finished Milton, importantly.

"Whom did she say that to?" inquired his mother, her curiosity getting the better of her.

"To Dan'l," replied Milton, promptly.

"Milton!" exclaimed his mother, severely, atoning for momentary weakness by renewed stringency, "you must never call an old man like Mr. Harwood by his first name."

"Every one else does," returned Milton, sheepishly. A light step outside the door and a quick little tap put an end to the discussion.

It was Eloise. "My dear, my dear," cooed the elder woman, embracing her.

"Dear Mrs. Glenn, I am glad to be with you once more," responded Eloise.

There was a high color in her cheeks, and a bright light in her eyes. She carried her proud head higher than ever, and moved more quickly. If she evaded Mrs. Glenn's sentimental suggestions, this was only natural in one of her sensitive temperament, so Mrs. Glenn told herself. Yet it was with a sigh that she submitted to having one of Eloise's roses put in her hair, and listened to the elusive chatter with which the girl filled every pause. Aunt Harriet and Philip were waiting for them in the rotunda, and they all went in together.

"Quite like a wedding-party," Mrs. Shipman whispered to her husband, "only the children ought to go ahead instead of behind, and scatter those roses which the bride is wearing. I suppose he gave them to her."

"He looks like a square sort of chap," commented Mr. Shipman.

"He is," replied his wife. "That girl may thank her lucky stars. I wonder if she'll keep on painting, or go right to getting ready."

This was what every one wondered while the weeks passed leaving Eloise still at her easel, showing no sign of her engagement save the brilliant jewel upon her finger. She worked with feverish restlessness, as if the future held no more than the pecuniary success which present needs demanded.

"What is it that you want?" Philip would ask, when he came upon his periodical visits and found her with the same questioning look upon her face. "What can I get for you? What can I do?"

"Nothing, Philip," Eloise would answer. "You do everything—much more than I deserve!"

"Don't talk about desert!" Philip would exclaim, making an impatient gesture. "Don't I love you? All I ask is to see you happy." Instead of doing this, he disturbed his own content, and went away with an unsatisfied look which was the reflection of her own.

"What is it, Eloise—aren't you happy?" Aunt Harriet would ask, fluttering around her niece with the offer of her whole helpless personality.

"Of course," Eloise would rejoin. "Haven't I everything to make me so; a dozen fresh orders, a full class of scholars, health, ambition—"

"And Philip," timidly supplemented Aunt Harriet.

"Oh yes," returned Eloise, carelessly. "And Philip, and you," she finished with one of her old, bright looks.

XV

It was hard for the Chicagoans to give up their White City. They made all sorts of impossible plans for keeping it through the winter, if not permanently: they detached special police to take the place of the Columbian Guards, they wrapped up the figures within reach, and boarded over the weak places; but every day the vision faded, every day some fragment fell, some bright wall clouded. It had always been incongruous in its beauty for beauty's sake, set among the tall, ugly buildings made to sell or rent, to do business in, to plot and plan in against poverty and disgrace, to be wretched and despairing in, and to make as much money in as possible.

They were beginning to crowd it, now; their puffing smoke blew offensively over its fair surfaces, where decay had already laid its finger as if saying, "Look here, and here; these proud structures are not immortal, after all!"

Still, there was a fascination about the place which drew throngs of visitors to it on every pleasant day. They came in carriages and drove slowly about, they came afoot, and lingered in the sheltered corners where the sun shone warm.

It had become a habit to "go to Jackson Park" whenever there was a holiday.

Following the universal custom, Philip and Eloise and Aunt Harriet celebrated Philip's mid-winter visit by driving thither in an open carriage. It was a glorious day. Only the bits of ice in the lake told that its brilliant tint was not the blue of summer. No snow had fallen, and the roads were hard as floors. The carriage rolled gayly along until they reached a central point, and then Philip called a halt. The walls yet standing showed no lessening dignity, in spite of the débris at their feet, but towered above it with the everlasting, imperial challenge of art.

"It's an awful shame," said Philip, cheerfully. "Got enough, Eloise?"

She nodded, then quickly turned her head, that he might not see the tears which filled her eyes. The struggle of the ideal with the real, of romance with reality, of art with the nature of things, brought emotions which choked and stifled her, emotions of sympathy and companionship. She longed to stretch out her hands to the beautiful, transitory things and cry, "I, too, am of your kind! I, too, struggle and suffer and aspire! I, too, defy that which I know is doomed to over-power me!"

"Don't the animals look funny, all done up so? There is a reindeer, his horns stick through the sacking," laughed Aunt Harriet, gleeful as a child. Her pink little nose protruded from her wraps like a crocus in the snow, and her innocent eyes roved in all directions, noting everything. Philip had taken such pains that the carriage should be easy and the robes plentiful; and he had such a nice way of tucking her in and asking, "All right, Aunt Harriet?"

Eloise hardly spoke. Her silence troubled Philip; he made clumsy, good-humored attempts to break through it and bring her out, "enjoying life" with himself and Aunt Harriet. Eloise was beginning to see that she had given him a right to do this. When she accepted him she expected and intended to go on living two lives: one outwardly, a part of the present world, the other inwardly, a part of the world of art which ever has been and ever shall be. Of course, Philip, who cared nothing for art, was to inhabit the outside world.

But if Philip did not care for art, he cared for Eloise and for all that concerned her. Into the penetralia of her hopes and joys he pursued her with the mistaken zeal of a lover, and professed his unbounded interest in everything there. At first she tried to be generous, and to tell him how she felt, but to her horror she found that she lost her fine fervors as soon as she described them. It was of no use, she told herself. She, too, must give up the White City of her dreams. "Nothing lasts which is beautiful," she said to herself, "Only the ugly and commonplace endure."

"Let's go down Midway!" exclaimed Philip.

"Shall we go down Midway, Eloise?" and remembering how many times she had lightened a heavy heart of its burden on the merry street, Eloise answered, quickly, "Yes, yes, drive down Midway."

But Midway was even more forlorn. Here deathless art had not reigned, but frail amusement that dies so easily. The dregs of wine, the tattered robe, the dulled and broken jewel, are not pathetic, but contemptible. Only the graceful little huts of the Javanese offered any temptation to the relic hunters, who pulled down the long grass which had thatched the roofs, and tore away the gay mattings from the walls, in spite of the policemen set to guard them. "You are tired, Eloise," exclaimed Philip, suddenly. "We will go home. Why didn't you tell me?"

"It is queer how Eloise gets tired over some things," prattled Aunt Harriet, "which don't tire me a bit."

The next day was Monday, the busiest in the week for Eloise. There were scholars from ten to twelve and from three to five. Philip was to go at six.

He came in at noon, having spent the morning hours with the Glenn children, and found Eloise still in her long brown apron cleaning her brushes. "How much longer do you mean to keep this up?" he inquired, anxiously.

"I don't know. Please don't hinder me, Philip," for he had taken the brushes out of her hands with the air of proprietorship which always annoyed her. Instead of returning the brushes, he took the empty hands in his and attempted to read her averted face. "Eloise, are you sorry that you said—that you promised—"

"Nonsense, Philip," she answered, letting her eyes meet his, for an instant.

"Then what is it? Why do you avoid me? Do I bore you?"

"Why, no; how foolish you are! I am thinking about my work. I have to, in order to succeed."

"Is it so necessary for you to succeed—now?"

"It is rather agreeable," returned Eloise, in a tone which puzzled him.

"I don't mean your painting, but the teaching and the fuss. I can't bear to think of your tugging along. You ought not to have to wrestle with the world."

"I like it," said Eloise, with a toss of her head. "If you don't let go of my hands I can't finish cleaning up, and we won't have any luncheon."

Philip released her with a sigh, comforting himself with the thought of the hour between five and six, when Eloise would be again at leisure, and he would renew the argument.

But at five came the alarm of fire, fire at Jackson Park. The Peristyle was burning. This was the first great wound, and all Chicago felt the hurt. Eloise and Philip hurried to the spot, but found thousands there before them. Along the dark streets of the Dream City men and women went in straggling groups, silently.

Silent, too, were the crowds that thronged the spaces along the lagoons, before the burning building. The Casino was ablaze when they reached the Court, and the flames were climbing the Triumphal Arch. Dense clouds of smoke hid the western walls and rolled up around the Quadriga. Above the smoke-wreaths, and seeming to outride their threat as his purpose outrode the storm of Western seas and the opposition of his enemies, the discoverer was to be seen in his chariot, radiant as Elisha's vision of his leader, and, like it, soon to disappear.

The helpless people recognized their helplessness. They had no enormous safeguards to protect the enormous structures they had reared. Pitifully inadequate were the streams of water thrown by the engines; hysterical their calls for coal; absurd their bold arrivals with prancing horses and clanging bells; disheartening the manner in which they were beaten back.

The wind was from the lake; it blew the smoke in their faces and blinded them. "Come around on the pier," cried Eloise, darting away, leaving Philip to follow. The pier was nearly deserted. A policeman was attempting to clear it completely; but an amateur photographer who had set up his trident in the very teeth of the flame, and a reporter equally daring, were deaf to his shouts and blind to the wave of his "billy." Eloise was close behind them. Philip drew her arm within his own. "Don't!" she cried, pettishly. "I can't bear—anything—now!"

Across the white pillars played the whiter flames, like sunlight upon snow. Every line was alive with a new and dazzling loveliness. Every figure sprang into prominence, swayed to the influence of the invading power, shone with the final benediction of its grace, and fell into the abyss. The roofless columns burned at the top like torches. In time they, too, fell, and their fall was like that of the forest tree when it yields to the axe, slow, stately, submissive. Under the roof of Music Hall, blown backward by the wind, swift, sinuous, the gray smoke clung like a restless drapery. Above and below darted the flames. It lit the figures upon the roof, standing as the Christian martyrs stood, or the victims of the French Revolution, awaiting the end with an ineffable dignity.

Suddenly there was a noise like that of a cannon, and the flame broke into a blaze. The adventurous people upon the pier hurried to a place of safety.

"You are cold ; your teeth are fairly chattering!" exclaimed Philip, folding Eloise's cloak more closely around her.

"It isn't the cold," she replied.

"And you have had no dinner. It is almost nine o'clock," pursued Philip. "You should have let me call a carriage. Here, s-s-t, boy! call me a carriage and I'll make it worth your while."

The boy turned, a dwarfish creature with an elfish face that leered at them in the flickering light.

"Can't git nothin' 'round yere. Everythin' taken—see?" Following the direction in which he pointed, they saw line upon line of carriages drawn up on the edge of the crowd. They threaded their way between them. There were vehicles of every description, old-fashioned wagons harnessed to animals that stood as if their hoofs had been driven into the soil, glittering broughams and victorias kept in constant motion by the fidgeting horses which champed their silver bits and clanked their silver chains in nervous protest.

It was the night of the Charity Ball, and the ladies had been taken out as they were. Their light dresses would be no more conspicuous, later, in the boxes than they were now in the fire-lit carriages.

"I will try again when we get out of this jam," said Philip. "Look out, there!" he caught an aggressive cob as his nose grazed Eloise's shoulder.

"What are you doing?" growled the coachman from his box.

"Minding your business for you," retorted Philip.

A man in a cape overcoat, leaning on the carriage window-sill, was thrown aside when Philip caught the rein. "What's the trouble?" he inquired, good-naturedly, but, without waiting for an answer, turned again to the window. The light had shone full on his face; Eloise saw him plainly. She saw also the face of the woman who sat in the carriage talking with him. The man was Mark Heffron. The woman was Mademoiselle Duvray. "Come," Eloise heard him say, "you must see the Golden Republic. She is grand, towering above the smoke!" and then he opened the carriage door.

XVI

Involuntarily Marguerite glanced down at her white shoes. Prudence had been a necessary virtue for the greater part of her life. Mrs. Burnham, who sat opposite, smiled significantly.

"The experience is worth a pair of shoes!" exclaimed Mark, holding out his hand, and she laid hers within it.

"I am really generous to furnish you such a figure to use against me," he said, as he led her through the crowd to the lagoon.

"What do you mean?" she asked.

"In our quarrel about 'the new woman.' You will be reminding me, after this, that severity of outline becomes strength in trying circumstances. There she is!"

The smoke cleared, permitting the majestic head to appear and the commanding arm. "Try any of your Venuses beside that!" cried Mark. "Isn't she superb in the calm of her invincibility? That conception of womanhood was impossible to the Old World of Art—do you know it?"

"Minerva?" suggested Marguerite, somewhat timidly.

"No, Minerva had to help out her followers.

For our Golden Republic men have been glad to die."

"And this ideal, this 'calm of invincibility,' you forbid to the modern woman!" she exclaimed.

"As an individual, yes. The proportions are too heroic. A real flesh - and - blood woman is ridiculous when she tries to be great in that way. We don't want our women to be goddesses."

"No, of course not," she retorted. "It's the same old song—man for himself, and woman for man. Why not woman for herself, also?"

"Because," he answered, looking indulgently down on her. "That deprives man of his inspiration and the end of his labor. Not woman for herself, but man for woman; it is the law of the universe."

"There is no progress in that," she answered, defiantly. "You said yourself, just now, that this conception of womanhood was impossible to the Old World of Art. The new woman has at least furnished an ideal to the artist."

"At the expense of other blessings," he finished. "You know and I know that the bond which holds between man and woman is not the new-fangled, Platonic, intellectual comradeship, but a feeling as primitive as the romance of Eden. It is the talk about the independent rights of women which has turned the world upside down." He squared his shoulders and his chin, and dared her to go on with the argument. This she was not ` yet prepared to do.

"Mr. French ought to see his creation, now," she evaded. "I wonder if he thought of her so, harassed and assailed?"

"A sort of artistic subconsciousness?" he suggested, accepting her evasion.

And then they talked of other things, mere "padding" such as makes up the greater part of all conversation. There were no pauses, and there was nothing said which either cared to remember, or which in anyway interfered with the train of thought carried on underneath. Marguerite was thinking, "Ever since I met this man last October he has tried to trip me. He shall not, and I will not run away as I did before."

Mark was thinking, "She shall not dodge me this time. I'll have her secret in spite of her." Both pairs of eyes flashed when they met in farewell, as swords flash before the fencing begins. Marguerite made a final effort to think of something which should make her feel less feminine and weak.

"I am going to lecture, day after to-morrow, on the Symbolists," she began, in an off-hand, business-like way. "Do you care to hear me?"

"Of course. What is the hour?"

"Four o'clock."

"I expect my friend Norton in the morning."

"'Joey?' Bring him, too."

They shook hands and parted, as two men might have done, and the carriage rolled away.

"How did you enjoy the Republic?" asked Mrs. Burnham.

"It was lovely," replied Marguerite, abstractedly, adding, with a laugh, "but I've ruined my shoes."

"There'll be plenty of time to change them," Mrs. Burnham, rejoined. "I suppose Mr. Heffron is not going?"

"No; he doesn't care for such things."

"So I should judge. Where are your flowers?"

Marguerite uttered a cry of dismay. "I had them when we started; they must be in the carriage."

"They're not. What will the Prince say? He was so careful to select your colors. You probably dropped them when you got out."

A feeling of annoyance altogether disproportionate to the loss of her flowers swept over Marguerite. To have forgotten where she was and what she was doing—it made her hot and cold by turns! She must pull herself up short and take a stand. The lecture would give her an opportunity—controlling an audience always helped her control herself. She hoped that he would come.

There was no uncertainty about his coming; he was as impatient for the hour to arrive as Marguerite herself. Joey went with him. Louise Ayer, who was a sort of prime-minister on such occasions, had been urged to see that they had seats near the front, but Louise was so occupied with Carl Dering when the two friends entered that they were in their places before she knew they were there.

The long room was filled with the cultured and fashionable women of Chicago—what is known as a "representative audience." Only a few men were present; they were too busy thinking of other things, in order that their wives and daughters might have leisure to think of the Symbolists.

A flutter of interest announced the arrival of the lecturer, who came swiftly in, and stood waiting until the applause of recognition had ceased. Between the rows of nodding bonnets, Mark caught a glimpse of the graceful figure, poised like a flower on its stem. "The calm of invincibility" he recognized with a smile, but instead of being properly overawed by it, was seized with a sacrilegious impulse to catch her up and carry her away, and fondle her and laugh at her until he should discover what human stirrings of heart lay underneath the calm.

Then she began to speak. It was a most artistic performance; the articulation, the accent, the clear, singing tones were perfect, and it was by these that she was to be judged, in the main. The names that she quoted were unfamiliar to most of her hearers, and of the poems which she recited there was no translation. But her French was exquisite.

The stories she told, and the descriptions she gave, were mystic and peculiar; they contained frequent allusions to death, moonlight, and vague unrest.

There was a hint, just a hint, of the voluntary production of ecstasy, but it was accompanied by the confession that the Symbolists often relied upon opium or hasheesh in the production of their fanciful compositions. One or two of the poets had been in prison for some petty crime, and one was an occasional visitor in the pauper ward of a hospital, where he received his decadent friends. It was all deliciously harrowing to hear about, and left a delicate impression of bewildering sorrow.

A murmur of appreciation and the clapping of gloved hands followed the close ; then every one turned to his or her neighbor and said it had been charming, delightful, and none ventured to say how or why. Professor La Motte bowed low over the hand which Louise Ayer gave him, and uttered his usual formula of French compliment, insisting that she reply in the same language. Carl Dering stood near, waiting for a final word with Louise. Mademoiselle Duvray had been surrounded by eager women as soon as she ceased speaking ; their sweet, shrill voices floated over to the corner where Mark and Joey stood. Joey glanced quizzically at Mark, but Mark was studying the Pompeian frescoes upon the wall. He was suave and gracious, for Mark, when in her triumphal progress down the room Mademoiselle Duvray came to the corner, and he spoke in flattering terms of her eloquence. Marguerite should have been content, but, after the full libations which her pupils had been pouring to her, his praise seemed poor and thin.

"I know you don't care for these things," she said, tolerantly, as who should say, "I see what you do not."

"What, 'the subtleties of sensation?'" he answered, caustically. "I think they're dangerous ; but if people like that sort of thing, it is their own lookout. It is two-thirds *pose*, anyway, with these fellows—they don't mean half they say."

When Marguerite had been taking her Symbolists altogether seriously, this was positively unkind. She welcomed the opportunity to exercise an admirable self-control. "I do not quite understand," she said with deliberation. "Do you mean that these new philosophers are not in earnest ?"

"They're anything but new," replied Mark, brusquely. "They combine the Pantheism of Bruno and the Idealism of Spinoza with just enough modern psychology to make their system appear new and scientific. It isn't new, and it isn't scientific. Science is accurate, it is clear. These emotional explorers are groping around in the 'misty borderland of thought,' making a great to-do over they don't know what. They'd better stop whooping until they're out of the woods."

"Don't mind him, Mademoiselle Duvray," interposed Norton, sweetly. "He has these attacks occasionally. If you had pitched into the Symbolists he would have sworn they were wiser than the Three Kings."

But Mark had no idea of being daunted in this fashion. "To be sure the universe expresses thought," he continued. "Most of us subscribed to that long ago, and to the doctrine that all things are subject to the same laws— 'We are all evanescent expressions of an eternal unity,' but you don't get any nearer to the eternal unity by playing tricks with the evanescent expressions. Scientific! Heaven forbid!"

"But, Mr. Heffron," pursued Marguerite, bravely, "as I understand the Symbolists, they do not pride themselves on their scientific accuracy but on their suggestiveness, which is a purely artistic quality. It may have no place in science, but it has in art, and art is as necessary as science—you grant that, surely?"

"No, I don't," replied Mark, bluntly. "People are bound to feel, anyway, and they won't think if they can help it. You don't need to hunt up their nerves and bear down on them in order to produce a sensation; teach them reason and self-control, and emotion will take care of itself."

Now, if there was anything in her instruction upon which Marguerite prided herself, it was the prominence she gave to reason and self-control. To be sure Mark had not seen her circulars, but he should have detected the quality of their spirit in their author. Marguerite was put on her mettle at once. It would never do to let that remark pass before the listening women who were her disciples. "Beauty is not unreasonable, Mr. Heffron," she said with dignity, "and there is nothing so subject to control as Art." With these words she virtually closed the debate, asking young Norton how long he was to remain in the city.

"You can't slug her, Mark," laughed Norton, as they walked down State Street, arm in arm, to avoid being separated by the crowd, "and she's the first woman I ever saw whom you couldn't. You needn't lift your eyebrows in that way. I've seen you pound the poor things all over the field, using words they couldn't possibly understand. If she doesn't catch on, you'll never know it, nor any one else. She won't own up to any limitations. That's the only fault she has, not to have faults; but that's a big one. Half the fun a man has with a woman is in laughing at her.

"You don't know what you are talking about, Joey," growled Mark.

"Yes, I do," returned Joey, positively. "She's an Ideal, take my word for it, Mark, she's an Ideal, and to fall in love with an Ideal is almost as bad as falling in love with a Type; it's too general in its application. You want something decidedly personal when you fall in love."

"Joey," pursued Mark, assuming a paternal air, "you are a nice boy, but you have one weakness; you talk too much."

"All right," returned Joey, submissively. "But

some one has to talk. I'll stop, and you say something."

Silence ensued for some seconds, and then Joey resumed in an injured tone, "What did I tell you? You won't say a blamed word when you get a chance. I say, Mark, don't you think it was rather pedantic for her to get off all those poems in French? Don't you think it was taking an unfair advantage—a sort of 'hiding behind the picket-fence of unintelligibility,' as she says the critics accuse these Symbolists of doing?"

"Probably to the majority of the audience it was perfectly intelligible," returned Mark, dryly. "It is hardly fair to impose our ignorance of French as a limitation upon Mademoiselle Duvray."

Norton stroked his pointed beard with his free hand and looked reflective. "There's another thing," he pursued, after a pause. "Did it ever occur to you that she was trying to get an influence over you—not as other women do, for their own enjoyment, but for your soul's good, and all that sort of thing? Now, women are perfectly welcome to my heart. That's on my sleeve, as any one of them can see for herself. But I carry my soul in my inside vest-pocket, and I'd thank them to keep their fingers out of there."

Mark did not even smile. "He's either hard hit or he thinks I'm a fool," mused Joey. "I don't believe he thinks I'm a fool.—You know they're all on to that sort of thing," he continued, aloud. "Circe up to date! She doesn't wave her wand over you and say, 'Begone to the sty!' She lifts you to immeasurable heights, and if you get warm and melt the wax which holds on your wings, it's your own fault. There is my car. Won't you come out to the house to dinner? Uncle says you haven't been there for an age."

"I have an engagement, thank you," replied Mark, coldly.

"Well, then, *au revoir*. I've been immensely entertained."

Mark walked on towards the bridge. He felt irritated. He was provoked with Norton, provoked with himself. What did he know about society women and their intellectual appetites? Marguerite probably gave them what was good for them. He had been like a clumsy bear putting his great foot into the lace-like web of her pretty fancies; he had destroyed their beauty, and what had been gained? She had been kind enough to permit him to be present when she spoke, and he had repaid her kindness by quarrelling with her before her friends. What business had he, anyway, airing his opinions? Who cared what they were? And yet, hang it all! she was mistaken all the way through; her ideas of life were absurdly false; some day she would find it out. That dissipated Russian who was dangling about last evening at the ball—for Mark had followed the carriage back to the city, contrary to his determination, and had stood for a full hour where he could watch Marguerite and her chaperon in their box—any one who knew the world could see what that fellow was; but evidently he stood high in her favor. Poor little thing! she walked in a cloud of beautiful ideas, and had no appreciation of the chasms which yawned on either side.

By the time he had reached his hotel, Mark had walked and reasoned himself into good-humor, and had decided that he would have a frank, friendly talk with Marguerite, and show her the fallacies with which she dealt.

XVII

"Pleasant, when you bring up Miss Gordon's dinner to-night, can't you stay and entertain her a little while, sing to her or something! She is rather down in her spirits."

"Yes, Mis' Larrabee, yessum," replied Pleasant, "I'll come up jes' as quick as I get thoo."

"Thank you, Pleasant." Miss Larrabee moved on with a sigh. It was a new experience to have strong, self-reliant Eloise an invalid. Half a dozen individuals stopped her on her way to the door to inquire for Miss Gordon. "Her cold is better, but she is weak and low-spirited," Miss Larrabee replied.

"Does she see folks?" inquired Mrs. Shipman.

"No, not at all—at least, only relatives, and near friends, and people on business," answered Miss Larrabee, trying to be truthful and prudent at the same time and making poor work of it.

"Do you think my music disturbs her?" asked a thin, dark woman, with a sprinkling of gray on her forelock which made her look like a Polish hen.

"I think not, Miss Thompson. No, there's nothing any one can do, Mr. NcNulty. It is six weeks since she was taken, that night at the Fair Grounds when the Peristyle burned. I will let you know, Mr. Armstrong, if there is anything you can do. Thank you all. Good-night." Miss Larrabee swept on, uplifted by the deferential attitude of her fellow-boarders. They had all been very kind, but she never knew when they would change and be disagreeable. However, when their interest lagged it was immediately stimulated by Mrs. Glenn. It was she who told Mrs. Shipman, who told several others, how brave and generous Eloise had been, actually refusing to have her lover informed of her true condition, because he had gone to the Pacific coast on important business which would detain him until spring. "It would break your heart to see her," declared Mrs. Glenn. "She sits up and writes to him when it is all she can do to move her fingers; and makes believe she is all right. She just *insisted* that we should not tell him."

Eloise had also added, "I will not have him here, he would drive me distracted;" but there was no need of telling people that.

"She is not herself, anyway," Miss Larrabee had whispered, after the two women had gone out into the hall to talk it over. "Why, she even gets provoked with *me*."

William Pleasant seemed to suit Eloise better than any one else did. She had discovered his capabilities by chance one day when he came up for a "pome" to speak at the club.

"What club, Pleasant?"

"The Lake View Club, Miss Gordon. It's a kind of littry and social club. We have debates and speeches, and the Happy Four Quartet sing. Mos' everything," Pleasant laughed by way of a period.

"What sort of questions do you debate?"

"Las' time we 'scussed whether a woman's brains or a man's was the best, and de time befo' that we 'scussed whether a feller'd save his wife or his mother if they's all shipwrecked together. Sam Jennin's and Jo Tarrents 'scussed that. Sam cried, he got so excited."

"Which side did he take?"

"The wife's side; but Jo, he said you could get another wife, and you can't never have but one mother. Tell you, Miss Gordon, that club's a big thing. There'd been less shootin' craps and more boys with overcoats if it had started sooner."

"You have a large number to choose from?" pursued Eloise, loath to let him go.

"Yessum," answered Pleasant, only too glad to remain. "There's one used to be an elder, he exhorts sometimes at the club; and an artist, he's doin' crayon po'traits to give away as prizes at a cigar-store; he's a perfesser—at least, if he ain't a regular perfesser, he's a perfesser of *am-er-chewer;* and there's a baseball player. Yessum, we've got a nice lot of boys."

"Don't you think it's a little reckless to let

Pleasant take Leigh Hunt's poems down-stairs?"
Aunt Harriet asked, afterwards.

"It's worth all the book cost to hear him say :

'King Francis was a *harty* king and loved a royal *spote*,
    And one day while the *lions* fought sat lookin' on de
       cote,'"

replied Eloise.

Neither Mrs. Glenn nor Aunt Harriet nor Carl, who came almost every day, could dispel from her face the pallid, bored look as could Pleasant, and Pleasant enjoyed the process as well as she did.

He came in to-night, after a modest tap at the door, with a respectful, "Bid you good-evenin', Miss Gordon," and took up her guitar, which he had fitted with new strings during his last visit.

"I'm goin' to play somethin' new," he said, with a chuckle, fondling the instrument as if it were a baby, and his own. Lovingly he ran his fingers over the strings, and struck into a melody whose every note was a caress, pathetic in its tenderness, joyful in its longing, giving all and asking nothing.

"What is it? It is perfectly exquisite!" cried Eloise, as the player stopped, and gave vent to another chuckle.

"I call it 'Pleasant Dreams,'" replied the boy, showing his white teeth.

"Did you compose that? Did you make that up?"

"Yessum."

"Pleasant, you're a genius. Play it again."

He obeyed, putting into the simple strain, if possible, more tenderness, more joy, and more renunciation.

"Pleasant," the listener asked, suddenly, after a pause, "what do you think of when you play like that?"

Pleasant giggled. "I was thinkin'—of a lady," he answered, continuing, confidently, "Miss Gordon, I wanter ask you what it is. I'm awfully fond of my folks, of my father and mother, but there are times when I don't go near 'em for a long while. But if I set out to go and see that lady, I'm goin' anyhow. And the nex' day I'm thinkin' 'bout it all the time. If I get a letter frum her, I'm boun' to set right down and answer it. Now, what is that, Miss Gordon?"

"You're in love, Pleasant."

"Oh, I sut'nly hope not."

"Why?"

"'Cause I ain't fixed to get married. I've always heard if poverty comes in at the do' love flies out at the winder. And I couldn't stand that nohow. If I couldn't get money by work, I'd do mos' anything, and then"— he put up his fingers and looked through them as through bars —"yessum, I'd steal, that's what I'd do, if I's sure to be shut up."

Eloise made no response, but the glance she gave him was so full of sympathy that Pleasant continued: "I feel 'sponsible for that lady as I do for my mother and sister. Now, times is so bad, I tell her to stay where she is, where her folks will take care of her." He patted the strings of the guitar thoughtfully for a minute; then remembering he was there to entertain and not appeal, he said, brightly, "Now I'll do a funny piece," and began to play the most doleful minor chords. The words which he sang to them were in broken English and German, and portrayed the sufferings of a young man at the hands of his prospective father-in-law. As the lugubrious wail went on and on the listener became fairly hysterical. At last it came to an end. "That's a funny piece," announced the player.

The entrance of Aunt Harriet relieved Eloise from an embarrassing position. Pleasant immediately said his good-night and withdrew.

Aunt Harriet looked uneasy. "I didn't mean to stay so long," she said, apologetically. "Carl has been here. He thought he wouldn't come up. He left his love."

"Thank you," returned Eloise, without looking at her.

"He wants me to go out with him to-morrow morning for a little while," continued Aunt Harriet, hastily—"that is, if you can spare me."

"Of course! Why do you ask?"

Aunt Harriet murmured some unintelligible response. If her niece had not been preoccupied she would have seen that Aunt Harriet had something on her mind, but Eloise was thinking of other things—of Pleasant and his "lady," and of the tenderness and renunciation of "Pleasant Dreams."

"Poor Pleasant!" she mused. "I wonder if Philip feels in that way. I suppose if he were any one else I should be sorry for him."

The early church-bells were ringing the next morning when Carl appeared to take Aunt Harriet "out" with him.

"Both of them seemed in a tremendous hurry," Eloise said to Mrs. Glenn, who was to sit with her during Aunt Harriet's absence. "Carl bounced in and talked all the time, and caught up Aunt Harriet and bounced out again. They are doing something which they mean to keep from me, but I don't know as I care."

It might have stirred her languid interest if she could have watched the pair enter Dr. Symonds's office, transformed for the occasion into a modest chapel. A slight young girl, with a far-off look in her dreamy eyes, was playing softly on the upright piano in the corner. Carl led Aunt Harriet to the front row of chairs near the preacher, who sat on a small platform behind a reading-desk. There was a vase of roses on the desk, and Aunt Harriet could not see his face until, with a gesture, he brought the soothing sounds to a close and stood up before his audience. He was of medium size, built slenderly and finely, like a woman. His eyes were large and dark, and felt out the faces of those before him like fingers, clinging where they touched. His sensitive nostrils palpitated when he breathed. A drooping black mustache hid his lips. The chin was well rounded, the brow was that of an idealist, full and white. There was no color in the cheeks, and the long, slender, pointed hands were also colorless. They trembled as he took up the Testament from which he read, and when he commenced to speak he put one of them behind him as if to hide its agitation. He was like a sensitive machine, thrilling to some invisible influence.

For an hour he talked straight into their upturned faces. As he proceeded his voice grew steadier and his hands ceased to tremble. He seemed to lose himself in his earnestness; whatever might be said of the theories which he advanced, there was no possibility of a doubt that he believed in them thoroughly.

It was all vague and bewildering to Aunt Harriet; she had not the remotest idea what the speaker meant, but listened because every one else was listening with absorbed attention. She was tired, body and soul; tired of care and worry, tired of combating the opinions and suspicions of the people at the hotel, tired of the uncertain and turbulent spirit of her niece. The atmosphere of the little chapel was restful beyond expression. It was as if her frail, cockle-shell of a body had been lifted by a giant palm and held above the swirl and dash of the waves where it had drifted. She settled back in her camel's-hair shawl with a sigh of utter content, feeling that for a few short, blissful moments she was freed from every responsibility, even from that of her own personal salvation, which was wont to harass her when she had nothing else on hand.

At last the speaker paused and said, impressively, "Let us unite in the Silence!"

Far down in the street the rumble of carriages and the tread of feet blended in a rhythmic murmur; a city clock chimed solemnly; there was no other sound. Aunt Harriet remembered no silence to compare with it save that which brooded over Max Gordon's great, handsome hall while he lay in it, dead, and they, his mourners, waited in the gallery above for those who came to do him final honor. The voice of the strange preacher blended with the calm.

"Now is every one taught of the Spirit," he repeated, reverently. "Now is every one led whither he should go. All problems are solved, all disquietude banished, and the peace which is past understanding is in every heart. Amen!"

The gentle musician was ready with her chords. The people sat relaxed and quiet, thrilling to the power which had played over them. When they looked up the preacher had gone, vanishing through a door in the rear of the room.

"Come, Aunt Harriet," whispered Carl. She stood up rubbing her eyes. The experience had been as a dream; she felt rested and refreshed, like one who awakes from sleep. Bird-like Mrs.

Symonds was shaking hands with this one and that as they went out.

She said she was glad to meet Miss Larrabee, and hoped to see more of her.

"There were a number of new people there this morning," said Carl, as they crossed over to the station. "The Rosses have succeeded in bringing their uncle at last."

"Who was the white-haired man who sat by the door?" asked Aunt Harriet.

"Mr. Norton; he has been a regular attendant for some time. Did you see the little woman who sat opposite us with the tall young lady? That was Mademoiselle Duvray. Louise Ayer was the one with her. I wanted to introduce you to them, but there are always so many waiting to speak to Mademoiselle Duvray that it is almost impossible to get anywhere near her. Some other Sunday perhaps I can do it."

"Some other Sunday?" repeated Aunt Harriet, timidly.

"Why, yes, you will go again."

"How bright you look!" exclaimed Eloise, as the two came in together. "I wish I could get out for a long walk like that. There is nothing like fresh air."

Aunt Harriet gave a guilty start, but Carl signalled her behind Eloise's chair to say nothing, and she obeyed.

XVIII

To women like Aunt Harriet the appeal from Cæsar is to Cæsar, from love to love. She could not have turned her back upon her niece except for Eloise's own sake. Whether Carl knew it or not, he was using the only argument of any possible weight with her when he told Aunt Harriet that she could bring home renewed strength to Eloise by attending the service at the chapel. It would seem that he spoke the truth. There was less friction between the two women day by day. Eloise certainly gained; her cough almost ceased.

"You must hold the right thought over her," counselled Mrs. Symonds, whom Aunt Harriet was beginning to seek out on week days at the office. "Say to yourself, 'All is Spirit and all is Good!'" And the obedient pupil went to sleep at night and awoke in the morning whispering the cabalistic words.

Timid as she was, Aunt Harriet never did anything by halves, possibly because she did so few things that she could afford to expend herself on each. She gradually relaxed her hold on the prayer-book, and tightened the tentative grasp with which she had received the books which

Carl gave her to read. The mystery with which they were bestowed and received enhanced their value. Many of them, when stripped of certain expressions which they shared in common, would have sounded not unlike the sermons she had listened to from orthodox lips all her life. But somehow they seemed more real, more her own. They gave her something to do and showed her how to do it. She had at last found a way to help Eloise. Her transparent diplomacy with the guests had been a failure, her anxiety to advance Philip's cause had only hindered it; this new, and, as it were, subterranean method of attack, "holding the right thought," was to accomplish everything. A tranquil look which Eloise had never seen there before gradually overspread Aunt Harriet's small, shrunken face. Moreover, in order to do her utmost by the "thought," she must talk less, and this, too, had a beneficial effect on her niece's nerves.

"She is certainly better," Aunt Harriet reported to Mrs. Symonds.

"I knew that before you came in," said Mrs. Symonds. "I felt that she responded to the treatment. Keep right on. Treat every one. That is the way to learn. You are going to do well with this line of thought. Don't you think you are ready for the manuscript lessons?"

Aunt Harriet colored and hesitated.

"You can pay when you feel like it," said Mrs. Symonds, generously. "Take One, Two, and Three to begin on. You can come back for the rest when you are through."

With a palpitating heart Aunt Harriet received One, Two, and Three, inclosed in huge brown paper envelopes, and, hurrying home, slipped them below the mattress of her bed. Already, volumes of her occult library made bunches beneath her when she slept; but, like the peas of penance in the shoes of the monks, they brought a comfortable consciousness of well-doing to soothe the discomfort they produced. When Eloise was busy with her scholars, for she had begun to teach again, the little books came from their hiding-place and were devoured eagerly by the new disciple. The manuscript lessons were not so simple in their language or so direct in their application. They had a great deal to say about the "First Cause, Unlimited, Infinite, and Absolute." By-and-by she might grow up to these. The tract on "No Evil" was more suited to her comprehension, and a thin, decorated booklet on "Perpetual Youth" went straight to her feminine heart. Warming to their influence she felt capable of any sacrifice. She longed to take a stand, to do something, to suffer something by way of an initiation into her new belief. She had passed beyond the attitude of investigation to that of espousal—had reached the state of mind which demands a catharsis, a baptism. What should it be? She had abstained from drugs ever since Carl told her they belonged to a lower plane of thought; but they were still in her possession. She opened the drawer where they were kept, and solemnly, as one looks into the face of the dead, examined the interior. There were bottles innumerable — bottles large and round, bottles small and flat, bottles wrapped in their own "directions" like a mummy in its cerements, bottles mysteriously dumb as to their contents and significance; and there were boxes daintily made and highly ornamented containing powders of various colors and tablets of curious shape. She fingered them affectionately. They were the silent witnesses to the long years during which, as Eloise said, "Aunt Harriet had been addicted to delicate health." They had been "closer than breathing, nearer than hands and feet," in time of trial, but they must go, every one. She gathered them up in her skirts and carried them to the open fireplace. The uncertain fate of the waste-basket would not serve. Reverently she poured them out on the hearth and set them afire. It was a heroic deed, and one which brought the light of determination into her dim eyes. Never again could she get up quietly in the night for a Dover's Powder or a dose of chloral; she must fight down her nerves unaided. Never again could she indulge her capricious elderly appetite with batter - pudding and spice - cake, relying upon Dr. Kendrick's Dyspepsia Pill to save her from the consequences of her reckless act. She had entered upon a new life of self-control and renunciation.

She was now ready to go forth with her modest banner and convert the blinded beings who were still "sitting in darkness, fast bound with misery" and material appliances. The music-teacher, Miss Thompson, was the first. She responded with a vigor of appreciation that was appalling. "I can't imagine what is the matter with Miss Thompson," said Eloise, wearily. "She used to be satisfied with three or four hours' practice, but now she is at it all day long. And she pounds so; you can't get away from the sound of her exercises."

"Miss Thompson *is* a good deal better than she was," replied Aunt Harriet, feeling guilty in spite of the righteousness of the cause.

Miss Thompson herself was delighted. "I can play pieces which I haven't been able to handle in years—that impromptu of Moszkowski's, for instance. It used to tire me to play it through once, and now I can play it over and over. It's a tremendously effective thing." She declared, almost with tears in her eyes, that Miss Larrabee's little books gave her what she had been looking for all her life. One, Two, and Three she swallowed with avidity, and was ready for Four, Five, and Six as soon as Miss Larrabee brought them home. Her progress made Aunt Harriet almost jealous.

Not all the interested individuals, however,

were ready for the "new thought." More than one scoffed openly; others led the devotee on to furnish them a choice variety of entertainment; a few, the sad and burdened ones, seeking the promised "means of escape," listened and questioned and tried to understand.

If Eloise had been on more intimate terms with her fellow-boarders she might have learned earlier and with less expenditure of nervous force the results of Aunt Harriet's crusade. It was through the Glenn children, finally, that her eyes were opened. They came in late to their drawing-lesson, after the other children had taken their places before their easels. Millicent had been crying, and coughed croupily. Milton had evidently been teasing her.

"Milton, what is the matter with Millicent?" asked Eloise, drawing the child towards her.

"Millicent has been denying God!" said Milton, promptly. "You stop laughing, John Somers, or I'll punch your head when we get out of here."

"Milton!" exclaimed Eloise, sternly.

"Miss Larrabee's doctor said so. He said any one who was sick denied God, for God is all-powerful and He is good, and there is no evil," repeated Milton, glibly.

"Take your seat, Milton," interrupted his teacher, suddenly realizing that this was not a case for public examination. "What could the boy mean?" she asked herself, while she arranged their work for the children, and directed their awkward hands. "Who could Miss Larrabee's doctor be?" Aunt Harriet had gone to the city on one of her peculiar, private expeditions. "Could it be that she had fallen into the hands of some terrible quack? Was this the reason for her sudden interest in something besides the bills and Philip and selling pictures?" The hour was a long one, but at last it came to an end. Hardly had the children disappeared before there came a business-like tap at the door. "I've come to see Miss Larrabee," said the woman who stood there, and whom Eloise recognized as one of the guests in the hotel. "I want her to give me a 'treatment.' I hear from folks in the house that she has wonderful powers as a healer. I've had a great deal of rheumatism."

"Miss Larrabee is not at home," replied Eloise, stonily.

"Oh, she isn't. Well, when do you expect her?"

"I don't know."

"I want very much to see her," pursued the would-be patient. "If she helps me, I'd like to have my daughter try her; she's been going to Dr. Budlong to reduce her flesh."

"I don't know when Miss Larrabee will return," said Miss Larrabee's unhappy niece, and, like a haughty princess, bowed the intruder from the door.

"Oh, Aunt Harriet," she cried, reproachfully, as the culprit returned, flushed and buoyant, carrying Seven, Eight, and Nine under her shawl, "what have you been doing? What dreadful things do I hear about you !"

"Now, Eloise," replied her aunt, seeing the rack before her, but determined not to apostatize. Her heart beat so stormily that it seemed to her to threaten to tear its way through her side, but she stood her ground. She began again, firmly : "Now, Eloise, don't talk like that about what has saved your life !"

"Saved my life !" repeated Eloise, bewildered. "What do you mean ?"

"Can you forget how you were four or five weeks ago? And see how you are now !"

"What has that to do with it?" demanded Eloise, almost fiercely.

"If it hadn't been for Dr. Symonds and Carl, and—*me*," replied Aunt Harriet, solemnly, "you would not be where you are to-day."

"Why, Aunt Harriet, are you crazy?" exclaimed her niece. "I never saw Dr. Symonds, and Carl I seldom see nowadays. I don't know what you have been trying to do to me."

"We have all been *treating* you ever since I went down to hear Dr. Symonds preach, six weeks ago," said her aunt, "and every one in the house has noticed how you have gained ; that is why they all want me to treat them."

Eloise stood speechless with amazement. Of all the irritating surprises of the morning, this was the crown. To hear that Aunt Harriet was

11

in collusion with a lot of fanatics, recommending their "science" to her friends, was like a blow between the eyes, but the news which had followed was even more crushing. Aunt Harriet as a healer! Aunt Harriet holding up her innocent and unconscious niece as an instance of her own extraordinary power! She rapidly reviewed in her mind the experiences of the past few weeks; so this was the explanation of Aunt Harriet's serenity and poise, and of her indulgent attitude towards herself. No one enjoys being deceived, even for one's own benefit. Eloise felt betrayed and entrapped; she whirled in a passion of anger and left the room. Aunt Harriet, more disturbed than she was willing to admit, went to put away Seven, Eight, and Nine. Her first impulse was to bestow them under the bed, but remembering that there was no longer a cause for concealment she laid them on the table, with a sigh.

The days which ensued were trying to both. Suspicious of the psychic attentions of Aunt Harriet and her friends, Eloise felt like inviting a relapse by way of defiance; but then they would say it was because she had rebelled against their influence. Either way, they had her at a disadvantage. She was not fighting against flesh and blood, but against principalities and "powers." She told herself that she did not believe a word they said, but their absolute confidence in their methods filled her with superstitious tremors; and they were so absurdly satisfied, so inanely cheerful—Mrs. Glenn among the rest ! "I thought you had more sense," Eloise said to her.

"You don't understand, my dear," her friend returned, indulgently. "If you had seen Millicent fall off to sleep, bathed in perspiration and the fever all gone, you would have felt, as I did, *there is something here which we want for ourselves and our children.*"

Eloise made no reply. When Mrs. Glenn intrenched herself behind her maternal duties the solitary maiden felt that she was outside the debate.

Meanwhile, Aunt Harriet's little bedroom bid fair to be turned into a consultation office. The woman with rheumatism came, and her daughter came, and there were other patients also. In vain Eloise expostulated. Aunt Harriet had emerged from the cocoon of her former existence ; it was impossible to pack the gauzy wings of her new ambitions and desires again in that limited space. Just as Eloise felt that she could no longer endure the changed appearance of her surroundings, the broad face of Mrs. Harwood arose like a shining sun on the horizon. "Why, yes, didn't you get my letter?" she inquired, cordially. "Dan'l's cousin's wife's died and left us his place up on Seventy-fifth Street. We've rented the farm, and have come to Chicago to live."

"Thank God !" cried Eloise, clinging to her. "Mrs. Harwood, the world's upsidedown, and my head has commenced to turn. Now you've come, I can keep it from going over."

XIX

"What on earth do you mean, child?" inquired Mrs. Harwood, anxiously, for Eloise clung to her, half laughing, half crying. "Is your aunt sick?"

"No; she's never going to be sick any more," replied Eloise, with a forlorn laugh.

"What do you mean?"

"Aunt Harriet has joined some religious body—people who believe there is no such thing as sickness. They're just like children; they make believe they are well, and that they have money and are happy—but that is easier. Happiness is mostly make-believe, anyway."

"Oh, you mean the Christian Scientists," exclaimed Mrs. Harwood, settling back in her chair with a sigh of relief. "They won't hurt her. Let her go it."

"But, Mrs. Harwood," persisted Eloise, "they're dreadful. They come to Aunt Harriet for 'treatment,' as they call it."

"Who, the Scientists?"

"No; the guests in the house."

Mrs. Harwood threw back her head and laughed heartily.

Eloise looked disconcerted.

"I can't help it ; it is too good a joke. The idea of their coming to her !"

"She said she and her friends cured me," pursued Eloise, ruefully.

"What if they did and what if they didn't ?" returned Mrs. Harwood, coolly. "You're well, ain't you ? What do you care how you got there ?"

This was an entirely new aspect of the question for Eloise. She had no answer ready.

"Look a-here, child," said the elder woman, laying her rough hand affectionately on the girl's knee, "I got my lesson about interfering with what doesn't concern me three years ago come summer, and I got it by making a fool of myself. I didn't know it, either, until the next winter, when I was studying art, getting ready for the Fair, and then it came over me all of a sudden. The very things I had rooted out of one garden I was cultivating in another. First time I called 'em weeds ; now they were flowers. It made me hot all over. Since then I've let alone what I didn't understand."

Eloise caught the hand upon her knee and pressed it.

"All I want to say," concluded the visitor, "is this : don't be in too big a hurry, and don't stick your elbows out ; give other folks their half of the road. Where is Miss Larrabee ?"

"Gone off on some mysterious errand," pouted

Eloise. "I never know what she's doing, and she used to think she couldn't. make a move without consulting me."

"She used to live and breathe through you, that's a fact," replied Mrs. Harwood. "She's beginning to find out she has got lungs of her own."

Eloise gave her a quick glance.

"Oh, I've learned some things besides letting other folks's pictures alone. When I broke my wrist I had to sit down and give up the responsibility of running the universe. I found it went right along. I fretted and stewed for a while, because I couldn't make folks see there wasn't any way but mine; but I couldn't, so that was the end of it. Things turned out about the same in the end. I must go."

"Don't," implored Eloise.

"Dan'l will think I'm lost."

"How is he?" inquired Eloise.

"Just the same," replied Dan'l's wife, "and always will be. What do you hear from Mr. More?"

Eloise colored. "We haven't been writing very regularly. He was well when I heard last. I will go over to the station with you."

They encountered Mrs. Glenn in the hall, and stopped so long to talk with her that Mrs. Harwood lost her train.

"I won't go back," she said, sinking into a large rocking-chair which faced the hotel clock.

"I know you don't like to sit down here, but—why, there's Mr. Heffron! Is he stopping here?"

Eloise started. Yes, it certainly was Mark Heffron, talking with the hotel clerk, who opened the register and showed him the list of names. Mark wrote on a card and handed it to him, then came towards them. He started in his turn when he confronted Eloise Gordon, whom he had not met since that eventful summer at Beau Lieu. If either of them had anticipated a meeting, neither had thought of it as taking place in the rotunda of the Lake View Hotel. But they did what any other well-bred individuals would have done under similar circumstances—shook hands and asked each other the usual questions. Mark explained that he was looking for his cousin's wife, who wrote him she would be at the Lake View, but had failed to keep her appointment, and Eloise proclaimed herself an old resident of the place. Mrs. Harwood he remembered at Beau Lieu.

Then who should come in but Aunt Harriet with her bonnet askew from an encounter with the wind, but looking so bright and satisfied that Mark scrutinized her curiously. Taught by her new philosophy to let bygones be bygones and live in charity with all men, she greeted her quondam enemy as if they had been dear friends separated against their will. This was more of a surprise than her color and briskness; but Mark met her half-way, and when she urged him to call declared that nothing would suit him better.

The next train south would be due in a few minutes, and as Mark had plenty of time to put Mrs. Harwood aboard before he started for town, they left together, watched from the doorway by Eloise and her aunt.

"How queer everything looks!" exclaimed Aunt Harriet. "I should say there was going to be a wind-storm."

Eloise hurried up into the studio and flung open the window overlooking the lake. It reflected the dull gloom of the sky. A thin strip of silver ran around the horizon between them.

The ships in the bay stood like phantom ships, motionless, with close-furled sails. The dark masses of water around them and the dense clouds overhead appeared to be strewn with ashes. On the shore not a leaf stirred. The trees seemed stiffened by fear. Everywhere there was an ominous silence, a tension as of a wild beast about to spring. She watched until the storm broke with a noise like the rending of stone walls and the outward rush of armed hosts. There was no rain, but the air was thick with flying dust and spray, and with débris caught up from the streets. She was forced to close the window, and tried in vain to peer through the whirling chaos outside.

By and by Aunt Harriet came in, full of stories told by those who had been caught in the storm.

"I hope Mrs. Harwood escaped," said Eloise, anxiously.

"She had probably reached home," replied Aunt Harriet, "before the worst; but Mr. Heffron must have landed in the midst of it."

All night the tempest raged. It was impossible to sleep. The roar of the waves was like the continual thunder of artillery. In the morning there was comparative calm on shore, but the lake had been stirred to its depths. Every one went out to see the waves, which ran lightly along the pier and sprang high in air. "Like a sportive mermaid," said Eloise.

"Not so innocent as that," returned Mr. Armstrong, who accompanied her. "Those beautiful things have done an incredible amount of damage since we saw them last. Boats were coming ashore at Twenty-second Street all night, I hear."

The girl looked up at him with bright round eyes in which there was no horror, only an intense interest. "Oh, I should dearly love to see a wreck!" she exclaimed.

"It would give me pleasure to take you down there, but I am sorry to say I cannot remain long," said her escort, politely.

"I am used to being alone," she responded, carelessly. "Wait, please, until I get a heavy cloak."

The train was crowded and ran slowly, as if to give the patrons an opportunity to view the wild scenes along the route. There were continual ejaculations, "Look! See there!" and men and women started from their seats, as with rhythmic regularity the incoming wave ran along the breakwater and reared a tower of foam far above their heads. The breakwater had given way here and there; and mingled with its ruin were broken masts and wrecked cordage and pieces of hulls torn to splinters, as if some monster had chewed them and spit them out. Over them frisked the untamed, untamable element; it was about its own business, in a savage play, building beautiful forms only to destroy them. Without life as we know life, without death as we know death, yet with the pulse of life and the coldness of death it went on, leaping and shining and tossing ashore whatever had been intrusted to it, ships and cargoes and bodies from which it had beaten the breath.

"Many of the boats put out to sea to avoid being pounded to pieces," explained Armstrong. "But, I declare, there's a schooner on her beam-ends. You will have your wish. We will get off here."

They perched themselves on a pile of timber commanding the lake. The wreck was in plain sight. They counted the men clinging to her side; there were eight of them. The crowds on the shore were gesticulating wildly, and shouting all sorts of advice which could not possibly be heard above the breakers. After a while there was a movement among the men on the schooner;

they were trying to throw a rope ashore. Again and again their efforts were ineffectual. At last it was caught by the men on shore, and a shout went up which must have made itself heard above the roar of wind and wave. Then, one by one, the shipwrecked sailors came ashore, and as each one landed that exulting shout went up.

"Quite a sight!" commented Mark Heffron, tiptoeing over the rails to the place where Eloise sat. Mr. Armstrong had just left her.

"Isn't it?" she responded, her face aglow.

"You must paint this!" he exclaimed.

"Do you think I can?"

"Of course you can. I won't give you any peace until you do. Look at those men hug each other! He's the last!"

They went home together, and Mark stayed to luncheon. In the evening Carl came, looking very sober. He had been watching the wrecks all day. "Some of you people who have such extraordinary power ought to get together and pray down the wind," said Eloise, mockingly. But Carl did not even smile. "It ought to be possible," he said, soberly.

The next morning was calm and lovely. Eloise sat down before her easel, determined, if possible, to reproduce the scenes of the preceding day. She painted all day, and for many subsequent days, whenever she had an hour to spare. "But it isn't good," she told Mark Heffron when he inquired how the picture was getting on.

"Let me see it," he urged, and after some demur she placed it before him.

He regarded it thoughtfully. "I don't know what the trouble is," he said, at length; "the perspective is all right, the figures are good, the water is superb. But somehow I feel as if you did not mean it."

"I don't," replied Eloise, frankly. "I wanted to. I felt it, in a way, as one feels the scenes on the stage; but not as if I were a part of it."

Neither spoke for some minutes, and then Eloise began again, "I wonder about this instinct for saving. I suppose it is a purely natural instinct. Dogs have it, without being trained. How eager they were! Any one would think they and the shipwrecked men were brothers."

"Yes, I saw them," replied Mark, quickly. "They'll knock each other over just as readily to-morrow, if they disagree, or cut each other's throats in a bargain. That's an instinct, too."

XX

"THAT Hindoo blackamoor started it," began Uncle Oliver, recklessly, "tellin' his yarns about folks goin' down to the banks of the Ganges and peelin' off their bodies like a suit of old clothes, holdin' up such doin's ahead of plain, common-sense, American livin'. Half the town went chasin' after him. Then came that Miss Duvray with a rigmarole about the *color* of a *tone* and the *heft* of a *gesture.* Whoop-halloo, off they went after her! Then a feller down at the Enterprise had 'em stuck on the *power* of *mind;* he explained the miracles so that any child could work 'em. They follered him up. Now, here's Nellie Heffron; she's got the whole business, and fortune-tellin' to boot. They'll tag along behind her just as they have behind the others. Crazy as loons, the whole caboodle!"

The Ross girls, sitting in a row before him, looked mutinous, but said nothing.

"It is *so,*" exclaimed their uncle, as positively as if they had contradicted him. "When I was young, girls wanted a real live *male man.*"

"Oh!"

"Oh!"

"Oh!" interrupted the three maidens, several-ly; and then they exclaimed together, "Uncle Oliver!"

"They did," replied the old man, doggedly. "But now there's a premium put on the most on-natural, nondescript kind of an animal that can be turned out. Let a feller come along who belongs to an Order or a Brotherhood, and who sets up to teach men there's a better way to live than to go straight ahead, tend to business, and look out for their families, then the girls sit down at his feet an' worship. Here's this Hindoo, told me he hadn't written to his own mother for seven years!"

"But, Uncle Oliver, when he broke those fam-ily ties it was to take upon himself larger re-sponsibilities," vouchsafed Julia, with dignity. "There are plenty to fulfil the family relation; there are few, like Haridass, who assume the mis-sion of *saving souls*."

"He needn't trouble himself about mine," re-turned Uncle Oliver, flippantly. "I don't want any one pullin' an' haulin' to keep me out of hell. I'll settle my own account with Him that made me."

Maud gave Julia a significant look. Mary opened her mouth to say something, but her uncle continued, "What's more, I don't think that fel-ler's so all-fired spiritooal as you girls try to make out. I noticed he knew how to make himself as comfortable as the next one, and he didn't spend much of his time fastin' an' prayin'. There's just one thing about it," and here he brought the fist of one knotty hand into the palm of the other with a crack like that of a pistol—"there's just one thing about it: when he comes back next month, as you say he's goin' to, I don't want you girls to have anything to do with him. As to your entertaining him, it is out of the question. I won't have it."

Now, whatever the Ross girls had of earthly possessions was under Uncle Oliver's care, and, deeply as they were interested in the unearthly goods offered by Haridass, they knew it never would do to sacrifice the one to the other. They temporized. Julia leaned forward in her chair with a constrained smile, and said, soothingly:

"Don't you think you are a little unreasonable, Uncle Oliver? Merely because you and Haridass differ on certain points of religious belief, are you going to forbid us to speak to him?"

"'Tain't that," returned Uncle Oliver, bluntly. "I've heard things that have been said. I ain't goin' to repeat them, but they made me mad clear through. He's no gentleman; that's enough!"

Here Maud took up the cudgels for the absent prophet. "Uncle Oliver, that is a serious charge," she began, in her high, clear voice, "and one that must be proved or—or rejected."

"Oh, I can prove it," retorted her uncle.

"Then why don't you?" replied Maud, flushing vividly.

"You surely cannot expect us to accept the statement without any further testimony," said Julia, who was of a judicial cast of mind.

Mary glanced furtively from one sister to the other.

"Well, if you will have it," cried Uncle Oliver, desperately—"no, I won't tell you. You can take my word or go without." He took his hat and cane and tramped sturdily out of the house, looking neither to the right nor to the left until he ran against another man equally unmindful of his way.

"Beg your pardon," he began, bluffly—"why, hullo, Jim! Goin' over to the house?"

Dr. Humphrey stopped and held out his hand.

"No, I wasn't. Any one sick?"

"Not exactly sick, but—"

"What is the trouble?"

Uncle Oliver coughed and swallowed and hesitated, but finally let out the story of the morning.

Humphrey threw back his head and laughed so heartily that the story-teller laughed, too.

"I'll tell you what it was," he went on, in a burst of confidence. "An acquaintance of mine met that feller on the street in Boston, and gave him some messages from folks here, our girls among the rest. Mr. Hindoo seemed to find it hard to remember who the Rosses were. At last he says, 'Oh yes, those old maids!' And he had lived on their bounty for three months! They did everything for that feller."

"I know they did," returned Humphrey; "but, perhaps," he added, slyly, "Haridass found it hard to express himself in English. Doubtless, in his own language, the remark would have read like a compliment. You know he thinks the single state is one of blessedness."

"Ye-es, they've got it all fixed up—no marryin' and no medicine. I hear they're cutting into your practice some, especially that preacher at the Enterprise."

"He did," responded Humphrey, with a shrug, "until I went down and found out how he did it."

"By George, that was a slick deal! But how about Dering?"

"Carl has to learn his own lessons," answered Humphrey, shortly. "He tried to teach me mine, what was more. I thought we'd better separate. Carl's brainy, but he don't know as much as he will some time. He's hardly the make-up for a doctor. I opposed his going into medicine, but his mother had her heart set on it. She's as superstitious for the profession as he is against it."

"You don't mean he's gone back on the profession?"

Humphrey shrugged his shoulders again, and lifted his eyebrows significantly.

"Humph!" ejaculated Uncle Oliver. "What in thunder is he livin' on?"

"On the proceeds of his outfit, I suppose."

"Sold out?" gasped Uncle Oliver.

"Everything; he had some wild notion of

throwing the things into the lake. He said they would do more harm than good; that as long as people were in bondage to the material, the spiritual would have no opportunity for development."

"The spiritooal!" shouted Uncle Oliver. "I want to *swear!* I'll go to Dering myself—I'll—hullo, here's Mark Heffron! Don't you know Mark? He's a sort of a cousin of mine. Dr. Humphrey, Mark. By George, I'm glad to see you, Mark! I've got some work for you to do. Excuse me, Jim, I've got to see Mark on business."

"What's up?" asked Mark, as the two men left Humphrey and walked on by themselves.

"Everything; that Hindoo fakir's been sassin' my girls, and Carl Dering's thrown up his job, and Nellie Heffron's holdin' forth on *occultism*—every one's goin' straight to the devil!"

"They think they're going the other way," responded Mark.

"Carl's as nice a boy as ever lived," continued Uncle Oliver, disregarding the interruption, "but away up in the clouds—his mother's that way; I used to know his mother when she lived in Kankakee. These folks have got hold of him—that Miss Duvray's at the bottom of it—and he's given up a splendid opening with Humphrey—that I was talkin' with when you came along. I want you to see Carl and have a good talk with him, and you must see Nell. Perhaps you had better begin with her, as long as she's in the family."

"And after I'm through with Nellie and young Dering I suppose you would like to have me drop in and straighten out your nieces," suggested Mark.

"'Twould take more'n one of you to do that," replied their uncle. "I'll let you off on the girls if you'll fix up Carl and Nellie."

"I went out to the Lake View to see Nellie yesterday," said Mark. "She wrote me she would be there; but they had heard nothing from her."

"No; the Lake View isn't grand enough," exclaimed Uncle Oliver, with an important sweep of his arm. "She's at the Cynthia — five rooms, French maid, the whole outfit; she's done well at this business." There was a regretful pride in his voice.

"Nell's as bright as a new pin," laughed his companion. "She'd do well at anything. Have you been to any of her lectures?"

"One of them," replied Uncle Oliver, looking sheepish. "I wanted to see what she's up to?"

"How did she look? What did she do?"

"Oh, she was all togged out, with a big round pin as big as a tea-saucer under her chin and a great long chain of these amethysts around her neck; she says they have the same vibrations that she does."

Mark laughed.

"Well, whatever she says *goes*," pursued the speaker. "There was a whole roomful of folks—

nice folks, too—and they swallowed every word she said. She arranged them according to their planets—Earth, Air, Fire, and Water folks together; that was on account of the vibrations, too. Oh, I can't begin to tell what she did. She got 'em all a-breathin' together, timed 'em, movin' her hand up and down, *so*. You could have heard 'em breathe half a mile off. One old gal liked it so well she wouldn't stop. I asked her some questions, and it made her kinder mad. She kept on snoring and wouldn't say a word."

"You excite my curiosity," cried Mark. "I shall certainly have to look her up." He took out his watch. "I wonder if she would see me now. I'll try it, anyway."

He held out his hand to Uncle Oliver, who shook it warmly, saying, "Drop into the office and tell me how things are."

"I can't do it—that is, not until late. Are you in the office after four o'clock?"

"After four o'clock!" sniffed the other. "This isn't New York. We don't crawl down to our work at ten and dig out at three; we begin work at seven in Chicago and keep it up until six. Good-bye."

Madame Heffron was in, but was engaged. Would the gentleman please be seated, and when madame was disengaged she would see him. Mark obeyed, making himself comfortable in a huge cushioned chair by the window, while the maid withdrew again to the outer room. The last time he had seen Nellie Heffron was soon after Jack's death. She had refused all offers of assistance then, although every one knew that she was in a tight place. "I don't want any help from you Heffrons," she had said, "nor from my people either. You called my poor Jack worthless because his will was not as strong as yours; I'll pay his debts myself." And she had done so, teaching music, and singing in a church at Columbus, where she lived. He had heard from her, now and then, thanking him for the music he sent her; but when he attempted to pay a bill of Jack's she promptly returned the amount.

He mused thus, looking out upon the park, where the trees were beginning to show the misty green of early spring foliage. Presently he heard voices in an adjoining room, and, glancing in the direction whence they came, saw the high-priestess herself seated in a big arm-chair, and receiving the confidences of a girlish devotee who knelt on a cushion before her. Yes, that was Nell; he recognized her wealth of golden hair and her plump shoulders.

"Let me look into your eyes," she was saying to the young woman at her feet. "Yes, you have more poise. You are learning the secret. Keep on with your exercises, the breathing and the recitations. I will see you again."

With an impressive gesture she dismissed her pupil by a side door, and turned to the room where Mark was waiting.

"I am so glad to see you," she said, extending both hands. "When did you come? How did you know where to find me?"

"No thanks to you," he answered, returning the pressure of her large, strong hands. "I went out to the Lake View, but—"

She interrupted him with a laugh. "You poor fellow!" she exclaimed, caressingly. "It was a shame to send you on a wild-goose chase. I found the Cynthia more accessible, and since I came here I have been busy every minute."

"So I understand. I didn't know as I could even get a glimpse of you for the crowd."

"I don't have a minute to myself," rejoined Nellie, with a satisfied sigh. "There are people here all the time, and really they take hold of it very well."

"Have you any of 'it' on hand?" asked Mark, quizzically. "Could you let a dog of an unbeliever get a scent of what 'it' is?"

"Now, see here, Mark Heffron," returned Nellie, sharply, "you needn't pretend to be so ignorant and unconcerned. You were the first to put me on to these things, years ago."

"O Lord!" ejaculated Mark, "here's another! This time I'll find out what 'it' is. Nell, for pity's sake, what form of 'it' did I ever have any dealings with?"

His cousin's wife burst into a hearty laugh. "Upon my word," she cried, "I don't believe you remember a thing!"

"I don't, upon my word."

"You don't remember coming to our house in Columbus one summer when Jack had gone off on a—a—time, and finding me all used up and crying my heart out? And you gave me a lot of books to read: *Cornelius Agrippa* and *Paracelsus* and *Jacob Boehme* and—"

"A light breaks in upon me! Poor little Nell, she sat down with the whole batch in her apron, and the fire went out in the kitchen stove and I got no dinner."

"Of course you remember that part, being a man," she retaliated, adding, earnestly, "Mark, those books kept me from going mad. Moreover, they helped me to pay up the old debts, and—"

"I tried to help you pay them," interposed Mark, sensitively, "but you wouldn't let me."

"The best way to help me was to teach me to help myself," returned Nellie, tranquilly. "All I needed was a starter. I could give you points, now."

"I don't doubt that."

"Wait a minute!" she exclaimed, and, going into the room where she had been with her pupil, returned with her hands full of photographs and circulars.

"That is my Rosicrucian teacher," she began, displaying the picture of a venerable man with a beard which covered him like a breastplate. "Isn't he a dear? And this is Haridass Goculdass. There he is again with a group of his followers."

"A moon-struck set !" commented Mark.

"They're concentrating their thoughts," explained the initiate, with a little giggle. "You see, they must look at one point and not move their eyes from that spot. If they do, their thoughts wander. They get marvellous effects from that concentration."

"I should think they might," returned Mark, grimly ; "and this is the prospectus ?"

"Yes, that is what I teach," she announced, complacently.

"Sun-breath, Moon-breath, Isvara," he read, "the influence of the stars, the influence of gems, the record of life written in the hand." As Uncle Oliver had said, she "had the whole business."

"Concentration, Isolation, Yoga," he continued.

"Haridass Goculdass says I am the only person in America who can teach Yoga," interrupted Nellie. "I make a specialty of that. There's a Mademoiselle Duvray in this house who pretends to teach 'Hindoo Deep-breathing,' but she is *away off*. Do you know her?" Something in Mark's manner made her pause and scrutinize him curiously.

"I have known Mademoiselle Duvray for several years," he answered, quietly.

"Oh, if she is a friend yours," apologized Nellie.

"Don't hesitate on my account, I beg," he returned, with one of his satirical gestures.

"Well, I'll tell you what it is," pursued Nellie, confidentially. "She won't come out with these things as I do. She covers up and plasters over and slides around, and then to call herself Mademoiselle, like a French governess !"

"What do you mean by not coming out ?" he demanded.

"You'll find out one of these days. She's a *Taurus*. The Taurus people are bound to rule. They take everything in sight. You want to look out for Taurus people. When were you born ?"

"The fifth of April."

"I thought so. You are an *Aries*—like me. I'm an Aries. *You* have great occult power if you would only develop it."

"How do you know I haven't ?"

"Well, you ought to do something with it—something to help humanity." A wistful look came into her deep azure eyes. "Mark, you'd be surprised if you could see the people who come to me for help. Honestly, I wouldn't care to live if I couldn't help people. It is the only thing worth living for."

"Very true, Nellie," he answered, seriously.

"There are plenty who do this to make money," she continued, with dignity ; "but I'm like Haridass Goculdass. I am working in the interest of humanity. Haridass and I are after souls."

"Pretty large game, Nell !"

"Yes, I know it is."

"And pretty small shot." He took up the prospectus. "Odyllic Force, Aura," he read. "How much do you really believe in all this, Nell!"

"More than you think," she answered, promptly. "You may call it *aura*, or you may call it *atmosphere*, it's *there*, and every scientific man acknowledges the fact. They have to have these things dressed up for them, Mark; they like the queer names; they think they are getting more in that way. And they have to have something to do — some little ceremony; the more unusual it is the more good it does them. Mark, you know there's a lot of truth in this, now, don't you?"

He held her eyes with his for a moment before he answered her. "It is just because I know there is so much in it that I hate to have you fool these people."

"If I do, I fool them into—into the *truth*," she cried.

"Ah, Nellie, Nellie, you are more Irish than the family you married into."

They stood up, laughing and holding each other's hands.

"Then you won't stay to luncheon and hear me speak?" she asked.

"I think not," he answered, affectionately.

She accompanied him to the elevator, chatting all the way of her triumphs and prospects, and of her delight in seeing him. "You will surely come again?" she asked.

"Oh yes, I will come again."

He sighed as he walked down the street under the tender green of the new spring foliage ; yet he smiled, too. It was all such innocent "fooling."

XXI

There was a young man talking to Uncle Oliver when Mark entered the latter's office the next morning—a tall young man with fair hair. As he turned Mark was struck by his resemblance to Eloise Gordon : he had the same hazel eyes with black lashes and brows, the same delicate nose and short upper-lip, the same winning smile. The absence of a beard enhanced the resemblance. Uncle Oliver introduced him as Doctor Dering, and soon afterwards made some clumsy excuse for leaving him alone with Mark. He was evidently very fond of the boy, whom he patted encouragingly upon the back as he said good-bye. "If any one comes in, tell them I'll be back in an hour or so," he added.

"There goes one of the kindest hearts in Chicago," said Mark, as Uncle Oliver closed the door noisily behind him to let them know he was out of hearing.

"Isn't he, though!" exclaimed Carl, enthusiastically. "I don't know what I should do without him. My own father couldn't have been more disinterested. And we are not connected, you know. He knew my mother when he was a young man."

"Your father is not alive, I take it," said Mark.

"Oh yes, he's alive. Did you think he wasn't? But there are no other children. That is why they make such a fuss over me." Again that winning smile.

"He is evidently a 'mother's boy,'" thought Mark. "Easy meat for the sharks; but I can't tell him that. What under the sun shall I say to him, anyway?" He was saved the trouble of deciding what to say by Carl himself, who continued, "She wrote to Uncle Oliver when she learned that I had determined to give up my profession."

"Why did you do that?" asked Mark.

"It seemed the only thing to do. I could not conscientiously go on."

"Why?"

"Because I had come to disbelieve in the method."

"In drugs?"

"Yes, sir."

"You have been in practice how many years?" asked Mark, with a quizzical look.

Carl blushed. "Nearly four years."

"And you are, I take it, about twenty-five?"

"Nearly twenty-six."

"With four years' practice and not yet in your twenty-seventh year, you have exhausted the virtues of Materia Medica?"

"I don't mean that," returned Carl, quickly. "But you must have seen for yourself—you are a thinker—that the recovery of a patient depends upon that patient's faith. You can't cure him if he does not believe in you and in what you give him."

"Have you learned," pursued Mark, "that you can always command the patient's faith without the employment of drugs—granting that the drugs themselves are without efficacy?"

"Sometimes I can," replied Carl, hopefully.

"In that case, do you not find it necessary to substitute for the dependence upon the drug a dependence upon yourself, a faith in your powers, a belief in your ability to do what you have undertaken?"

"Why, yes," granted the young metaphysician; "but that is faith, that isn't drugs."

"Exactly; but do you find yourself so much more nearly infallible than the drugs are? Isn't it substituting one prop for another, and don't you wish at times that you could give up the responsibility, and whip out that old black leather case to operate for you?"

An illuminating smile broke over Carl's sunny face. "You come pretty near to the truth," he answered, ingenuously. "But is it right to deceive the patient?" he questioned, the smile disappearing. "Have I a right to say 'This will cure you' when I don't believe the drug has anything to do with it?"

"Have you a right to say 'I will cure you' when you feel a similar uncertainty?"

"I don't say exactly that."

"What do you say?" The question was put so frankly that there was no resenting it, even if Carl had been inclined.

"I say, 'God is Good and He is Absolute,'" he replied, like a child saying his lesson. "'There is no evil. This idea of sickness is a misapprehension. The truth is that you are well. Now, you must realize that truth, and manifest it.'"

"Do you say that aloud?"

"Oh no, it wouldn't do."

"Any more than telling a patient, 'This pill or this powder isn't of any use, but if you brace up and have some confidence in it, it will pull you through, because of the marvellous effect which confidence invariably has upon the human mind.'"

Carl looked thoughtful. "Sometimes you can say what you mean aloud," he persisted. "There are some patients who want you to tell them how to get hold of this for themselves."

"Among the unenlightened," responded Mark, "weren't there a few who could bear to be told the truth?"

"Why, yes. Oh, I see what you mean plainly enough."

"My dear boy," exclaimed Mark, laying his hand affectionately on the boy's arm — no one could help being affectionate with Carl—"I admire Truth as much you do; I've followed her trailing skirts this many a year; I've lain low and listened for her footsteps; I've cherished every

far-off glimpse of her, every faintest whisper.
Let me give you a warning : she has no use for a
lover who blabs her secrets. Keep what she tells
you and use it. Don't think you must tell every
one you help how you do it. Don't think you
must formulate your belief ; unformulated belief
is the best, because it is alive; the formulated
things are dead. And don't think you must foist
your opinions on the rest of the world ; their opinions are just as good—for them."

"And you believe—"

"I believe your own profession is the place for
you. Give just as little medicine as you please ;
use just as much faith as you can ; you will find
plenty of room among scientific men for the truth,
however novel its application. Among these new
friends and teachers, have you found such unquali-
fied welcome of the truth as truth ? Can you tell
them what you honestly think ? Will they hear
'a plain, unvarnished tale' ? Do you never find it
necessary to flatter and soothe them with pleasant
words which mean little or nothing ? Have the
women no vanity, the men no self-conceit ?"

Carl looked sober. "That troubled me more
than anything else," he acknowledged. "I found
I was getting back into the old ways. It was so
magnificent to say just what you meant. But of
course these people aren't perfect."

"Even if they do say, ' All is Spirit and all is
Good,' " concluded Mark. "No, I am not laughing at them. They had a work to do, and they

are doing it—in the church, in the professions, in society. The power of thought would never have been recognized and taken advantage of as it is if it had not been for them. They have my best wishes, and so have you. How are you off for funds?"

It was as impossible to resent this question as it had been to resent those which preceded it. Carl looked confused, but answered, readily enough, "I am pretty nearly 'strapped.' I've been trying to get work for some time. Dr. Symonds thought there would be plenty of his sort of work to do, but I don't feel prepared to undertake it in just the way he proposed."

"Not quite ready to claim infallibility?"

"He doesn't claim infallibility," returned Carl, quickly, "except for the Principle. He says that if you will fulfil the conditions you will accomplish what you undertake."

"That's liberal, I'm sure," said Mark, "to all concerned. What advertisements have you answered?"

"All sorts. Some of the people I saw, but none of them wanted me."

"Any more than you wanted them. My dear fellow, there's only one thing for you to do. Go back into Humphrey's office. Eat humble pie, if it is necessary; he is older than you are, and has had more experience."

"I can't," exploded Carl. "He called me—an unmitigated ass!"

"What if he did?" returned Mark, trying not to smile. "That was his way of putting it. I'll tell you what I'll do: I'll go over and see him myself, and explain matters. I'll venture he'll be glad enough to get you back again. Where is his office?"

Carl gave the address. "But I know it is of no use," he said, dejectedly.

Mark disappeared, and Carl sat down to wait for him, surprised at his own agitation. A picture of the pleasant office rose before him; of his own desk and the instrument-case which he had bought by means of such self-denial, both on his own part and his mother's. How fondly they had arranged the shelves together, wrapping each shining implement in its chamois-skin envelope embroidered with his initial by her devoted hands! How carelessly he had parted with them in his zeal for the "development" which he seemed somehow to have missed, after all!

He sprang to his feet and walked the narrow room to and fro, to and fro. How could he expect Humphrey to overlook his defiant attitude and personal thrusts? And what should he, could he do if Heffron's mission failed? His fruitless search for work had taught him its scarcity and his own lack of preparation for anything outside his medical training. The other, the spiritual substitute, had appealed to his love of beauty and goodness; it had been a courtesy to his friends, a graceful mannerism, a lofty mode of life; but as a means of winning a livelihood it had always appeared out of place. It seemed impossible now, since his talk with Uncle Oliver's friend. He dreaded Mark's return, and trembled when, at last, he heard a footstep in the hall. One glance at Mark's face encouraged him. "Is it all right?" he faltered.

"Of course it's all right," replied the mediator. "You're to go right over. He has an operation at St. Luke's this morning, and you're to go along with him to assist. 'Jones is N. G.,' Humphrey says; 'he's as honest as a cooper's cow, but his fingers are like sticks.'"

"That's Humphrey all over," laughed Carl, delightedly. "He always liked my hands." He spread them out before him — Eloise Gordon's hands: long, slender, shapely, full of skill and sympathy.

"What's the matter now?" demanded Mark, for Carl had suddenly stopped with a face full of consternation.

"I haven't a thing," he cried, tragically, "not a thing. I sold every book and instrument to Jones when he took my place; I haven't so much as a needle."

"That's all right," said Mark, coolly. "Humphrey bought them in. He always expected you'd come back some time."

"Blessed old Humphrey!" ejaculated Carl. "I'll fall on his neck."

"I wouldn't do that," advised Mark, "and

what's more, I'd keep a good lot of self-respect handy. I told him you'd been investigating mental science for the benefit of the profession, and you had some very valuable material—as I think you have. You needn't undertake to teach him the explanation of the origin of evil or the personal characteristics of the First Cause."

"He took Dr. Symonds's course himself," returned Carl, "and bought the manuscript lessons ; I found them in his desk. That was what the row was all about ; I told him he ought to come out and show his colors."

"Oh, you did, did you ? That was politic. Well, I wouldn't offer any more advice if I were you. Hurry up now ; don't keep him waiting. I'll stay here and 'tend store' till Uncle Oliver comes back. Don't stop to talk ; I understand."

Carl gave him a grateful look and hurried away. He had not been gone many minutes before Uncle Oliver came bustling in.

"By George, Mark !" he cried, seizing his hand, "I'll never forget this morning's work !" He took off his glasses and wiped them, and blew his nose violently. "A better boy never lived," he went on, earnestly, " but he's no more fit to wrastle with the world than a chickadee—his mother right over. She was the prettiest, smartest little thing you ever saw when she was a girl, and she's married to a great, selfish lubber."

Uncle Oliver wiped his glasses for the second time, but he still seemed to have difficulty in seeing through them. "Everybody likes Carl," he continued. "Our girls think the world of him—adaptable, you know—goes right in. He's got a cousin out south of here ; I sent the girls out to look her up — poor girl — teaches drawing or painting, or something of that sort ; I thought they'd work her in. They took lessons of her, but never got any further—not but what I respect her full as much for it as if she grabbed every chance that come along, like that Miss Duvray."

Mark frowned. "You seem to have a grudge against Mademoiselle Duvray," he said, caustically.

"She's too almighty successful," growled Uncle Oliver. "You and I know what success means. Some one has got to go down to let us go up. We expect a man to pile up his feller-beings and climb over them, but we don't expect a woman to do it. There's another way, to be sure," Mark started to speak, but Uncle Oliver hastened to add, "I don't say she's one to take it ; she isn't. She'd dodge before it came to an actual experience ; the other feller'd get the experience. I tell you, Mark," he continued, earnestly, "it made me mad to see that boy mooning around after her and that leftenant of hers, Louise Ayer. They played on that sensitive nature of his just as they would on fiddle-strings. 'Tain't right; 'tain't right."

Mark shrugged his shoulders. "You can't follow that boy around and cry 'Hands off !' to every one who touches him.   If he can't protect him-self, he'd better learn how.   I must go."

"Come and have some lunch with me."

"Can't do it.   I want to catch a man before he leaves his office.   Good-bye."

"Good-bye, Mark.   Hullo! I nearly forgot Nell. Did you see her?"

"Yes, I saw her."

"How was she?"

"Plump and pretty as ever."

"Did you—did you have any talk with her?"

"An hour or more of it."

"Well, was she—was she *reasonable?*"

"She thought she was.   Reasonableness is a relative quality."

"You know what I mean.   Is she going to quit her nonsense, and settle down and behave her-self?"   Uncle Oliver was becoming impatient, but his impatience was but as the sputter of a match to the explosive light in Mark Heffron's eyes.

"See here, Mr. Ross," he exclaimed, wheeling in his walk towards the door, and facing his com-panion, "I'm not a special policeman detailed to look after other people's business.   I have some affairs of my own, and it is high time for me to be attending to them.   Good-morning !"

"Of all the peppery Irishmen !" ejaculated Uncle Oliver, standing where Mark had left him in the middle of the room.

To tell the truth, Mark had in his pocket at that moment a letter relating to "other people's business " which troubled him not a little; it was from young Norton, and ran somewhat as follows :

"I wish you would see my uncle. I hear in a roundabout way that he has withdrawn his stock from the B. & O., and goodness knows what he has done with it. He doesn't favor me with his confidence, but he always thought you knew more than any one else did. When I was in Chicago, a few weeks ago, he seemed hurt because you had not been out to see him."

XXII

It was some distance to Norton's office, and Mark had already traversed it twice that day, intending to leave Uncle Oliver until afternoon; but Norton had been out. He was out now, and there was no office-boy to tell where he had gone—nothing but a small card stuck into the sash of the door and saying briefly, "Back at two."

Mark looked at his watch. "Just one. I'll get something to eat, and come back in time to catch him," he decided. He hurried along the street, trying to find some clean, attractive place where he could obtain "a bite" to last until dinner-time. Suddenly, out of the earth beside him, as it seemed, started up the very man he sought. Norton had a guilty look; Mark eyed him suspiciously. "I have been to your office twice," he said, with some severity.

"Is that so?" replied Norton, shamefacedly. "The fact is, I—well, to tell the truth, I had an early breakfast; I was a little faint for food."

"Nothing criminal about that," returned Mark.

"Why, no; nothing criminal," said the old

man ; "but I meant to be in. I got your note. You haven't been to lunch ?"

"What's this place you went into ?" Mark scrutinized it curiously—as much of it, at least, as appeared above-ground : a large plate-glass window inscribed in black and gilt letters, "Cafetira," and a stairway, up and down which men and women were passing.

"It is *clean*," said Mr. Norton, hesitatingly, "but there's no style about it. Don't you know what a *cafetira* is ?"

Mark confessed his ignorance, adding, " But I'll be wiser very soon."

"Perhaps you won't like it," suggested his companion.

"If it's good enough for you, it's good enough for me," replied Mark, and led the way down the steps. Within the door, at the bottom of the stairway, a man sat at a turnstile and handed long slips of paper to those who passed. Before another turnstile stood the cashier's desk, where the same slips were handed in and the amount settled. Mark looked at his list ; upon it were printed the names of the articles of food, with the price opposite the name.

" You want to set your table," directed his companion. " There are the cups over there and the saucers ; the plates, knives, and forks are opposite."

Groups of young girls were preparing a table together, chatting and laughing as they went to and fro with their dishes. The men who were in the room seemed more inclined to be solitary, and walked soberly to their seats with their cups of coffee and sandwich plates.

"You get what you want and they punch the list," counselled Mr. Norton, and Mark obeyed, marching from coffee-urn to salad-stand, and feeling, as he told himself, "tired of the whole business" before he commenced to eat. Overhead, the ground-glass windows of the roof reminded them that they were under the street. Small parallelograms of shadow glided over in pairs when men passed, and large waving triangles when the women's skirts went by. Mr. Norton affected a cheerful indifference to the discomforts, assuming a jovial, picnic-seeking air which was entirely foreign to his pensive, ponderous nature.

"He isn't doing this for the fun of it," mused Mark, "but I won't say a word now." He talked of business and the "depression," computed the possibilities of better times, discussed the threatened "tie-up," and all the while watched the old man before him narrowly.

"I never saw him look so alive. I suppose it is the fever of the gambler," he mused. "Poor old duffer! He'll tell me all about it when we get back to the office."

But when they had reached the office and were settled in their respective chairs fronting each other, Mark found it difficult to open the discussion. Either Mr. Norton had determined to be wary in his confidences, or he feared Mark's disapproval of what had been done. In vain Mark led him diplomatically around to the question of investments, and invited his faith by vouchsafing all sorts of information about his own affairs. The old man shied away from his tempting suggestions as a horse shies from the salt-box when there is a halter behind it. Yet he detained Mark, and evidently wanted to say something.

"Why doesn't he out with it?" mused Mark, uneasily. "I've hung around here as long as I'm going to." He arose and held out his hand, saying, "If there is anything I can do for you, Mr. Norton, let me know."

"Don't go," implored the old man. "Don't go. I—I want to talk with you."

Mark sat down and waited, with some impatience. "I've wanted to talk with you for some time," pursued his companion, diffidently; "but you always seem in such a hurry. I wanted to consult with you before I took any decided step; but when I recalled our conversation of a year ago, I knew you'd approve of what I was doing —what I meditated doing."

Mark stared. What could he have said a year ago which could possibly be construed as having any bearing on investments or the B. & O.?

"And so I went ahead," pursued the other. "Then afterwards I learned from Mademoiselle Duvray herself that she was the little French girl you told me about, and I remembered you said she was a living example of your opinions. She always had plenty of time to talk about these things, and she knew just what I wanted. Mark, that woman has been an angel of light to me!"

"She told me you two were good friends," replied Mark, civilly.

"Friends!" broke in the old man, "she has been my salvation! You see, Mark," his voice took on a forbearing tone, "your way is all right for you; some have to get it one way, and some another. But I knew that night when you were talking about faith being founded on reason that we never should understand each other. She's a *woman*, all intuition and sensitiveness. I don't have to explain a word to her. She understood without my saying anything, and she led me back into the path from which I strayed years ago. Mark, do you remember my telling you that I'd give all I possessed to feel as I did then? Well, the Lord has taken me at my word!"

A sudden horror seized Mark Heffron. "You don't mean to say," he exclaimed, "that you've given up all your property to Marguerite Duvray? What is she, to do this thing!"

"Why, no," replied the old man, tranquilly, "she doesn't want money; that is why it comes to her. She never lacks for anything, and neither shall I, now that I've learned how to live. It's all in the universe, enough and to spare. Put yourself in the right attitude, and it flows towards you."

All this was interesting, but furnished no explanation of the disposition of Mr. Norton's stock. Mark pushed on, seeking a solution. "What am I to understand," he asked, bluntly, "by the Lord's taking you at your word?"

"Just what I said," replied his companion, with a bright look. "I've given up carrying on business in the old way. I've undertaken to help spread a gospel which is going to revolutionize the world." The speaker started to his feet, and paced up and down the office. "Mark," he said, earnestly, coming to a standstill before the young man's chair, "what are people after? *Happiness!* What is the cause of all the trouble in the world, the struggle, and the misery? *Unhappiness!* Make people happy and they'll be satisfied. Show them that happiness depends on their being kind and generous, and the rich will divide with the poor; everything will even up; there will be no poverty. Show them that health depends upon thought, and every one will learn how to think rightly, and will be well in consequence. Prove to them that sin is a mistake, that it is acting upon a misconception, and does not bring happiness, and people will cease to sin; they will *change their thought*, that is what *repentance* means. Why, don't you see, Mark, this is only carrying out your own theory, the controlling power of thought?"

Mark saw, only too plainly. "Who is going to do all this?" he inquired, dryly. "The world isn't exactly clamoring for these ideas."

"It is more ready for them than you suppose," replied the other, calmly. "There are institutions for the propagation of this teaching all over the world. The little paper which we publish goes to France, Germany, even to India."

"Who are *we?*" asked Mark. "You and Mademoiselle Duvray?"

"Why, no," responded Mr. Norton, quickly. "Dr. Symonds is in charge of the work here in Chicago—a most able man. I wish you would go and talk with him, Mark."

"How did you get hold of him?"

"Mademoiselle Duvray took me there. Didn't I tell you? I told you that it was through her that I found the Light!"

"And Dr. Symonds represents the Light!"

"You wouldn't speak in that tone if you knew him." Evidently Mr. Norton's feelings were hurt. He began to draw himself together and away from the scoffing visitor, who saw the mistake he had made and hastened to repair it.

"Forgive me, Mr. Norton; I spoke ill-advisedly. As you say, we look at these things differently; I was born without a bump of reverence, and time has not filled in the hollow. But I am interested in whatever concerns you."

"But this concerns *you*," interrupted the other. "The first thing I thought of when I began to study with Dr. Symonds was how pleased you would be to know that your theories were being verified, were being *practically applied.* Why, Mark, it is magnificent!"

Mark remained silent. Mr. Norton sat down with a sigh. A young man who could theorize so glibly, and yet resent the application of his theories, was a being beyond his comprehension. But neither theory nor application absorbed his visitor just then. He was saying to himself, "How in thunder shall I find out what has become of that fifty thousand dollars?" It would never do to write Joey that his mission had failed.

While he was still puzzling over the next move, Mr. Norton began again. "I know what you think ; you think because you never heard of this man that he is without influence or position. When you see a big brownstone building go up, right here, on the lake front, devoted to the offices and halls of those interested in this movement, you will see what Dr. Symonds has accomplished."

Mark pricked up his ears. "Has it really gone so far as that ?" he asked, temperately.

"Wait, I'll show you something !" exclaimed Mr. Norton, jumping up and going to his desk. "There, what do you think of that ?" he asked, triumphantly, unrolling a huge sheet of thick blue paper such as architects use. "That" was a drawing of a façade, lofty and beautiful, adorned with many quaint and graceful symbols, each significant in itself, but all subordinated to the artistic glory of the whole.

"It is very fine," said Mark, "and represents a great deal of money. It will take a pretty wealthy association to put up such a building as that."

"Fifty thousand dollars has already been subscribed," said the old man, rolling up the plan, with a chuckle. "Other subscriptions are coming in fast. It's a good investment, Mark. A building like that pays its stock-owners better than almost anything else that they can go into. Didn't you know that?"

"Sometimes," replied Mark, absent-mindedly. He was wondering what he should say next. If the money had gone, that was the end of it, unless he could induce this unknown apostle, Symonds, to relax his hold, which was improbable, to say the least. If the money was still uninvested, there might be a chance of saving it.

"I wouldn't be in a hurry to go into that sort of thing if I were you," he said, assuming a carelessness which he did not feel. "And don't trust your Dr. Symonds too far; you don't know anything about his antecedents."

Mr. Norton turned upon him a pitying smile. "That's all right for you, Mark—for all of you who trust to reason and logic, and who make a man explain and prove what he is; but to those of us who have learned to trust a higher guide, Intuition, there is no possibility of being deceived. I *feel*, I *know* the integrity of that man. Mark, if ever a man was inspired, that man is; I wish you'd go and have a talk with him."

Argument was useless, that Mark saw. The quiet obstinacy which is the strength of dependent natures fortified the large, loose figure before him. Direct attack would be hopeless; whatever methods he employed must be indirect and unsuspected by their object. He would see Marguerite and have a plain talk with her. This matter must be sifted to the bottom, whatever whirlwind of influence was brought to bear. Either she, too, was deeply deceived, and must be warned, or—no, she was true to her ideals, however they might have led her astray.

XXIII

It was not easy to obtain the coveted interview with Marguerite. Twice Mark went to the Cynthia, only to learn that she was not at home; the third time he found her surrounded by the men and women of her little court.

She flushed as he took her offered hand, but made no attempt to detain him by her side; he maintained his position there by sheer persistence, and even then did not succeed in driving the others away. Prince Vladislaf openly disputed the field with him, and some young men from the university took turns in claiming the attention of their hostess. The women whom Mark had seen at the studio were there; they were always there; he had grown to dislike them for their constancy. Their ease and their grace palled upon him, and the concord of their sweet voices "made his ears ache," he told himself, "for a good old Yankee twang."

What they said was as annoyingly accurate as their manner of saying it; they discussed art and music and the drama from the standpoint of the artist, the musician, and the actor, free from the illusions of the unsophisticated.

Yet with all this parade of disillusionment, they were themselves as illusory as sylphs or lorelei, diffusing the atmosphere calculated to bewilder and intoxicate. Mark felt, as he watched them and listened to the clever things they said, and which seemed to occupy them almost to the exclusion of interest in his reply, that his hand would go through their dainty draperies and delicate bodies and find nothing mortal there, if he were bold enough to attempt to grasp them.

They handed him on from one to another with the dexterity born of training and experience. His resistance was utterly ineffectual when opposed to their devotion to the social game. He realized that he was drifting farther and farther from the spot where Marguerite stood, and that he would soon be swept out of reach as certainly as Professor La Motte and rosy little Herr Meinzer. Their backward, unreconciled glances filled him with dismay. He decided to make a stand, and to this end planted his feet so firmly and looked so grim that the woman into whose hands he had now fallen inwardly exclaimed, "What a Berserker!" His frown changed to a smile as he recognized Mrs. Burnham, and she smiled, too.

"It is too bad, Mr. Heffron," she said, soothingly. "I know you want to see Mademoiselle Duvray, and you come so seldom. That is the penalty a man must pay for admiring a popular woman."

Her eyes kindled as they fell upon her kinswoman. "Isn't she like a rose?"

Like a rose, indeed, appeared the perfect little figure. Rose-colored was her gown, and soft as petals lay the folds from which emerged the small, shapely head with its low, loose coils of bright brown hair. To this side and that she turned with sympathetic interest, listening, replying, suggesting, leading every one to do his or her best.

"She certainly is very charming," replied Mark, soberly, adding, as he saw Mrs. Burnham's eyes rove around in search of some one to whom she could intrust him, "I do want to see her. I have something of importance to say to her—something she ought to hear."

Mrs. Burnham's eyes came back and dwelt upon him steadily. "It is almost impossible to obtain a personal interview," she replied. "You know she lectures every morning except Saturday, and afternoons she means to be by herself. The evenings are like this, unless she is at the theatre or at some reception."

"It is a matter of business," began Mark.

Mrs. Burnham's attention focused immediately; if there was anything that she loved more than the world of flattery and fine apparel, it was that protean shape which lurks behind the Exchange.

"Some investment?" she inquired, framing the word almost without uttering a sound.

"It has to do with an investment," replied Mark, evasively.

"You know I take care of Mademoiselle Duvray's business," explained Mrs. Burnham, drawing nearer and becoming more friendly. "I am a sort of relative of hers. We have lived together for nearly three years now."

"My business is with Mademoiselle Duvray herself," returned Mark, decisively. "If you cannot obtain me an interview with her it will have to wait, that is all."

"I will see what I can do," replied the lady, her eyes beginning again to roam. "Ah, here is Louise Ayer; you remember Miss Ayer?"

As Mark turned to the young girl he was conscious of a feeling of relief. She was looking pale and worried, and there was a seriousness in her manner extremely grateful after the refined gayety of the company, like a cloudy day after weeks of unvarying sunshine. He greeted her with a cordiality which made her innocent blue eyes open wide, but when he tried to enlist her sympathies sufficiently to carry a message to Mademoiselle Duvray, she shook her head.

"I can't; I'm so sorry," she said. "The fact is I am in disgrace with Mademoiselle Duvray myself."

"Impossible!" exclaimed Mark.

"No," said Louise, mournfully, "it is true. It was, of course, my fault. I offended her."

"She must be more easily offended than I dreamed," said Mark, gallantly.

"No," exclaimed the girl, tragically, "I knew

better.   I knew it was the one thing she would not forgive.   I—" a ripple of light, feminine laughter followed by a hearty masculine explosion burst in upon her words.   Mark turned to see his cousin's wife enter, in evening dress, her fine neck and arms bare even of the amethysts.   Something she said had sent her escort, a portly, elderly gentleman, into a fit of laughter that made him quite purple in the face.   All along her path she dropped her jests, like pebbles in a quiet pool, until the gentle waves of influence setting out from Mademoiselle Duvray were all broken and disarranged.   If Marguerite felt any chagrin she did not show it, but graciously presented the prince and a young Italian musician who had been timidly attentive for the past ten minutes.   Nellie received them good-humoredly, but allowed them to slip from her, together with the elderly escort, while she turned to Mark, who was not far away.

"*What are* you doing here, Nell?" he inquired, in a low tone.

"It's all right," she answered, cheerfully.   "She left a card one day when she thought I was out.   I came to-night because I knew she was in.   There are some people here that I want.   Give me your arm to that fat woman on the sofa, the one with a fistful of diamonds under her chin.   She came to one of my lectures and did not show up afterwards ; I've got to lasso her over again."

There was nothing to do but obey.   Nellie forthwith ensconced herself beside her truant disciple on the sofa, which their voluminous skirts filled to the rim. The tide of interest set steadily in their direction ; the generous vitality of the new-comer, her prompt overriding of conventionality and form, her droll remarks addressed to every one in general as well as to some one in particular, drew like a magnet. The prince began to listen with one ear for the cause of the laughter which came with periodic regularity from the sofa in the corner ; the young Italian had deserted at the first peal. Mark recognized his opportunity and took it ; the prince bowed and withdrew.

"Mrs. Heffron is a cousin of yours, I believe ?" said Marguerite, glancing towards the corner.

"A cousin's wife," corrected Mark.

"She is very clever," said Marguerite, civilly.

"In her way, yes," he replied, and then, fearing another interruption, he continued, hurriedly, "I have tried to see you several times lately. I have something of importance to say to you."

Marguerite assumed a listening attitude, her pretty head bent.

"Not now !" he exclaimed.

She questioned him with her eyes.

"There is too much of it ; it is too personal."

"I am usually very busy," she pursued.

"Yes, I know," he replied, with some impatience. "But this concerns friends of yours and mine."

"What is it ?" she demanded, with an imperious little gesture. "No one will hear us ; they are listening to Mrs. Heffron."

Mark paused. Should he enter upon a discussion, that required leisure and his best effort, in a crowded drawing-room, where he might be cut off at the most inopportune moment? Yet, when could he be sure of having her to himself again even to this degree? He hesitated, and she pressed her advantage. "Go on, please."

"I want to talk with you about old Mr. Norton," he began, speaking rapidly, and in a low voice. "I had a long conversation with him a few days ago, in which he confided to me the story of his relations with a certain Dr. Symonds. He said you took him to Dr. Symonds's office in the first place. He seems to have given himself up utterly to the influence of that man."

Marguerite had changed color at his first words, but it might have been from irritation rather than from embarrassment. She was almost herself when she answered, quietly, "What do you wish me to do?"

This return of the responsibility to himself abashed Mark for an instant ; then he answered, bluntly, "Isn't it as much your affair as mine?"

"It appears to me," replied Marguerite, coldly, "that it is neither your affair nor mine, but Mr. Norton's."

"It would be, perhaps, if Mr. Norton was perfectly able to judge for himself," continued Mark, "but I don't think he is. It seems to me a case which calls for interference. Unless I am greatly mistaken, Mr. Norton has given this man a hold upon him which is out of all reason."

"Mr. Norton has an impulsive manner of expressing himself; you probably exaggerated the importance of what he said," returned the clear, cool, silvery voice of the woman beside him. She was quite herself now, and speaking with the utmost composure.

Her ease annoyed Mark; he felt impelled to break in upon it, ruffle it, hinder and prevent it, if by the roughest handling. "When it comes to relinquishing one's fortune to a rascally fakir," he began, and then paused, having accomplished his purpose. The slender figure beside him trembled with indignation. "Take care, Mr. Heffron," she said, warningly, "Dr. Symonds is my friend."

"Friend or no," replied Mark, coolly, "he's got to explain his methods, or I'll show him up to the public. This isn't the first time I've run afoul of them. He's a dangerous individual; I've seen enough to convince me of that."

Marguerite made no reply. Her agitation had subsided; she had withdrawn into herself, and wrapped about her a veil of reserve impalpable as air but absolutely impenetrable. Mark made one or two futile efforts to conciliate her and then retired.

Louise Ayer was waiting for him near the door. "I wanted to finish what I was saying to you," she said, anxiously. "It was all my fault with

Mademoiselle Duvray. I knew that she never allowed any one to meddle with her affairs, and that was what I did. It was my own fault, and I am perfectly wretched." Her eyes were misty with unshed tears as she looked at him.

"Don't worry, child," he answered, comfortingly. "She'll come out of it."

"Do you really think she will ?" inquired Louise, eagerly.

"Of course," he replied, in a matter-of-fact tone.

"I don't know what I shall do if she doesn't forgive me," exclaimed the girl. "It would just about kill me."

"She will, she will," returned Mark, cheerily. "She probably wants to give you a lesson, that's all." He hoped that he was speaking the truth.

The guests were beginning to leave, led by Mrs. Heffron, who had wound up the triumph of the evening with a telling jest, and made her exit, followed by applause. She slipped her hand confidingly within Mark's arm, and made him take her to her room.

"I've had a beautiful time," she said, gayly, as they walked down the long hall, " and it did them good, too. Live men and women want something besides art and elegance ; they like to be waked up and set agoing. I told six or seven hands and hit it right every time. They'll all come in to the lecture to-morrow. I think you might come, Mark."

"Can't possibly, Nell ; I've got important business on hand for to-morrow. I'm glad you enjoyed yourself. Good-night !"

But Nellie laid a detaining hand upon his arm. "Remember what I told you about Taurus people," she said, prophetically. "They'll never give in ; there's no use in trying to make them."

"How about Aries people ?" he asked her.

"Oh, they're set in their way, but they're reasonable, and when they become enlightened they're the *salt* of the *earth !*"

"How you encourage me," he cried, mockingly, and, squeezing her plump hand, flung away down the hall.

She watched him with a sigh, then rang the bell and was let in by Marie.

WHAT Mark had said to her encouraged Louise Ayer for a while. She went to sleep trusting his assurances that all would be well, but when she awoke in the morning it was with the undefined dread of something which had happened, or would happen, of harm. "What is it?" she asked herself; and then it all came back—her imprudent questionings, Mademoiselle Duvray's displeasure, and the wretched realization that she was shut out from the favor of her beloved guide and friend. The tears would come in spite of her. After breakfast she made her way to the park, hoping to escape from the dull ache at her heart.

Sitting on a bench under a spreading maple, she was aroused from her reverie by a fresh young voice. "Aren't you early?" it asked.

She looked up, and held out her hand to Carl Dering with a smile. "I'm *so* glad to see you," she said, warmly; "do sit down."

Carl responded with the alacrity of one whose desire approves his action. "I suppose I ought to hurry back to the office," he said, by way of apology; and then, scanning her face, "you've been crying!" he exclaimed. "What is it, Louise?" The past year had been equivalent to many years, in their friendship, and had made them "Carl" and "Louise" to each other.

"Nothing — that is, nothing much," she responded, blushing.

"You're not the girl to cry for 'nothing much,'" said Carl, positively. "Come, out with it. You helped me carry my load once upon a time ; now give me a turn at yours."

"It was my own fault," said Louise, humbly.

"I don't believe it."

"It was ; I knew better ; I meddled with what did not concern me."

"I don't believe that, either—at least, I don't believe you meddled."

"Oh, I did ; it didn't concern me in the slightest degree, and the person never will forgive me."

"I'll bet I know who the person is," said Carl, sagaciously. "It is Mademoiselle Duvray."

Louise looked conscious.

"Now I know half you may as well tell me the rest," pursued the inquisitor.

"Oh, I *never* will !" cried Louise, betraying her secret by the very vehemence with which she guarded it.

"Now I *know!*" he exclaimed, triumphantly. "You quarrelled over *me*."

Louise blushed furiously, but made a desperate attempt to throw him off the track. "You conceited creature !" she exclaimed; "don't you think we have anything better to talk about than you ?"

"That depends," returned Carl, not a whit disconcerted. "Now, Louise, tell me what she said."

"Talk of the curiosity of women !" cried Louise. "It is nothing beside that of men !"

"But this is excusable," returned Carl, persuasively. "It is necessary for me to know how Mademoiselle Duvray feels, so that I can tell how to behave when I meet her."

"You told me that you shouldn't go near her again."

"So I shall not, unless she asks me ; but I may meet her at the Rosses, or at your house, or lots of places. Really, Louise, as a friend, you ought to give me points ; I'm all in the dark."

"Well," granted Louise, reluctantly, "she said you were too mental. Now I shall not tell you another word."

"What did she mean by ' too mental ' ?" asked Carl, looking puzzled.

"Don't you know—' mental, emotive, and vital ' —the chart—the three sides of the triangle—oh, dear, how shall I explain ? You know there are three primitive colors—red, blue, and yellow— red, green, and violet, some say now ; and three notes in the major chord—C, E, and G. So we are made up of three kinds of forces—mental, emotive (or moral), and physical ; the mental becomes the spiritual, you know. I'm afraid I can't tell you how it is, Carl!" She stopped in despair.

"Yes, yes, go on!" he urged.

"Well, you see, whatever we do has to have all these forces in it—you must think, you must feel, you must act; do you see?"

"Yes, go on."

"That's all, except that when she said you were too mental she meant you thought out these things, but you didn't feel or act them."

"Much she knew about it," returned Carl, sulkily.

"There, I knew it wouldn't do any good to tell you!" exclaimed Louise, "and I've gone and betrayed her confidence."

"Nothing of the sort," returned Carl. "She told me the same thing herself."

"Then why didn't you—" began Louise, and stopped.

"I'll tell you why I didn't," returned Carl. "She and Dr. Symonds wanted me to 'treat,' and I didn't want to do it. It's too—too—*personal.* It made me feel queer."

"Perhaps you would have felt differently if you'd gone on," suggested Louise. "I suppose you would have become accustomed to it."

"I don't want to become accustomed to it," he replied. "I'll tell you, I felt—I felt as if I had made love to those girls whom I treated; I believe love is a kind of 'treating.'" It was Carl's turn to blush now; he was scarlet to the tips of his shapely ears.

There was an embarrassing silence, during which Louise poked holes in the sand with her parasol.

"What else did she say?" demanded Carl, at length.

"I am not going to tell you," replied Louise, firmly. "I am sorry I said a single word."

"I knew it all before," responded Carl. "She said the same thing to me, and that I lacked force of character and stability; that she was disappointed in me; that she had granted me favors she rarely granted any one, and I did not appreciate them; and that if I trusted to the Principle it would take care of me."

"And I told her," finished Louise, starting to her feet, her eyes flashing, "that it was not right to get you out of your profession when she had not the slightest idea what to do with you. Oh, dear, what have I said?" She sank back on the bench and covered her face with her hands.

"Don't, Louise," pleaded Carl; "don't feel so."

"I am a traitor!" murmured the girl, behind her handkerchief.

"You're *not!*" exclaimed Carl. "You're the bravest, truest girl I know. Don't go back on yourself in that way; you will be a traitor if you do that!"

Louise smiled through her tears. "You see, Carl," she said, pathetically, "Mademoiselle Duvray has been everything to me. I was a delicate, dependent, helpless thing, and she has taught me

how to take care of myself and be a help to others.
You don't know what she is to her scholars; it's
no wonder they worship her. I've thought—I used
to think that I wouldn't ask for any greater happiness than to be just like her and help people
as she does."

Carl wondered what had wrought the change
in her ambition, but forbore to ask.

"I realize, now, I never could do it," pursued
Louise, with a sigh. "I am so weak; I cannot
keep my centre; I get interested in people and
away I go." Her blue eyes were sorrowful with
self-reproach as they looked at him.

"Of course you can't do it," he returned, briskly. "You're human, and she isn't."

"Oh, Carl!"

"She isn't. She told me it was her constant
aim to 'maintain the impersonal relation with
every one'—that isn't human; human beings don't
hold each other off in that way. You can't do it,
and I'm mighty glad you've stopped trying."

A wandering breeze came near at his words,
and all the leaves of the great maple over their
heads rustled a faint applause. Through the
branches a ray of sunlight slipped, like uncon-
trolled laughter, and ran along the walk. The
two young things felt the influence of the sound
and the sparkle. Their seriousness vanished, and
they smiled at each other for the sweetness of
the spring day and the joyousness of it.

"Don't you see, Louise," cried the young man,

eagerly, "God didn't stop making trees and flowers when he began to make animals, and he didn't stop making animals when he commenced on man; I don't believe we are meant to give up what we had because we have something more."

"But you surely believe in developing the spiritual side of us," pursued Louise, anxiously.

"H'm, yes, I suppose so."

"Oh, Carl, you haven't given up the Principle? I was afraid that would be the result if you went back into medicine; that was why I said so much to Mademoiselle Duvray—I was fairly desperate."

Carl gave her an appreciative glance. "You were awfully good to try to help me," he said, affectionately. "But honestly, Louise, I like this a lot better; that always seemed to me a kind of old woman's work, going round lecturing and healing—it did, really."

Louise looked thoughtful. "Of course," Carl continued, hastily, "I know there's a great deal in it, and I do try to hold on to the Principle; but, as Mr. Heffron says, 'You needn't tell all you know.'"

"Did you talk with him about things?"

"Didn't I, though! If it wasn't for him I'd be in the street now. He saw Humphrey, and persuaded him to take me back into the office. I tell you what, Louise, that man knows what he is talking about!"

"Who—Dr. Humphrey?"

"No, Mr. Heffron; and he doesn't think it is

necessary to shut yourself off by yourself and keep every one else at arm's-length. I'd like to hear him go for Mademoiselle Duvray!"

"She won't let him," said Louise, sententiously.

"How do you know?" inquired Carl.

"He tried to make me take a message to her last night, and of course I couldn't under the circumstances. He managed to get a chance to talk with her, but she had that way she has when she won't let a person get hold of her."

"I know," returned Carl, sagely, "all about 'the way.' Louise, she doesn't dare have it out with him. It would be the best thing in the world for her if she would marry him."

"Oh, Mademoiselle Duvray doesn't believe in marriage," replied Louise, quickly, "except—"

"Except for those who cannot get along without it, I suppose," interrupted Carl, with warmth. "That's a nice thing to teach her girls."

"She doesn't teach them anything of the sort," responded Louise, with equal warmth. "Carl, you do her injustice. She only tries to make her girls independent enough so as not to give up every bit of their individuality to the first man who comes along. You know how girls are."

"Some of them," answered Carl. "But I notice that the girls who get so independent of the men turn around and fall in love with her. They do, you know they do, Louise; they send her flowers, and make her presents, and wait on her just like lovers."

Louise looked hurt. "I suppose you mean me."

"Partly," he confessed. "It provokes me to see you revolving around her when you ought to be the one yourself to have some one revolve around you."

His words and the gesture with which he illustrated them brought a smile to the pensive face beside him. "People have to like each other," he continued, philosophically. "They can't help it; they're made that way. If it isn't one, it's another; only I don't believe the other can ever take the place of the one. I don't think it's necessary or right to fight such feelings; I believe we are meant to do some of the things we want to, or we wouldn't want to so much."

"Then you don't pray to be 'delivered from all inordinate and sinful affection'?" inquired Louise, archly.

"Who would believe you remembered so much of the old prayer-book!" he exclaimed, humorously. "No, I don't think affection is sinful, and if it's inordinate the best thing to do is to examine it carefully and find out what to do with it; nothing is inordinate when you find a use for it. Oh, I've thought about these things," for Louise was looking at him curiously. "I'm about ready to think, as Humphrey does, that chemical affinity becomes natural selection higher up, and natural selection becomes sympathy—the same law; think of it, one force to hold the world together!

Why not call it one name—Love?" Carl's honest face was all aglow.

"We keep saying 'God is Absolute and Infinite,'" he continued, "'and as limited and finite beings we cannot comprehend Him,' and never realize that He keeps putting Himself before us in a way we can understand. It's of no use to stand on tiptoe and try to stretch up to be like Him, but He comes close to us and shows us how to be like Him right where we are. I tell you what, Louise, I'm awfully tired of trying to be a *spirit;* I'm going to try to be a *man* for a while." He ceased and drew in a long breath of the splendid spring air. Louise did not dare to look at him; she saw, without looking at them, the strong young figure and the winsome face. She felt the vigorous pulse beating sturdily and true to the true heart which directed them; and her own heart gave a queer little turn, like a somersault.

"I must go home," she said, faintly, and arose, still looking away from him. Carl made no attempt to detain her, and they walked, side by side, in silence, along the leafy aisles of the park. The breeze blew over them, and the leaves rustled, and the sunbeams romped like playful hounds on the path before their feet, but upon the gravity of their self-consciousness, and consciousness of each other, these childish influences could not intrude.

At her home door he left her, bidding her good-bye with the brevity which promises a prompt return, and she responded with the gentleness which assures a welcome. Then she sped on up to her own room.

Before the mirror she stopped to interrogate the face she saw there—shining eyes, parted lips, cheeks in which the color came and went; whither had vanished the dolorous maid of the morning? She recalled Carl's words, "I believe that love is a kind of ' treating.' "

The girl in the glass smiled back at her.

"Isn't he the queerest boy in the world?" she asked this girl.

"Yes, he is," the girl answered, adding, with a blush, "and the dearest."

Then came a pang of remorse as she remembered how frankly she had discussed Mademoiselle Duvray with one, like herself, out of favor with the absent friend. During the remainder of the day these two emotions divided the empire of her heart—remorse for the changed relation between herself and her beloved mistress, joy for the new love to which the old had yielded, as fantastic moonlight yields to the vitalizing influence of the sun.

"I wish she could feel like this," she sighed, as if the wish were somehow a reparation, "but I don't believe she ever will," and the girl who had sat at the feet of Mademoiselle Duvray actually pitied the object of her former admiration.

XXV

Mark's threat to make Dr. Symonds explain himself was not an idle one. Proving this, he sallied forth early the next morning in pursuit of the healer, so early that there was no one stirring in the Enterprise except a sleepy elevator boy, who was quite positive no such person as Dr. Symonds roomed in the building. Cross-examination divulged the fact that he became an elevator boy only yesterday, and the chances were against the reliability of his testimony.

Mark traversed the long, dim corridors, floor by floor, growing more determined and more belligerent with each one. The darker the corner the more active his anticipation of coming upon the hoary villain whom he sought. "Bring on your occult forces," he muttered, stiffening his biceps and shaking his fists. "I'm bound to do you up!"

After all, it was not in the shadowed and musty by-ways of the old house but in the full radiance of the top-floor skylight that he found the door bearing the inscription, "J. G. Symonds, Metaphysician."

He rapped, but no one answered; there was

not a sound within. He opened the door and entered the room; there was no one there, even behind the screens, for he examined them to make sure.

He tried the door into the adjoining room and found it locked; then he sat down to wait, glancing here and there at the contents of the modest apartment. There were books behind glass doors and brown paper envelopes in piles by themselves. On a small table stood a contrivance for taking reprints. Folding-chairs, a piano, and a desk of ecclesiastical pattern were all the furniture besides the screens; there were two of these, some seven feet high and coming down to the floor.

The minutes passed. Mark grew impatient, and had very nearly decided to relinquish his quest when the door into the adjoining room opened softly, and a slender, dark-haired young man in clerical dress appeared. "How can I serve you?" he asked, advancing courteously, and then stopped with a startled look in his large black eyes.

Mark sprang forward and caught him by the arm. "Jack Symonds!" he cried, in tones of surprise and disgust, "for God's sake, don't say it is you who are running this infernal faking machine!" Here was an entirely different encounter from the one which he had planned.

Symonds was the first to recover himself. "That is a singular salutation from you, Heffron," he returned, calmly. "Is that all you have to say?"

His affectation of unconcern nettled Mark. "No, it isn't," he answered, doggedly.

"Come in here," said the healer, leading the way to the inner room.

The two men sat down and looked at each other curiously. The years had made a breach between them which neither could have crossed if he would. To the unimpassioned seeker after spiritual truths the vehemence of his companion represented a phase of existence from which he shrank—a phase to be feared and avoided. To the virile wrestler, hand to hand and foot to foot, with the greed of the world and its dishonesty and cunning, and with the temptations entangling his own five senses, the other was a coward and a renegade. By stretching out an arm they could have clasped hands, yet they were worlds apart and spoke in different languages. Each eyed the other with the instinctive dislike which one animal feels for another seen for the first time and not yet tested, the balance of the antipathy being on the side of the one who was physically the stronger.

Again Symonds was the first to break the silence.

"What did you mean by your words just now?" he inquired.

"I might modify them somewhat," replied Mark, obstinately, "but they would mean the same thing. I'm sorry it is with you that my quarrel lies, but I can't back out now."

"What is the quarrel, Mark?" asked the other, quietly.

"Hang it all, Jack," blurted out his visitor, "if you want to be a 'magus' and parade around in a long-tailed robe, with a tiara on, do it and be darned, but don't go into it in this dead-earnest fashion, fooling honest people, and playing fast and loose with—with—the mysteries of life."

"When the veil of the temple was rent it was in token there should be no more mysteries," responded the healer.

"And so you invite in the American public to lift the lid of the ark and finger its contents?"

Symonds colored like a girl. "Nothing of the sort. I shall train up men and women to defend the ark because they appreciate its sacredness."

"You won't do it with 'manuscript lessons' or a course of 'treatment.'" Mark was getting his bearings. There is more than one way to bully; he had several at his disposal.

Symonds colored again more vividly. "What do you know of my methods?" he asked, defiantly.

"Considerably more than your scholars do. What do you suppose young Dering knew about what he was up to? You needn't shrug your shoulders; you can't throw off a responsibility in that way. You influenced him to give up his profession, and for—what?"

The healer's pallid face kindled with indignation and remonstrance. "For opportunities which a king might envy him. I placed young Dering where, if he had made the most of what I gave him, he could have controlled his destiny. If he did not do this I am not to blame."

"You pushed him into situations for which he was unprepared, and then blamed him because he was unprepared," rejoined Mark, sturdily. "You can't force human beings as you would tomato-plants. You ought to have known that if you didn't. As to controlling his destiny—bosh !"

The hall door of the outer office opened to let in a small, fair woman carrying a travelling-bag. From her manner, as she stepped briskly into the room, Mark guessed that she had a right there ; from Symonds's manner, as he hastened to meet her, he was quite sure of it.

She listened to his softly uttered explanations with the air of one high in authority, and replied in a voice which recognized neither fear nor favor. "If he isn't here on business, get rid of him. You have no time for ordinary callers. Besides," and here the voice dropped, "you'll take his thought."

"You'll take it, too, if I get a shot at you," mused the pugnacious visitor. "I wonder if I can hit you at long range."

But the little woman ignored his presence and bustled about, arranging the papers on the table and placing the chairs in orderly rows, suggesting as plainly as possible, without words, that this was a busy office, affording no foothold to idle, unnecessary people, who only got in the way and interfered with important work.

Dr. Symonds tiptoed back to the inner office, and, with a deprecating glance behind him, noiselessly closed the door. "Was it on Dering's account that you came to see me?" he asked, as he took his seat.

"Not entirely," confessed Mark. "I was more disturbed on account of old Mr. Norton."

The healer lifted his eyebrows questioningly. "Mr. Norton is certainly much improved in health," he said, "and happier."

"But he hasn't had fifty thousand dollars' worth," was the blunt reply.

"Who said anything about fifty thousand dollars?" demanded the healer.

"I did," replied Mark, coolly; "and I have reference to the sum which Mr. Norton subscribed to the new building you mean to erect on the lake front." He watched Symonds closely, but the latter showed no sign of discomfiture. "I suppose he was willing to pay that much for another 'change of heart,'" he pursued, significantly. Still there was no response. "But any common hypnotist could have given it to him much cheaper," he finished, with a sneer.

Dr. Symonds sprang to his feet, his dark eyes flashing. What he intended to say Mark never knew, for the door suddenly opened and the small sentinel of the office demonstrated that she was still on guard.

"Dr. Symonds," she said, warningly, "you have an engagement at ten, and it is now two minutes of."

"Is there any one waiting?" asked the healer. He was trembling from head to foot.

She beckoned him to her. "Are you crazy?" she whispered. "That man is exhausting you. Send him away."

He made some inarticulate response.

"Then *I* shall." She placed herself before him and assumed a threatening air, not unlike that with which a brave hen-sparrow defends her nest.

"Sir," she said, authoritatively.

"My name is Heffron," interposed Mark, with a twinkle.

"Mr. Heffron," she repeated, "you will have to wait till another day. Dr. Symonds is very busy this morning."

Mark walked to the door of the office and looked out. There was no one in the outer room. He walked back and sat down.

"He has several absent treatments to give," she explained; "besides, it is contrary to our custom to sit and talk. If you want anything of us in a business way, please state your errand."

Mark smiled upon her quizzically. "I think I'll wait until Dr. Symonds gets through," he answered, easily. The little woman went out and shut the door.

For full half an hour Mark was left to his own reflections, and he found them enormously entertaining. The whole affair had gradually assumed for him the proportions of a huge joke, and it was in this spirit that he took up the thread of the discussion when Dr. Symonds returned.

"Your wife tells me," he began, cheerfully—"I suppose she is your wife, or would be on our 'plane of thought'?"

Dr. Symonds inclined his head in affirmation.

"Your wife tells me that I am making an unusual demand upon your valuable time ; that you do not allow your influence to drip away in prolonged interviews, but condense it into occasional acts of mercy. Don't you think that is rather going back on ourselves, to develop into isolated intelligences which only come in contact for the discharge of some beneficent function ? What is to become of all the delightful gossipings, the comforting convivialities ? Many of us have to become warmed up by prolonged intercourse with our fellow-beings before we can give out anything ; what is to become of us ?"

Mark was enjoying himself after his own fashion, but the imperturbable healer did not abate his seriousness. "What is to become of the kingdom of heaven which we are to seek 'first of all' ?" he asked.

Mark was saved the exposure of his ignorance on this point by the return of the little sentinel, announcing impatiently, "Dr. Symonds, there is some one here who wishes to speak with you !"

In his exit Dr. Symonds left the door ajar only an instant, but in that instant Mark caught a glimpse of some one who was really there this time. He saw quite plainly the trim gown and jaunty hat which suited their wearer as its plumage suits the bird ; he recognized the low, loose coil of bright brown hair, the compact, well-poised figure ; and his jesting mood left him.

Why was Marguerite there ? Was it her custom to consult this psychic guide ? Good heavens, what a pull he had, combining the influence of the physician with that of the priest ! How complacently he smiled as he returned to the inner office ! Mark's fingers tingled to lay hold of him and squeeze the smile out of him.

"It won't do for you to carry this thing too far, Symonds," he began, superciliously. "There are too many people taking aim for you. I have in my pocket now a letter inquiring about that fifty thousand dollars you took from Norton."

"I took no money from Norton, except a small fee for attendance," interrupted the healer.

"The money you intend to take," corrected Mark, adding, to himself, "Thanks for that much information."

"Is that all you have to say ?" inquired Symonds, with dignity.

"All but a word of caution. Fly low. Don't soar so high that you can't get to cover ; and take care how you meddle with souls; it's risky."

"Take care how you meddle with my soul and its mission!" retorted the healer, spiritedly. "I can't understand you, Heffron. Years ago, in college, you agreed with me that this thing ought to be done, that philosophy, science, and religion should join hands, and faith be made a working principle. You said—"

He paused, for the scowling face before him had changed like an April sky, and was all sunned over with smiles. "Don't stop!" cried its owner. "Don't stop! Go on. What else did I say?"

"You said, 'It is the thought of the world which creates its atmosphere; unhappy and unwholesome conditions are made by the mind; the realities are beautiful and good, and if all would see them so we could work on a common basis and bring out into form the beauty and goodness which exist as spiritual realities.'"

Mark gave a sigh of satisfaction. "That's it; that was the hobby I kept moving until I went into business in New York. Business killed it. What are you going to do about business, Symonds? Did you ever do business on that basis?"

"It is the only way to do business properly," responded Symonds, with confidence.

"You try it," returned Mark, with a bitter laugh. "Try it, Symonds—but don't take Norton and his fifty thousand dollars along with you." He grew grave as he thought of the trusting old man, graver yet as he remembered Marguerite. So it was his own philosophy, warmed over, which drew her to Symonds, and Symonds probably worked the vein for all it was worth. He eyed him suspiciously.

"Of course we did not determine then how religion should become an applied science," Symonds was saying, "and I never heard it discussed at the theological seminary, although we were confronted by the words, 'Heal the sick and preach the gospel.' While I was in charge of my first parish Mrs. Symonds was taken very ill. We did everything; I carried her everywhere; but the doctors declared nothing could be done. Finally we fell in with some people who believed as we did. We studied with them, and *Mrs. Symonds recovered by the application of this Principle.* Of course the case attracted public attention. People came from far and near for treatment. We were fairly forced into the work."

"So Mrs. Symonds was really the means of your conversion," said Mark. "She had to apply your theories for you." He was still thinking of Marguerite, and wondering if there must always be a woman to lead a man where he would go.

"Mrs. Symonds has been and is of great assistance," returned the healer. "I know of no one who is so helpful in the—the Realization."

"Realization of what?" inquired Mark.

"Of the Principle," replied the healer, "of course."

"How do you know it isn't the realization of Mrs. Symonds?" suggested Mark, with a smile.

The healer started as if he had been stung.

"You seem so cocksure of the whole business," pursued the irreverent visitor. "How do you know, when you get these telephonic communications, where they come from? You needn't get angry over it!" for the healer had again started from his seat. "You've brought this on yourself. You've set yourself up as an authority on these matters. You *know;* you're a ' *Gnostic* '; now, *how* do you know?"

The face of the healer changed as he stood there before his accuser. A look, reminiscent and tender, passed over it. "I *know,*" he said, with gentle emphasis, "because I have *experienced.*"

Mark felt the power of his patience, and because he felt it and knew that it must have had an influence over others struck out against it brutally.

"That's all right for you, yourself," he exclaimed, harshly; "but when it comes to having experiences for other people, that's another thing. We've got rid of kings—in this country, at least; we've got rid of priests—some of us; we've got to get rid of creatures like you, who step in and offer to save people from the consequences of their own acts. Who are they that come to you, anyway? A lot of silly women, some doting old men, and a few green boys. What do you know about how a *man* feels—you, without any red blood in your veins? Because your little pint-pot of desires is full you needn't think you can satisfy the cravings of others with—lake water and a pinch of snuff." Mark had begun to rant, and he knew it. "I must go," he said, hurriedly, looking at his watch. "We should not agree on these matters if we talked a thousand years."

"No," responded the healer, gravely. "You do not understand ; you will not understand."

There were two women and a child waiting in the outer office. The child carried a crutch. Mrs. Symonds was talking with them, and did not look up when Mark tramped heavily through the room. As he reached the entrance of the building and passed out into the street he drew a long breath and shook himself as a big dog shakes himself upon emerging from the water. "By Jove," he murmured, "I'd like a Martigny cocktail and a strong cigar. I never felt so conspicuously and predominantly *animal* as in that atmosphere of condensed spirituality."

It was not until he had drunk the cocktail and was puffing vigorously away at the cigar that he attempted to recall what Symonds had said of his own long-lost philosophy. "It sounded very pretty as he got it off," he mused, "but I can't remember a blessed word of it now. Well, he's welcome to all he can make out of it. I believe I've had about enough of the—Symbolists."

He finished his cigar and wrote a long letter to Joey full of Mark-Heffron-isms.

XXVI

It was by no means in accordance with the habits of Mademoiselle Duvray to seek an interview with Dr. Symonds at his office early on a week-day morning. No one was more surprised than Dr. Symonds himself when he saw her standing by the office table, nervously turning over a paper which she found there. She looked up at his approach, and he saw that her eyes were heavy.

"I have not slept," she said, hurriedly. "I am very nervous, and I must lecture at eleven to-day. Will you help me?"

Dr. Symonds promised to do his best, trying to keep down a climbing exultation which threatened to mount into his voice and the expression of his face. She had come at last—this independent woman who wanted his philosophy, his rules of conduct, his incentives to faith, and who cheerfully sent her friends to partake of his psychical medicine, but who had always disclaimed for herself any need of such assistance.

"My battle is not with aches and pains," she had said, "and I have no nerves; what I want is something to live by." She had taken his various

"Courses of Instruction," had bought his manuscript lessons and his little books, but of his personal, professional attention she knew absolutely nothing. He had thought he detected a doubt in her attitude, and it had increased what might have become a doubt in his own heart if permitted to develop. This proof of her confidence sent him back to the inner office fortified to meet what awaited him there.

She looked after him irresolutely, half tempted to call him to her and withdraw her commission, and then she saw through the half-open door the broad shoulders and massive head of the man who was sitting there.

"Did you want to speak to the doctor?" asked Mrs. Symonds.

"No, thank you," replied Marguerite. A childish impulse seized her to run away. It was with an effort that she walked deliberately out of the room, followed by Mrs. Symonds, who kept up a blithe chatter as long as it could be heard. Empty of meaning as the twitter of the sparrows without, it came to Marguerite's ears. She was more disturbed than she cared to acknowledge. To find in her last refuge the menace to her peace threw her back upon herself—a feeble, fluttering self, shaken by unwonted sleeplessness and apprehension. Hardly knowing what she did, she walked rapidly down the street and turned her face towards Lincoln Park. It was not long before the exhilaration of the exercise had brought back her self-command. By the time she reached the green sward and the trees she had commenced to think coherently and reasonably.

This was really nothing new, she told herself; it was merely an old conflict resumed. If her belief in the principles which she advocated and attempted to apply had been sure, she would not have run away from Mark Heffron at Beau Lieu; she would have stood her ground and let him say what he pleased.

The evasion had been only a postponement of what must come sooner or later; she could not always run away. Besides, she no longer stood alone. There were her pupils and her friends dependent upon her—dependent upon her theories. She had proved that she was right by her success, by her helpfulness, by the happiness she had enjoyed until now. Then what did she fear? Why did the sight of Mark Heffron in Dr. Symonds's office fill her with perturbation? Why was she unwilling to have her new teacher examined by her old one? Was it entirely because she sympathized with the gentle, sensitive nature of the metaphysician and hated to have it hurt, or was it partly because she could not bear to have his comfortable words disproved? She pulled herself up short with a feeling of irritation. Why should she examine her motives and analyze her thoughts in this fashion? She was losing all her buoyancy, all her relish of this good and beautiful world. That aggressive personality which she could not walk away from was to blame for this. She looked back over the months since she met Mark Heffron ; how secure and how free she had been then ! Now even her teaching had grown petty and irksome. She was continually asking herself the use of it, and if she really meant what she said. The women who followed and imitated her seemed so many puppets whose strings she pulled. The men who admired her were vainly marshalled to preserve the balance of power. The elegance of Prince Vladislaf and the learning of Herr Meinzer had become alike wearisome. A laughing face looked at her over their shoulders and a mocking voice derided what they said.

Mrs. Burnham had been a better bulwark ; behind her matter-of-fact attitude Marguerite had often intrenched herself. But Mrs. Burnham partook of the New Thought only as a means of social advancement ; its virtue, in her eyes, was that it paid.

There were others who claimed Mademoiselle Duvray as of their number—not openly, but in their meetings among themselves. They were for the most part intellectual or religious Bohemians, having little to relinquish in the way of authority or tradition. But they recognized the necessity of caution on her part, and, proud of her position and influence, took care not to hazard these by imprudent allusions to her in public.

It was not until recently that she had felt responsible for her acquaintance with these people, although it had been a comfort to turn from them to leaders like Haridass Goculdass and Dr. Symonds. In the services conducted by the latter she had found her greatest help, especially since the Rosses and the Ayers, Carl Dering, and old Mr. Norton had become regular attendants. The little chapel had appeared sometimes to pulsate with warmth and radiance from the sympathy and the devotion which were concentrated there.

Of late there had been a change in the atmosphere—a shadow and a chill, an uncertainty, a foreboding, as of an approaching crisis. They were all conscious of it. Carl Dering no longer sat with bowed head, but tipped back in his chair and measured the words of the preacher. Old Mr. Norton, who used to go out of his way to say good-morning, shuffled in and out without stopping to speak to any one. There had been discussions among the women, of ways and means, and talk of a bazaar to raise funds for necessary expenses. The machinery had commenced to creak and to call attention to the fact that it was machinery. Hitherto the vehicle of worship and benediction had seemed a live thing, sustaining itself. This had all happened since Mark Heffron came to Chicago. Something must be done; some one must withstand this unfriendly influence. Thought against thought, will against will, faith against doubt, the battle must be fought, and by whom but herself? It was to her that he came first with his questions and criticisms. He had gone to Dr. Symonds only when she refused to talk with him.

She began to review the argument for the non-existence of Matter and Evil. Every word of it was familiar to her, she had quoted it so many times to those whom she was trying to convince. It had always been received without dispute, yet now with feminine timidity she held it up to the light and looked through it suspiciously. The rest of Dr. Symonds's system of philosophy was not unlike Mark Heffron's own belief in the power of thought, but how could one get a resting-place for this lever on a slippery world of Matter and Evil? "Have you got away from Matter?" had been a favorite question among her metaphysical friends, and, absurd as it might sound in the ears of the uninitiated, it stood for a most important emancipation. Some of them spent hours "denying" Matter and Evil, enemies she found it easier to ignore, as she found it easier to run away from Mark Heffron. Possibly this was the reason of her unrest. If she would only face it out with her antagonist and settle, once for all, the grounds of her belief, then she might go on to radiant heights of perfection. The thought steadied her and gave her peace. "That is it," she decided. "That is the solution of the problem. Who knows? It may be given to me to lead him into the right path. I will see him. I will talk to him fearlessly." Light of heart again, and light of foot, she retraced her way through the park, no more a weak, timorous woman, but a part of the Universal Harmony. As such, the resources of the universe were at her command. She looked around, ready to appropriate whatever was needed. Moving leisurely along towards the entrance came — not the manifestation of her exalted thought, but a boy in blue uniform sprinkled with brass buttons. She beckoned him to her, and gave him the portentous words written in pencil on a visiting-card and enclosed in the envelope he furnished her: "If you will call upon me at the Cynthia this evening I shall deem it a favor." Her hand trembled as she addressed the envelope to Mark Heffron at his hotel, and the boy looked interested. This was not the first romantic episode which had been outlined before his keen eyes. "Where'll I bring the answer?" he asked, briskly.

"There will be no answer," she replied, and wheeled abruptly. He gazed after her inquiringly for a minute, and then went off whistling.

In her haste to be rid of him she had turned down the nearest path and did not pause till the sound of voices stopped her. Not twenty rods away, on a bench under a spreading maple, sat Louise Ayer and Carl Dering, too much occupied in what they were saying to notice her approach. She heard distinctly, in Louise's clear soprano, "I told her it was not right to get you out of your profession —" and waited to hear no more.

So this was the way these two, whom she believed to be her devoted pupils, met to criticise and condemn her! A fierce glow eclipsed and superseded the white light of inspiration in which she had been enveloped. When she arrived at the studio it had burned through to heart and brain, and utterly effaced the argument for the non-existence of Evil.

Unfortunately, it is the fate of philosophy as well as of romance to be put to the test by the very world it would escape and which cunningly applies, not the mighty blows which philosophy and romance are prepared to meet, but the pin-pricks which they cannot endure. Not only was Louise Ayer absent from class, but the Ross girls also failed to appear. The hour dragged in spite of the lecturer's best efforts, and while it dragged who should appear but Madame Heffron, smiling and serene as the sunlight without, and attended by two large, determined-looking women who had an air of being present to see fair play.

Nellie had not come uninvited. There had been plenty of talk about her and her methods among the various representatives of the New Thought; for there are degrees of orthodoxy among the unorthodox. Marguerite had been asked, " Shall you call on her? Shall you invite her to hear you speak?" and, assuming a generosity which she did not wholly feel, she had declared her intention of calling and extending the courtesies of the studio. On the whole, this was

the wiser course. Some of Marguerite's pupils
had gone to Nellie, and some of Nellie's to Marguerite. One well-meaning woman had done her
gentle best, by repeating whatever each said that
was kind of the other, to reconcile the two leaders.
She was present this morning and effusively con-
ciliatory.

Madame Heffron was fully as prominent as the
mistress of the studio; she had led her companions to the most conspicuous seats in the room.
Marguerite looked unusually girlish as she stood
up before them.

The lecture was over, and the half-hour which
should be devoted to personal application was already due. The instructor proceeded with some
misgivings, for the class were on the gesture
chart, and were to illustrate it with sight-read-
ings from "As You Like It." She longed for
Louise Ayer and the Ross girls, but Louise Ayer
was sitting under a maple-tree at Lincoln Park
with Carl Dering, and no one knew where the
Rosses were. She called on Grace Merriam, who
was not always to be depended on, but occasionally surprised herself and every one else by a
brilliant performance. Alas, poor Grace became
hopelessly entangled in upward curves and downward curves, and finally came to a standstill. " I
cannot do it, Mademoiselle Duvray," she said, despairingly.

"You went through all this only a week ago,"
exclaimed her teacher, betraying a rare annoy-

ance. Madame Heffron and her big attendants seemed to fill the room. It was impossible to send over or around them the influence which should draw together the straying interest of the class. Mrs. Bateman, the woman with peace-making ambitions, hurried to the rescue, losing her head completely in her zeal to be of use. She asked foolish questions and made pointless remarks, until Marguerite felt a most unphilosophical desire to take her by the shoulders and put her out of the place. Finally she begged Mademoiselle Duvray to read something. Madame Heffron seconded the request and settled herself comfortably in her chair, preparing to be entertained.

Marguerite could not refuse without appearing ungracious. She looked about her for a book, and picked up the first which came to her hand. It was the *Spectator*—a most unfortunate selection. Waves of anguish crossed Mrs. Bateman's face. Why could it not have been one of those dainty Dobson things which Mademoiselle Duvray read so cleverly, or the *Portrait,* or even dear old *Sandalphon*—with that she could have lifted her listeners to the very gate of heaven!

Marguerite ploughed gallantly on through the involved sentences, stopping now and then to emphasize an example or apply a rule ; but, despite her musical voice and accurate inflection, the reading was tedious—a new experience for the studio. Every one was glad when it was over, with possibly the exception of the unwelcome guest, who could not be expected to mourn the discomfiture of her rival. Half the class turned to her, ready for the audacious sallies which they had learned to expect from her lips. The other half, with defiant loyalty, rallied around Mademoiselle Duvray. Thus the two women met. Madame Heffron opened the ball with an allusion to Addison's great-great-grandniece, whom she had met. Mademoiselle Duvray responded with a description of Addison's great-great-granddaughter, whom she knew quite well. Madame Heffron spoke of the English schools which she had visited, and Mademoiselle Duvray was ready with a comparison of English methods with German. Then they both tried France, and found they were equally at home there. The group of young girls and matrons listened attentively, and with the impartial mien of a jury.

"They would throw me over in a minute," thought Marguerite, bitterly, "if they considered it for their advantage to do so; if they believed she could give them wider opportunities, showier attainments, more ease in society, more influence at home. The impudence of her, coming into my studio to steal my scholars!"

Quietly but firmly she asserted her superiority over her visitor, who with equal firmness, if not so quietly, asserted her superiority over her hostess. Both displayed a remarkable familiarity with the business methods of women, which, compared with men's more desperate efforts to bear each other down, are "as moonlight unto sunlight and as water unto wine." The jury was divided, and when the evidence was all in went off in pairs to consider it.

Marguerite was left to reflect upon the singular misfit of human emotions and the situations in which they find themselves. If she had been less in earnest, the inapplicability of the argument for the non-existence of evil to the exigencies of the occasion might have sent her into healing fits of laughter; but she took herself and her moods too seriously for that. She went home hurt and sore, wondering over the trick which Fate had played her, lifting her to heights of divine illumination only to drop her into the midst of the scuffle which attends success in all professions, even with those dealing with spiritual demand and supply.

A pile of letters waited on her table. She selected one bearing a crest, and opened it with a feeling of expectancy. She read it slowly, as one tastes a tempting dish. Mrs. Burnham watched her hungrily.

"It is from Prince Vladislaf's sister," said Marguerite at length, trying to keep the triumph out of her voice. "She invites me to visit her at St. Petersburg."

She read the letter to Mrs. Burnham, who interposed pious ejaculations of delight.

"Of course you will accept!" she cried, in conclusion.

"I think so," replied Marguerite, temperately, "and I think I shall go abroad earlier than I proposed. Let me see, May 20th. We have engaged passage for June 30th. Write and exchange it, if possible, for the 9th."

"Can you finish your work by the 5th? We shall have to start by then."

"Oh yes," returned Marguerite. She was already arranging the words in which she should inform her pupils of the alteration in their schedule, necessitated by her engagements at Paris and St. Petersburg.

Her spirits rose as she began to plan for the summer, and to picture to herself the brilliance and the charm of the world into which she was going. That was her life—the life of elegance and of art. In the very thought of it all her pruned and lattice-bound instincts began to stir and strive, and to stretch out tendrils of hope and gladness.

"Oh, I forgot to tell you," said Mrs. Burnham, suddenly; "Dr. Symonds was here just before you came in. He wanted me to call him up on the telephone and tell him how you were. He wanted to know about continuing the treatment." She did not look at her cousin, and delivered the message in an offhand manner, but Marguerite was evidently annoyed. "What shall I tell him?" asked Mrs. Burnham.

"Tell him," replied the fair convalescent, "that

he need not attempt anything further. He did not help me a bit." She went off to her own room with the princess's letter, and evidently found its influence most tranquillizing, for she reappeared at dinner-time looking more like herself, Mrs. Burnham told her, than she had in a month.

It was late when Mark Heffron's card was handed her. He had gone out after writing to Norton, and had not come in again until after dinner.

"Why do you try to see him?" asked Mrs. Burnham, as Marguerite made a gesture of despair.

"It is an engagement," faltered her cousin.

"What if it is? I can tell him you are all tired out, as you are. If you keep on at this rate, wearing yourself out over other people, you will be a broken-down old woman. You were a perfect wreck this morning." Marguerite glanced at her image in the neighboring glass. "You look better now," pursued her companion, "but you will lose it all if you talk and argue with that man. I'll make it right with him."

She patted her gray curls into place, pulled out her sleeves, and left the backsliding advocate of the non-existence of evil to nestle among the cushions of her divan, murmuring, "I believe I *have* had about enough of those Heffrons for one day."

Mrs. Burnham left nothing unsaid in the way

of apology or explanation, and Mark received her pacific messages with the utmost magnanimity. Examining his mood, as he left the Cynthia, he was surprised to find, first, that he was not disappointed; second, that he was not displeased.

XXVII

Philip More had been away five months—yes, it was five months since the Peristyle burned; that was in January and this was June, a superb June Sunday—one of those days in which Chicago atones for weeks of bad weather by one dazzling hour, and goes on piling up unlimited credit for weeks of bad weather to come.

Philip contrasted it with the day he went away. Then, smoke and fog, mixed to a paste, had been daubed upon everything ; they built a wall over which the towers and domes at Jackson Park stared helplessly, while the Ferris Wheel seemed to bowl along the horizon in a murky cloud. Now what remained of the White City came out, like a regained ideal, fairer than ever. The day was in sympathy with his mood—was he not going to the woman he loved ? He was glad it was Sunday ; Aunt Harriet would be at the Enterprise and Eloise would be alone. He had stopped down-town to remove the traces of travel, but it was not yet ten. How surprised she would be ! He could see her dark-fringed hazel eyes open, and could hear her say, " Why, Philip !"

Five months ago he would not have ventured

to come thus unannounced, but she had altered in her manner towards him of late, writing him long, confidential accounts of Aunt Harriet and Carl and their doings, confessing that she felt very much alone since the defection of her kinsfolk.

In his turn he had been encouraged to employ greater frankness concerning his own affairs, persuaded that his cause did not lose thereby ; for he had succeeded in his business, and had made friends with men and women both. Eloise might as well know that others thought well of him. He sent up his card and waited impatiently in the reception-room, walking to and fro and glancing at his image in the glass. He had never looked so well, or weighed so much, or worn so becoming a suit of clothes.

These are not puerile considerations. Smaller factors than a man's weight or the fit of his coat have told for or against him in a woman's favor.

After what seemed an interminable time the bell-boy returned with the undelivered pasteboard.

"De do' am locked ; guess Miss Gordon gone out," he drawled. "But her key ain't in de office."

"See if Mrs. Glenn knows anything about her," directed Philip, and waited again while the boy scoured the house, only to bring back word that Miss Gordon was not to be found. Mrs. Glenn had gone off with Miss Larrabee, and so had Miss Thompson. The Glenn children were out somewhere with somebody—no one could tell where or with whom.

Philip bought a Sunday *Tribune*, and sat down with it in the rotunda. Eleven o'clock came, but no Eloise. Of course it was not her fault, but that did not lessen his disappointment. If he could have found some one to talk with, the time would have passed more quickly, he told himself; but the hotel was nearly deserted. The bell-boys sat in a row opposite the office-desk, undisturbed. The great clock over their heads ticked solemnly in the silence. A breeze came in through the open door, gently rocking the empty chairs standing there. Something else came in also—a fluttering white figure which hesitated but an instant, then darted towards him. It was Millicent Glenn, her blue eyes shining like stars, her golden hair streaming back like a nimbus, her lips parted in a smile.

"Mr. More! Mr. More!" she cried, and flew straight into his arms.

He strained her to his breast—the warm, happy, loving little creature! There was something strangely comforting in the contact with her clinging, yielding form and the clasp of her arms around his neck. He hid his face in her soft curls, murmuring the tender words he would gladly have given to another, and she kissed him frankly on cheek and chin, and told him he was "nicer than ever."

She asked him a dozen questions in a breath. How long could he stay? Was it hot in California? Were there any little girls there? Did he like them as well as he did her?

She showed him the golden heart he gave her, hanging by its chain around her neck. There was another band there—a silken cord, at which she tugged in vain for several seconds. It had something tied to it ; she drew it up with difficulty from under the tiers of ruffles which stood out like wings from her dimpled shoulders—something bulky and cumbersome. It came in sight at last—a bag of yellow silk put together with long, awkward stitches.

She opened it and took out a sheet of writing-paper folded small to just fit the bag. Philip recognized it with a smile; it was the letter he wrote her one dull day in Sacramento, when a man who had promised to meet him did not come and there were six hours in which to do nothing. It was brief, only half a dozen lines, beginning "My darling little Millicent," and ending "Yours faithfully, Philip More ;" but Millicent knew them by heart—she repeated them to prove it.

Philip was glad that he could produce her reply, in huge printed capitals wandering over the entire page without much reference to one another. Millicent scanned it critically. "I can do lots better now," she said, viewing with contempt the immature efforts of a month ago. "I can write ' *Millicent Glenn, Lake View Hotel, Chicago.*' Want to see me ?"

Philip avowed his anxiety to witness such a finished performance, and to further its inception produced a tablet from his pocket and a small silver pencil. The latter pleased her mightily.

"That isn't much like a man's pencil," she said, tentatively.

"No, it isn't," granted Philip. "I won it as a prize at a card-party."

"I didn't know but somebody gave it to you," she pursued, turning it over with admiring glances.

"No one gave it to me. Would you like it?"

"Oh, I should *like* it!" she exclaimed, clasping it rapturously to her bosom; "but I didn't ask for it, did I?"

"No, you didn't ask for it. What is more, I am going to make you earn it. You can have it for your own when you have written 'Millicent Glenn, Lake View Hotel, Chicago.' Here, use my arm for a writing-table."

The small scribe went promptly to work, bowing her head until her curls swept his arm. She tossed them back impatiently. "I wish you'd hold my hair till I get through," she said, plaintively. "I can't do a single thing."

He obeyed, grasping gingerly the handful of silken locks, conscious of a curious thrill as he did so. His coarse, masculine palm had never come in contact with anything so fine, so soft, so full of life.

"Ouch!" cried Millicent. She had drawn back quickly to inspect her work, forgetting how she was held.

"I am awfully sorry," he exclaimed, penitently.

"It isn't very good," was her irrelevant reply, mindful only of her work. "Sometimes I do better, when I can get both elbows on the table. Oh, dear, there's Miss Gordon!" She slipped to the floor and Philip stood up, brightening visibly.

Eloise came leisurely towards them, holding out her hand. "How do you do, Philip?" she said, composedly. "This is quite a surprise."

There was nothing in her tone to indicate it, he thought, with some chagrin. This, then, was the result of his eager anticipation—a commonplace greeting in a hotel rotunda; and she seemed in no hurry to take him where she could give her welcome a more personal application. She stood and chatted with him of the weather and his journey, while the guests of the hotel came in and the bells began to ring and the bell-boys to rush about, for the Sunday forenoon rest was over. After a while Aunt Harriet appeared, followed by her flock. She, too, greeted him perfunctorily, and seemed to have her mind on something else.

Millicent had claimed her mother's attention for the silver pencil, but Mrs. Glenn put her aside, murmuring, "Yes, yes, child; there, run away now," and held out her hand stiffly to the traveller.

"Confound it all!" mused Philip, angrily, "what have I done that they should treat me in this manner? I wish I had stayed where I was."

In his turn he became dignified and unapproachable, and by the time he was left alone with Eloise, for Aunt Harriet went out soon after luncheon, their conversation was as formal and stately as an old-time minuet.

She put polite questions to him and he gave them polite answers. Then they reversed the figure; he questioned and she answered in the same manner. Each felt innocent and injured, and neither would ask the other, "What is it?"

Once Philip arose, declaring that he must be interfering with her siesta; but Eloise assured him that she had given up all her old Southern ways, and the minuet went on, more stately and more dignified and more cold, until Philip could contain himself no longer.

"This is a delightful meeting after an absence of half a year!" he exclaimed, with bitterness.

"I don't know who is to blame," replied Eloise, sensitively.

"Millicent Glenn is the only one who seems glad to see me," he continued, in a hurt tone. "Miss Larrabee used to be fond of me, but she has gotten bravely over it."

"Aunt Harriet is not herself to-day," said Eloise, firmly. "Something has happened; I don't know what."

"And I suppose Mrs. Glenn is not herself," retorted Philip.

"She does act rather strangely."

"I don't care how they act," he exploded. "If

you had shown any feeling, they might have turned their backs for all I'd care."

Eloise looked mutinous. Love does not come by recrimination. A woman is not teased into being tender.

"I'll tell you what, Eloise," pursued Philip, "I'm getting tired of living on hopes."

"It was your own proposition," she responded.

"I know it was. I thought—the more fool I—that my devotion would soften you; but it doesn't. Then I went away. I said to myself, 'Perhaps she will miss me a little—'" He stopped and swallowed hard, choked by emotions of disappointment and self-pity.

Eloise made no reply, and he began to be angry with himself for thus yielding. "It's all right, of course," he said, proudly. "I am sorry I have bothered you so long, and—"

"You have not bothered me," interrupted Eloise. "Can't you understand, Philip, that I have much to think of—many cares, many duties? I can't sit down and be sentimental. I must have my wits about me to meet the world and conquer it."

There was a pathetic ring in the girl's voice, to which his heart responded chivalrously; but when he considered what she said he hardened. The keen business life he had been living had taught him to challenge words and demand their full significance. She need not have cares and duties, she need not meet the world and conquer it. This was no excuse.

"You see, Philip," she went on, lightly, "that old saying about 'man's love' being 'of his life a thing apart' is beginning to apply to us women as we come to have individual occupations and interests."

Philip remained silent. He could have met a rival with sword or pistol, he could have wooed an unresponsive mistress longer than he had wooed Eloise; but for a woman who looked him coolly in the eye and laughed when his heart was breaking he had no resources. Grieved beyond measure, he stood up, straight and tall and white, to say good-bye, barely touching her hand as he did so.

A wild desire seized her, as the door closed behind him, to run after him and bring him back. She resisted it, but could not drive it away. He was all the lover she had, and life without a lover is a dull thing for a girl; unutterably dull her life would be with only her work to comfort her, and her few friends.

And Philip had been so patient and so true. Her heart began to plead for him. A man is inclined to dislike the woman he has wronged; consciousness of wrong-doing makes him surly. A woman pities the man she has hurt, and becomes almost loving in her remorse.

She told herself he would return the next day, and stayed in, all the long, lovely afternoon, expecting him; but Philip did not come.

Day after day passed and brought no sign of him. Aunt Harriet finally emerged from her abstraction sufficiently to inquire if there was any trouble, but returned to it when her niece gave an evasive reply.

"That shows how she is wrapped up in her mysticism," thought Eloise. "But I could never have told her about Philip—or anything else. There is only one woman in the world I can tell things to, anyway. Bless her old heart, I'll go there this minute!" It was a wet morning, and there was nothing doing in the studio—no diversion from the grinding monotony of regret. She put on her mackintosh as if it had been armor, and with desperate eagerness started for Seventy-fifth Street.

"Come right in," said Mrs. Harwood, cheerily. "I'll take your umbrella and open it in the kitchen ; it'll dry better so. Give me your cloak, too. Sit down ; I'll be right back."

Eloise mechanically surrendered the umbrella and the cloak, and seated herself in a large cushioned chair which had been covered by its owner with one of her discarded dresses. Most of the chairs in the room wore Mrs. Harwood's old clothes, but that made them seem so much the more hospitable and inviting. They were like reflections of herself, standing about, prepared to do her will.

There was nothing in the flat which had not survived several reincarnations. It was Eloise's wont to find entertainment, when Mrs. Harwood was occupied, in wondering what the carpet and curtains used to be. To-day the most that she demanded of the place was its wholesome atmosphere of calm and common-sense.

She was not long alone; Mrs. Harwood soon returned and sank into the lap of another arm-chair as plump as herself.

"Now let's hear all about it," she said, taking up her knitting. It is always easier to tell one's story when the listener looks the other way. What penitent could pour out his secret at the confessional if the priest presented his eyes as well as his ear?

Eloise watched the twinkling needles, and felt as if they led her on. Not once did the knitter look off her work until the story ended with an outburst of self-reproach; then she glanced up sympathetically.

"You can't make two things fit by rubbin' 'em together," she began, tersely. "No more can you two people. I didn't know but you'd stop rubbin' after a while and get the consolations of matrimony along with its trials. It's dreadful handy to have a man around." She shifted her needles and resumed her knitting.

Eloise laughed and then she sighed, as if she had no right to be amused. "You make me feel a little less like a—homicide," she said, pensively. "I'd begun to think that I could make any sacrifice to atone for not loving Philip—"

"And you'd felt more an' more so as time went on," finished the elder woman, quickly. "You're a great deal more apt to sacrifice yourself to a man if you don't care as much for him as you think you ought to. It's a sort of salve to your conscience, like giving money instead of sympathy." Mrs. Harwood looked conscious, it seemed to Eloise; but Daniel and Philip were not the same. Again her heart softened towards her absent lover.

"I have thought sometimes I would write to him," she pursued, "and try to be more generous, more kind."

"Don't you do it," warned her adviser, "unless you can be kind the way he wants you to. Let him wrastle it out, man-fashion. Don't keep a-feelin' of the sore spot to see if it is sore."

"But I cannot do my work," confessed Eloise. "I am there with him, thinking of his hurt."

"That's a big mistake, too," replied her friend. "If you try to live somebody else's life you'll miss of livin' your own."

"But don't you think I ought to suffer for making him miserable?" asked the girl, between a laugh and a sob.

"The Lord 'll take care of that," said Mrs. Harwood; "He set the thing a-goin'. You don't gain anything by trying to punish yourself. You'll have to take the regular retribution just the same —that is, if you've done wrong. I don't say that you have. You ought to know."

Counsel like this is stimulating—at least, in the presence of the counsellor. When, walking along to the station, Eloise tried to repeat the helpful words over to herself, they seemed to have lost their efficacy.

How could Mrs. Harwood or any one else understand?

The rain had ceased, and all along the street the piazzas grew gay again with bright cushions and carpets and with the light summer dresses of those who had nothing of graver importance to do than to shield themselves from bad weather and come out with the sun.

One tall, blond youth not unlike Philip stopped to pin a red rose on the gown of a girl not unlike herself.

XXVIII

ONLY once more did Mark Heffron meet Marguerite Duvray, and that was on the eve of her departure for New York. He had an affable little note from Mrs. Burnham, telling him of their proposed absence from Chicago and repeating Mademoiselle Duvray's apologies for having failed to keep her appointment with him. They were to be at home to their friends the evening of the 5th, and should be glad to see him, if he were not otherwise engaged.

Mark was not engaged on the evening of the 5th; if he had been, the chances are that he would have broken the engagement, so curious was he to "see what she would do next," as he phrased it.

He found the pleasant drawing-room filled with men and women who expressed their regret at the coming separation, according to their kind—the men by a jocoseness hinting at repression, the women by open and emphatic lament. There were farewell bouquets everywhere, and farewell gifts in tinted papers—books, trinkets, whatever could be thought of in connection with travel.

The object of these attentions received them

graciously, maintaining the level of appreciation towards all, but vouchsafing subtle, personal acknowledgments to each one. Mark watched her for some time at a distance, and found it impossible to withhold his admiration. "It would be a pity to limit her," he decided. "She ought to have both hemispheres to operate in, and perhaps the planet Mars; I'll bet my bottom dollar she could cover it."

He took this tolerant mood with him when he addressed her, and she responded with the frank cordiality which signalized her welcome when he first came to Chicago.

"But you have not told me why you wished to see me," he said, when she had blamed a headache for her non-appearance the evening he called, and he had assured her that his sympathy for her outweighed his disappointment.

"I wanted to continue our conversation about Dr. Symonds," she answered carelessly, "but now that he is gone—"

"Dead?" ejaculated Mark, in tones which caused his nearest neighbor, a thin, nervous woman, to turn upon him a look of indignant remonstrance.

"Why, no, I suppose not," she replied, lowering her voice as a signal for him to lower his, "but he has disappeared. Mr. Norton had a note from him, saying that he felt he was not doing his best work here and should go elsewhere for a while. He gave no address, and nothing has been heard from him since. I thought you knew."

"Not at all," Mark responded, earnestly. "I haven't even heard his name for three days. It is strange."

"Very strange," said Marguerite. "Ah, good-evening, Herr Meinzer. I thought you would not let me go without a word."

Herr Meinzer murmured several words over the hand she gave him, but only himself knew what they were. His glances were more intelligible; his pale blue eyes gleamed at her through his spectacles like street-lamps through a fog.

"You remember Herr Meinzer, I am sure, Mr. Heffron," protested Marguerite.

Mark acknowledged the acquaintance and retired to the background of his own thoughts. "Symonds go down and Meinzer come up! 'All is Spirit and All is Good,'" he reflected. "Great is philosophy! I suppose he 'gives her the right thought.' How she would like to have me go away!"

But Marguerite showed no sign of wishing to be rid of him. She made the conversation triangular as far as she could, and divided her smiles equally between the two men.

"I wonder if she ever has any preferences or predilections," mused Mark, "and what she does with them when she has them."

Herr Meinzer was too happy for reflections; those would come later, when he should smoke his long pipe and call up the image of the gracious fraulein. One cannot enjoy to the utmost and reflect upon it ; that is to hinder joy. If the dark man Heffron chose to be moody because he had not the beautiful lady to himself, that was not the fault of Herr Meinzer. Alas, there were more than the dark man Heffron to contend for the honor of a chat with her—the Russian prince and the Italian and some strange youths. The joyful moment was over. "A happy voyage, madame, *Auf Wiedersehen !*"

"A happy voyage," echoed Mark, holding out his hand. Was there a reproach in his eyes as they encountered hers? Was there a regret in hers ?

"We shall meet in October," she said, gayly, and he answered, "If the gods are kind."

It seemed to him, as he made his way out of the room, that there were a number of new people present, and he did not see the Ayers or the Rosses or the Merriams ; where were they all? Mrs. Burnham called out to him, "What ! going so early ?" He stopped to shake hands with her and wish her a pleasant journey.

"It is always pleasant for me to travel with my cousin," she answered. "You know I am devoted to her."

"She is most fortunate," said Mark, with unusual gallantry.

"How charming of you to say so !" she exclaimed. "Of course I am the fortunate one, but I like to think she depends upon me somewhat."

"She will need you more than ever now that

she has lost her 'ghostly comforter,'" said Mark, wickedly.

Mrs. Burnham gave him a searching look. How much did he know about the matter?

"Although she seems to take the loss very philosophically," he concluded.

"She always thinks everything is for the best," responded Mrs. Burnham, quickly. "That is her creed. I fancy you yourself are not easily disturbed," she added, returning the thrust.

"No, I am not," he answered. It was the trait in himself that he most approved and cultivated; but our own virtues are less agreeable just as our own faults are more obnoxious when we find them in some one else.

"If I were easily disturbed," he went on, flippantly, "just think what a state I should be in now! That young Italian over there is actually wiping his eyes. I must make my escape before the contagion reaches me!" He bowed low with mock emotion, and left her looking after him.

"He either cares more than he'll confess," she decided, "or else he's glad to get out of the whole thing."

As an actual fact, both conjectures were correct. Just what Mark expected to find in Marguerite and why he was disappointed he could not have told; or why, with his soreness of heart, he felt such a sense of freedom when he went from the crowded drawing-room at the Cynthia into the open air. Equally paradoxical appeared to him his indignation at the ease with which she dismissed Dr. Symonds from her thoughts; had he not tried to bring about that very result?

"Queer that I hadn't even heard his name!" he said to himself.

He heard it often enough the next morning; indeed, it seemed to him that he heard little else.

Julia Ross was on the car when he went downtown. She said Maud and Mary were quite prostrated. She herself did not believe in depending entirely upon one teacher. Of course Dr. Symonds was a remarkable man, but she had not found much in his system which was new to her. She had hoped to have Haridass Goculdass return for another course of lectures, but had not been able to arrange it. And now that people were beginning to go away for the summer, she should have to wait until fall.

"Do you think Dr. Symonds will return?" inquired Mark.

"He may and he may not," replied Julia, guardedly. "We are never left alone for long. There will be some one—there always is."

"That is a comfortable way of looking at it," vouchsafed Mark.

"It is the only way," was the determined reply.

Carl Dering, whom Mark overtook on State Street, was less inclined to philosophize. "You see," he said, confidentially, as he fell into step, "it has such a bad effect on the people. I went out to the Lake View yesterday to see my aunt, Miss Larrabee. My cousin sent for me. My poor old aunt has hardly slept since Symonds went away."

" Could you do nothing for her?" inquired Mark. " What has become of your mental influence?"

" I tried it," said the young fellow, honestly, " but she was too much for me. I'd quiet her for a while, and then she'd start right up again. She will have it that some enemy has driven him away ; she says she can feel that he is suffering."

Mark looked annoyed. " How do you explain Symonds's behavior?" he asked.

" I don't explain it," returned Carl. " He was doing well, I believe. Perhaps some patient sent for him. He never told his business."

" He may return," Mark suggested.

Carl shook his head. " He will have to come soon if he is going to help Miss Larrabee," he said, with a sigh.

Mark walked on alone, trying to convince himself that it was none of his affair. He went over in his mind the interview with Symonds at the office. " Symonds certainly thought he had the better of me in that argument," he said to himself. " It is all a put-up scheme to increase his popularity. He'll descend unexpectedly, in a blaze of glory, some day, and tell his disciples that he has been upon a mountain somewhere getting spiritualized."

But, despite his cynicism, Mark felt uneasy, and returned early to his hotel.

"Ben a gentleman here to see you, sir," said the deferential clerk. "Ben here twice. There he is now, sir."

It was young Norton, who advanced without a smile, and looking pale and worried.

"What's up?" asked Mark.

"I'll tell you presently," was the curt reply.

"Anything the matter in New York?"

"No."

"What the deuce is it?"

"I'll tell you when we get to your room."

They filed solemnly down the hall, and Mark flung open the door. "Have a cigar?" he inquired, laconically, as Joey seated himself in the nearest chair.

"No, thanks; I won't smoke. Mark, what under the sun did you kick up such a rumpus for?"

"What rumpus?" growled Mark, resenting the tone as he had resented the manner, since he landed, of the man who would never be anything but a youngster to him.

"With Uncle Eli," replied Norton.

"Now look here, Joe Norton," began Mark, firing up, "please remember at whose request I 'kicked up a rumpus,' as you call it. You wrote to me and begged me to interfere, and I did so."

"But, by Jove, you might have left him a leg

to stand on," returned Joey, impetuously. "You didn't spare him an atom of faith in himself or in any one else ; and now that What's-his-name that he thought so much of has cleared out the old man is sick abed. He's really in a bad way, Mark."

"You talk as if I'd set deliberately to work to finish him, instead of trying to save him from making a pauper of himself."

"But he says he gave you to understand that he was only considering the investment."

"Gave me to understand nothing !"

"And, really, I'd give fifty thousand, if I had it, to put him back where he was when I saw him last."

Mark made no reply.

"He says this man is the only one who has understood him," pursued Joey, "except Mademoiselle Duvray, and she has avoided him lately. He says you haven't been near him for weeks."

"Good thing," put in Mark, grimly, "if my influence is so bad."

"Well, really, Mark," persisted Norton, who was still inclined to be disagreeable, "you don't realize how you carry people along with you. If I wanted to keep a conviction I wouldn't mention it before you. I used to envy you the power you have over people, but I've come to the conclusion that I don't want it."

"Thanks, awfully," returned Mark, cut to the quick by these home-thrusts. "Anything more ?"

"No, I don't think there is," replied Joey, with a faint smile.

"I hope you feel relieved."

"I do."

"Perhaps you'll have a smoke now?"

"I don't know but I will," and he took to his solace as a fretful baby takes to its bottle after a cry.

They talked of business, and lamented the existing condition of affairs, as every one in the commercial world was lamenting it at that time—discussed the railway troubles and computed the probabilities of a general strike, hoping their freight would get in from the East before there was a tie-up. The angry current which had surged between them seemed to have iced over with an enduring peace. Joey began to test it to see if it would bear his weight.

"If it hadn't been that business was so dull I couldn't have come on," he said, amiably. "Uncle Eli's housekeeper telegraphed me there was trouble. You know I am his only relative, as he is mine. I'm awfully fond of the old fellow, and I'd do anything for him."

Mark made no reply by word, look, or gesture, and Joey skated on. "I wish I knew what to do with him," he said, anxiously. "Is there anything you can suggest?"

At this the ice gave way. "Not much!" exclaimed Mark, with emphasis. "I'm through suggesting."

Joey floundered out as best he could. There was no need of getting into a huff—he was sure he meant no offence—he hoped before they met again that Mark would have forgiven him if he had said too much. He stood up to go.

"There's nothing to forgive," said Mark, bluntly. "If that's the way you feel, I'm glad to know it. But don't ask me again to give advice; I'll do anything but that."

"I did want to ask you—" began Joey, and stopped.

"What is it? Go ahead!"

"I'd like to change places with you until Uncle Eli is better."

"Thunder and guns, yes!" exploded Mark. "Nothing would please me better than to get out of this confounded hole!"

"I'll speak to the firm about it. You're awfully kind."

"No kindness; it suits me as well as it does you."

So, after all, they shook hands and parted friends.

XXIX

MARK had plenty to think of besides his talk with Joey in the days that followed. The "sympathetic strike" had become a certainty, and business was at a standstill. The freight expected from the East might be stopped outside the city. He haunted the telegraph-offices in company with a number of other business men, like him sending and receiving messages all day long. Uncle Oliver Ross was among them.

"It does seem as if the devil was on top!" exclaimed the old man, cheerfully. "I never saw the beat."

He mopped his face energetically, reducing the general griminess to a few well-defined smirches.

"Let me help you," said Mark, producing his handkerchief and plying it vigorously.

"Much obliged," said Uncle Oliver. "There, I guess that'll do; a little dirt, more or less, don't count."

"So you Chicagoans always say," returned Mark, good-humoredly. "I believe you enjoy a muss. I never saw anything like the way you take this strike."

"We always did kinder thrive on excitement,"

said Uncle Oliver, complacently, "and we ain't afraid of emergencies. Brought up on emergencies, you know; they come natural. If those South-siders have to ride in town by the cable or on a tug-boat, it will only get their blood up; it makes 'em feel good to be overcomin' circumstances. Besides, there ain't any business; they might as well spend their time that way as any other."

"That's all right for now," returned Mark, significantly; "but you wait until property is destroyed and acts of violence are committed. These strikers aren't in it for the fun of the thing."

"Oh, we'll take care of 'em, we'll take care of 'em!" cried the old man, gayly.

He left the office and started off down the street, then came back suddenly. "Did you know Nellie Heffron had left town?" he asked.

"I thought she went some time ago," replied Mark, indifferently.

"No; she stayed over, she was doing so well—pockets full, big dinners, presents;" with a comprehensive sweep of his hand Uncle Oliver included whatever other gains he had not time to enumerate.

"You're the man who wanted me to stop her before she began," laughed Mark.

"I don't say now that I approve of it," returned Uncle Oliver, quickly. "But I believe she means all right."

"Is she coming back another year?"

"That depends. She's afraid the bicycle craze 'll knock her business higher 'n a kite. When it comes to bicycles and bloomers, I tell you what, I'd rather have Nellie Heffron!" He started again, and again returned. "I suppose you've heard about that feller leavin'—that preacher at the Enterprise?" he asked.

"Dr. Symonds?" returned Mark, shortly. "Yes, I have."

"What do you think of it?"

"I don't think."

"Seems strange; but then you never can tell what a feller like that will do."

Mark made no reply.

"Our girls are all broke up over it. I declare, if I'd known where he was I'd ha' gone to him, there, one spell, and brought him back."

Mark smiled. "I expect to hear next that you are entertaining Haridass Goculdass," he said, satirically.

"No, sir!" cried Uncle Oliver, straightening himself. "I draw the line at that Hindoo."

He marched off without another word, and this time he did not return.

Mark felt annoyed, he could not tell why, and spoiled two despatches before he wrote one to suit him.

As he had prophesied, things grew from bad to worse. Day by day one body of workmen after another "went out." All over the city there was an ominous silence, except where the cable cars were running. The platforms of the Illinois Central stood bare and deserted and the tracks lengthened out, shining in the sun, unoccupied, save where a shrieking locomotive darted up and down carrying news, or drew with deliberate purpose cars filled with gray - coated policemen.

Ominous reports came from the suburban towns, where anarchy was gathering to a head. Idleness and discontent had given rise to desperate efforts to win or lose all. The women raged like Furies. The very babes were taught to creep under the cars and apply the incendiary torch.

"What do you think now?" asked Mark, the next time he met Uncle Oliver. The old man hung his head. "It's too bad," he murmured— "too bad. I'm sorry for the rascals. They've got hold of the blade instead of the handle, and only cut themselves. I'm sorry."

"*Sorry* for the hounds?" cried Mark. "I'm surprised. Come along with me and see the soldiers; that's where your sympathies ought to be."

"I'd just as lief go and see the soldiers," replied Uncle Oliver, "but I wish there hadn't been any need of their comin'. It's too bad!"

They strolled slowly along Wabash Avenue towards Van Buren Street. "Mark," said his companion, "you never was a working-man. You went to college and then into business; you didn't have to do day's work for day's wages. I did. I know how working-men feel, and—I'm sorry, I'm sorry."

Mark made no reply. The compassionate words of the old man were to him the expression of a sentimental tendency increased by age. To answer them according to their substance would be to employ an unwarrantable harshness. For the sake of their kindly spirit it was better to let them pass unheeded.

As the two pedestrians turned into Van Buren Street they found their way obstructed by a dense crowd of silent, sullen men, who stood and stared at the white tents before them, attempting neither to advance nor to retreat. The open space along the shore of the lake, hardly to be dignified by the name of park, was appropriated entire by the encampment. At one end the horses were corralled. Cannon pointed up every street, and a sentinel stalked up and down keeping back the curious and defiant.

"Hullo! there's a woman trying to get through," exclaimed Uncle Oliver. "They've hauled her back, but she ain't reconciled, not by a long chalk!" Sure enough, on the edge of the parade-ground, gesticulating earnestly with the umbrella which she carried, stood a woman, evidently trying to persuade the sentinel to let her through the lines. Mark took note of the ample, motherly figure and benignant face.

"I know that woman," he said, positively.

"Perhaps I had better go and see what the trouble is."

"Yes, yes," agreed his companion; "go ahead! I must get back. It's most noon. Come around when you can;" and he dove through the crowd.

Mark advanced towards the disputants. "What's the matter, Mrs. Harwood?" he called out, encouragingly.

Mrs. Harwood turned and held out both hands, burdened with the umbrella and several brown-paper parcels. "Oh, Mr. Heffron, you always come at the right time!" she cried. "Do tell this man I ain't carryin' powder or information, and all I want is to ketch that boat and get home in time for dinner. I'll be left as sure as the world!" She glanced despairingly in the direction of the dock, where the *Pilot Boy* was puffing and screaming preparatory to being off.

"'Tisn't that I think you're in league with the strikers, madam," replied the soldier, patiently, "but our orders are strict. You can't expect us to relax our discipline."

"Then why can't you give me an escort and go the whole figure," demanded the intruder, "if it's discipline you want? That boat's going to get off, as true as you live!"

Mark glanced back at the crowd, scanning it closely; then he beckoned. A newsboy ran forward. "*Tribune! Herald!*" he called—"all about the strike!"

"Give me a *Tribune*," answered Mark, and

while the boy was making change added, in an aside, "Do you see that boat — the one that is backing-down there?"

"Yes, sir, that's the *Pilot Boy;* runs to Seventy-fifth Street."

"Stop her, and I'll give you a quarter."

The urchin was off like a dart. Between the very legs of the soldiers he slid nimbly while shouts arose—"Come back! I'll fire!" But the gamin did not come back and the soldiers did not fire, and Mark led his companion leisurely around the encampment to the pier.

"I'm for law and order as much as any one," said Mrs. Harwood, as he arranged her among her bundles on the shady side of the boat, "but the idea that I'd got to get left just to give them practice in military discipline! Why didn't he send an escort with me, that's what I'd like to know! You going, too?" For Mark had seated himself beside her.

"If you don't object," he replied, with a smile.

"Of course I'd like it," she exclaimed, "if you can spare the time."

"At present there seems to be more time than anything else," he answered, dryly. "Besides, I think the change will do me good."

The *Pilot Boy* reeled tipsily out of the slip and headed for deep water, where it pitched and tossed as if in the midst of heavy seas, although the lake was like a mill-pond.

"Do you suppose the boat is safe?" inquired

Mrs. Harwood, not timorously, but as one inquires for information.

"I don't suppose it is," he replied, carelessly, "but nothing is safe nowadays ; and you couldn't very well walk."

"No, I couldn't, that's a fact," she returned, comfortably. "It's real pleasant going this way. The houses on the shore look like the pictures in the old geography."

"Only Chicago never would stand still long enough to have her picture taken," he suggested.

"Ain't she just like an uneasy young one !" cried Mrs. Harwood.

"But you like the place ?"

"Yes, I *do*, and I vowed and declared I'd never live in it ; but if you vow and declare you'll never do a thing you're sure to do it before you die. There's more of the young one's performances," as they passed the pathetic ruins of the Fair and the gaunt black skeleton of the Spectatorium. "No old, grown-up city would ever have started to act out such a fairy story. You ain't going back ; no, sir, you've come thus far, and you've got to go home to dinner with me. I won't hear two ways about it."

Mark made a slight show of resistance and yielded, only too willingly. "Dan'l" had gone up to the farm, where he appeared to spend most of his time, and there was no one in the flat. Mrs. Harwood bustled about, opening the doors and windows which she had frugally closed before setting out for town. "You make yourself at home, and I'll have dinner on the table in half a minute," she promised.

Left alone, Mark surveyed his surroundings with friendly interest. "Talk about being taken into the bosom of the family!" he mused, rocking softly to and fro. "Most families haven't any; but there's no doubt about this. Why don't other people live into their belongings, and let you have the benefit of it? There's flesh and blood in that sofa-cushion. What a thing it is to be a woman! I wish Mrs. Harwood had a daughter. I'd marry her and go to housekeeping to-morrow. What is it, anyway—Kansas, or W. C. T. U., or Beau Lieu? I wonder if St. Ursula and the Eleven Thousand Virgins are still abroad in the world and unattached; I'll ask her."

He did so, when he had eaten and praised the beefsteak, fried potatoes, and johnny-cake with which she had heaped his plate.

"Susan—Susan—what was her name? Susan Gray ought to know how to make johnny-cake. I wonder if Susan would have me?"

"She's married," replied his hostess. "Married a college professor with four children. He was at Beau Lieu last summer lecturing on biology. But any woman with brains can make johnny-cake. Are you through? We may as well go into the other room. I'll let the table stand." She rose as she spoke.

"Perhaps they can, but they won't," returned

Mark, following her; his mind was still on johnny-cake—"and they wouldn't do their sewing up in tidy bundles like that;" he pointed to her "mending," lying, neatly folded, on the table. "My mother used to do her work up like that," he added, wistfully. "I was only nine years old when she died, but I remember distinctly her— I suppose they would call it femininity, the quality they're trying so hard to get rid of nowadays." A hard tone had come into his voice.

"They can't get rid of it," said Mrs. Harwood, quickly, "and I don't believe they want to."

"Perhaps not," returned Mark, abstractedly. He had taken a large photograph from the table and was looking at it critically.

"Those are the scholars at Beau Lieu last summer," explained his hostess. "Do you recognize any of them?"

"I see the Reverend Billings," replied Mark, with a smile, "and, upon my word, his wife is with him! How did that happen?"

"She's been going out more the past two years," said Mrs. Harwood, drawing her chair up beside his. "There's Susan Gray that was, Mrs. Tinker that is. That's her husband with the bushy side-whiskers, and those are the four children; nice children, too. Susan makes a first-rate mother. There's Miss Gordon; I suppose you recognize her. It's a good likeness."

"Yes, it is," agreed Mark. "She's a fine-looking girl."

"She had it taken to please the Glenn children —they're with her. She doesn't think much of that sort of thing herself. Have you found me yet? There I am, over there, and Dan'l's just behind me. Oh, I want to ask you while I think of it if you've read this book." She caught up a volume, into which she had folded a piece of newspaper to keep her place, and laid it on his knee.

"'*The Ascent of Man*,'" read Mark. "H—m! who set you at work on this?"

"We had a list of books given us to look over before we go to Beau Lieu this summer," she replied, "and that's one of 'em. The Reading Circle are on Evolution this year, and seems as if I couldn't wait till I get there. I'm just crazy to talk it over with some one."

"Then you haven't tried Dan'l?"

"Oh, it's all monkeys to Dan'l," she answered. "I undertook to explain it to him, but I couldn't make him let go his grip on old-fashioned ideas. Perhaps its just as well; he might have dropped into — Nothing, between lettin' go and catchin' hold again."

"Then you don't think Evolution detracts from the dignity of the Divine Purpose?" pursued Mark, leading her on.

"Detract! My, it's the biggest thing! Seems as if I'd—smother—sometimes, I'm so full, when I think of it."

"How about the Bible?" he questioned.

"The Bible's full of it!" she cried. "Did some one come up the walk? Yes, there's the bell! Now you sit right where you are. I ain't half through. There are some questions I want to ask you."

She was absent several minutes, and when she returned she was followed by a tall young lady whom Mark did not at first recognize. As she emerged from the dim hall and came straight towards him he saw that it was Eloise Gordon.

XXX

The manner in which Eloise Gordon approached Mark Heffron was that of one who has a disagreeable duty to perform and would have it over as soon as possible.

"Mrs. Harwood told me you were here," she said, briefly, "and I made up my mind to ask your assistance. My aunt is in a critical condition from lack of sleep. She will not take medicine or employ a physician. Will you hypnotize her and put her to sleep?"

Only twice in his life had Mark Heffron been thoroughly routed by surprise: the first time was when he saw Joe Norton in the prize-ring; this was the second. He found himself at a loss for words, and stood before Eloise Gordon coloring like a school-boy, until she caught the infection and began to color, too, all over her fair face and white throat.

To hide her confusion she turned to Mrs. Harwood, whose shrewd, searching eyes were taking in every detail of the situtation.

"I discovered a new Chicago to-day. I came over here in an omnibus," she said, with a nervous laugh. "There is one which runs every hour." And Mrs. Harwood made the answer she was wont to make when she had nothing to say—"Is that so!"

Then they both turned to Mark, who realized that he was in an embarrassing position.

To deny his ability was useless; she knew it too well. To refuse to exercise it was to appear unfriendly and unkind. If she had only made the request as if he was a friend and this was a kindness; but, "confound her, she asked it as if I were a barber or a chiropodist," thought Mark, with chagrin, "and she wanted a piece of work done which was in my line of business."

There was an awkward pause which Mrs. Harwood, as hostess, felt in duty bound to fill. "I'm sorry Miss Larrabee's so bad," she said, sympathetically. "I guess from what I hear that a good many of Dr. Symonds's folks are in the same fix since he went away."

At this Mark found his tongue. "Mental suggestion ought to be taken out of the hands of these ignorant creatures and intrusted to scientific men," he said.

"I dunno about that," said Mrs. Harwood, reflectively. "The 'babes and sucklings' are not half so apt to cut up didoes with it as the 'wise and prudent;' they das'n't. Besides, what have the 'wise and prudent' found out that amounts to anything? They don't know what it is or where it comes from."

"Then they had better let it alone," said Mark, severely.

"But can you let it alone?" asked Eloise, who had been doing some pretty steady thinking on the subject of late. "Doesn't 'suggestion' depend on influence? Surely influence exists and ought to be exerted for—for good." She hesitated, and her eyes fell. To her and to Mark Heffron this was a personal discussion.

"Exerted!" he cried. "Heaven forbid! If you have any influence, bottle it up; seal it hermetically; bury it fathoms deep! Then it will get away in spite of you."

"I don't think Dr. Symonds was a bad man," put in Mrs. Harwood, with no particular pertinence, but fearing another pause. "He was 'occupied with good works' more than he was with preaching. I should think most ministers would preach away all the religion they've got."

No one responded and the dreaded pause ensued. Eloise looked at her watch. "My omnibus is nearly due," she said, rising. "Good-bye, Mrs. Harwood. May I depend upon your assistance, Mr. Heffron?"

Mark rose also. "You had better let me get a horse and take you home," he said, considerately.

"It is wholly unnecessary," she returned, coldly—she did not want him to be considerate—"unless you object to the omnibus," she added.

"Not at all."

They set off together, watched from the door by Mrs. Harwood until they were out of sight. "Both of 'em need the same thing," she soliloquized. "But they can't either of 'em give it to the other. This is a queer world—I must go in and do those dishes."

Since that fatal summer at Beau Lieu these two had not been alone together until now; there had always been some one else present to interpose as a shield. They congratulated themselves that it could not be for long ; there were sure to be other passengers in the omnibus. Suddenly it turned the corner, three blocks ahead—a big black vehicle enveloped in its own dust and defended by its own noise, impervious alike to signal and shout. After a few ineffectual efforts to stop it, Mark gave up the chase. "Here is a livery-stable," he said, turning to his companion. "If you will wait in the office—"

"It isn't far to the Lake View," she protested. "I have walked much farther."

"If you will wait in the office I will order a carriage," he finished, and she obeyed. To do otherwise would have appeared like childishness, and if ever Eloise desired to appear mature and dignified it was now. She had not long to wait. Very soon she heard the sound of wheels and went to the door to meet the carriage. It was a coupé.

"I can sit with the driver," said Mark, answering the expression on her face as he helped her in.

"By no means," she responded, quickly. "Have I been rude? I beg your pardon," and she drew aside the skirt of her gown to make room for him.

"Not rude," he replied, taking the seat beside her; "but of course I know you would rather be rid of me if circumstances permitted."

"Yet I am asking a favor of you."

"As you might ask a dentist to pull a tooth. There was no one else to do it."

"Is it strange," she asked, defiantly, "that I am—that I feel—"

"Why can you not forget that piece of boyish nonsense?" he exclaimed, impatiently.

"You were not a boy and it was not nonsense. Besides, I choose not to forget. I choose to remember that I am weak, easily influenced, liable to be played upon by any one who wishes to amuse himself with that sort of experiment!" The passion in her voice betrayed what she had suffered.

Mark Heffron gazed at her with amazement. Emotions of pity and self-reproach were depicted on his face. She did not see his face, but she detected the change in his voice as he ejaculated under his breath, "Cursed fool! cursed brute! clumsy fool!" and she knew he was belaboring himself.

"What shall I say? How can I explain?" he continued to her.

"There is nothing to say, nothing to explain," she answered, proudly. "You revealed me to myself. It has taught me to keep myself in a— straight-jacket ever since."

"A straight-jacket!" exclaimed Mark so loud- ly that the driver opened his window with an obsequious, "Beg pardon, sir?"

"Nothing. Go ahead!" shouted Mark.

"Hey?" asked the driver, who was somewhat deaf.

"*Nothing!*" roared Mark, and slammed the window in his face. Eloise smiled a wintry little smile, and Mark took courage. "Do try to see," he began, eagerly. "It is not weakness, but the artistic temperament which makes you sensitive, susceptible. I was a brute to take ad- vantage of it. But I wanted to see you. I had something for you. I did not really expect to succeed. I never thought of your taking it so seriously."

She bit her lip in self-restraint.

"Will you forgive me?" he pleaded, humbly, tenderly. Alas, he was too humble, too tender. She stiffened where she sat. "Of course," she answered, frigidly, and he was quite sure she never would.

They spoke no more until they reached the hotel, and then she asked, courteously, "You will dine with us?" but he answered, "No." Her face fell; he had not yet acceded to her request. "I will return," he added.

"You are very kind," she said, warming a frac- tion of a degree.

"Not at all," he answered, cooling to the same extent, "and I may fail."

"Oh no!" Her lip curled.

"She hates me as if I were the devil," said Mark to himself, as he rode away. "I wish I had never touched the confounded thing."

People were going in to dinner when Eloise entered the hotel. Through the open doorway of the dining-room she caught a glimpse of William Pleasant on the lookout for her. He ran forward, calling, "Oh, Mis' Gordon! beg pardon for hollerin' at ye, but Mr. Dering says you're to eat dinner befo' you go up-stairs."

"I don't want a mouthful, Pleasant," she answered, putting from her with a gesture the very offer of food.

"Oh, please, Mis' Gordon!" Pleasant begged as if interceding for a life. "I've got it all fixed up nice, for ye. Jus' come an' look at it, Mis' Gordon."

Unwilling to disappoint him, she went into the dining-room and took her seat. With joyful alacrity Pleasant removed the covers from the dishes and presented them for her approval one by one.

"Very nice, very nice indeed, Pleasant," she repeated, absent-mindedly, and made a show of tasting this and that.

"But she ain't eatin'—only jus' play!" groaned Pleasant. He racked his brain for entertaining gossip to spur her laggard appetite. "Guess you ain't noticed the boys got on dress-suits, Mis' Gordon," he began, anxiously.

"Why, yes; so they have!" she answered, arousing from her reverie. "How did that happen, Pleasant?"

"The boys over at the Wilmin'ton had 'em on since May," explained Pleasant. "Our boss had to come to it. Can't let the Wilmin'ton boys get ahead of us." He chuckled as he spoke, and tripped lightly to and fro, changing the dishes.

"Consid'able many of our boys gettin' married," he pursued, encouraged by his success. "They think they might as well, when they got their suits."

Eloise smiled in spite of herself. "I suppose you'll be going after the lady you used to think about when you played 'Pleasant Dreams,'" she suggested.

Pleasant shrugged his shoulders. "She went off with another feller," he answered. "That's all right; there's another lady. But I ain't goin' to get married. Won't you have some ice-cream, Mis' Gordon? It's very nice this evenin'."

"Oh, I can't, Pleasant; I've done my best;" and she threw down her napkin.

"Jus' picked a little, like a chicken!" muttered Pleasant, discontentedly. He shook his head as he released her.

"She's goin' to be sick again, sho's the world," he grumbled, as he gathered up his neglected dishes and shuffled with them down the long dining-room ; nor could he have understood had he known the value of his ministrations.

"A servant is much better than a lover," said Eloise to herself, and smiled all the way to the elevator.

Carl met her in the studio, leaving Aunt Harriet's room as she entered. "Come into the hall," she whispered, and they tiptoed out together.

"It's of no use, she hears everything," he said, when they were outside.

"We'll go farther away, then," said Eloise, with determination. "She must not know. Mr. Heffron is going to put her to sleep."

Carl danced a quickstep, noiselessly. "Good for *you!*" he whispered. "Where did you run across him ?"

"At Mrs. Harwood's. Go down now to your dinner, and leave word at the desk, when Mr. Heffron arrives, to let you know. You can bring him up as a friend of yours ; then she won't suspect me. He can sit in the studio where she won't see him, but he can see her."

"Eloise, you're a brick !" exclaimed her cousin, solemnly.

"Hurry !" she urged. "Don't stop to talk. He may be back any minute ;" and she glided from him into the studio.

Aunt Harriet was lying precisely as she had lain for days, staring with wild, wide-open eyes at the ceiling. Her gray hair was tossed like spray about her face. Her thin, pointed little nose looked thinner and sharper than ever, and her small mouth was puckered like that of a child who resolves not to cry.

Eloise longed to take the pathetic little figure up in her strong young arms, but the formal relations which had existed between them since Aunt Harriet became a "healer" and she herself a girl with a broken engagement rendered such a move out of the question. There must be many a subtle change in both before they could meet on the old terms.

"Can I do anything for you?" she asked, gently, and Aunt Harriet shook her head.

With a sigh, Eloise seated herself by the window and folded her hands in her lap. As she did so they came in contact with a letter which she had put into her pocket that morning, unopened because it was from Philip, and just then she could not bear any added burden of sorrow or regret.

She broke the seal and read it now by the fading sunset glow; not that her heart was lighter than before or less anxious, but something was about to happen, and something had happened; between the two experiences, it would be easier to forget.

Philip wrote in a direct, manly way of his plans and purposes; he was going to Idaho on a prospecting tour with some friends, and should not return until he could be satisfied with her friendship, and could offer her his own without a pang.

She must not blame herself, he wrote : he was the only one to blame for presuming upon her generosity. She had tried her best to care for him and he appreciated the effort, even if it had been useless.

There was no address. Evidently he expected no reply. She longed to send him some word—dear, noble Philip, he deserved a better fate than to devote his life to her! With all her heart she longed for his happiness and success, at the same time emphasizing her resentment against Mark Heffron as if it were a virtue. She could have been as hard on him, just then, as she tried to be on herself.

Slowly the rose of sunset faded, and the city streets blossomed with lights as thickly as a May meadow with bluets. Eloise watched them thoughtfully. "God's light is withdrawn; we must make what substitute we can," she said, and arose with a sigh, for she heard Carl at the studio door, and knew that Mark was with him.

"I'll go and prepare her," whispered Carl; and, waiting in the hall, they heard the low, inarticulate murmur of his voice and the querulous response of the invalid.

"Is he a regular healer?" asked Aunt Harriet. "I don't want any animal magnetism;" and again, "Eloise cannot be in the room. I shall feel her opposition."

The soothing murmur went on, and the feeble complaint grew feebler, until at last they heard her say, " Well, I'll try him, to please you, but I know he can't help me."

Then Carl came out into the hall. "She doesn't take much stock in it, but she's willing to try," he whispered. " You'll have to sit away from the bed, Eloise; she doesn't want you too near. Mr. Heffron is to sit in the studio as we proposed. You can let him know when she goes to sleep. I've got to get back to town. Humphrey will be crazy; I promised to meet him at half-past seven. Good-bye. Good-luck!" and he was off.

As quietly as possible they took their places, Eloise by the window, where a ray from the hall came over the transom and gilded her hair; Mark in the shadow of a huge easel, where, with his bowed head and bent shoulders, he could not be distinguished from the couches and chairs about him. The mystery of silence settled down upon the place. They heard the rumble in the street below, they heard the clock tick on its shelf in the studio, they heard the beating of their own hearts; but the unknown utterance of the city, the homely voice of the clock and their own throbbing pulses were alike remote and unrelated to them.

Aunt Harriet gave a happy little sigh ; she recognized the silence, and the power which governed it. Eloise would have sighed, too, if she had not strangled the fluttering breath as it escaped. Mark was too much occupied in what he was doing to notice either of the women, fascinated, now that he was fairly at it, by the production of that strange anæsthetic which is generated by the contact of two human wills, the will to yield, sometimes known as faith, and the will to command and control. He could feel the force go out from him, and he exulted in his mastery. He could feel the fragile creature upon the bed relax and soften and become like clay in his hands; and a great tenderness filled him—the tenderness of responsibility for the life intrusted to him.

Another force he felt, drawing and mastering him.

He stood up suddenly and confronted Eloise, who bowed her head and laid her finger on her lips. He glanced at the bed; the patient was sleeping like a child. He did not want to go, he wanted to linger and look at the girl before him, transformed as she was, at that moment, by the exaltation of her mood.

"I have heard that it affects some of them in that way," he mused, as he went down the hall, that radiant white face following him. He decided that he himself felt "queer"; there seemed to be a cloud around him, and his own steps jarred him as he walked. He went to the hall window and looked down upon the boulevard lights, strung like beads, in two even rows, as far as eye could reach. There was a balcony outside; he stepped out upon it, and sank into a chair which he found there.

By and by the cloud which had hung about him

and hindered his movements unfolded and floated away. His head became clear again, with a peculiar clearness. He felt ready for any intellectual effort, and free from the limitations of the body. Then the body came back also to its full consciousness, and he was himself again ; so much himself that he laughed as he went down in the elevator at a certain humorous phase of the situation which struck him now for the first time. He had been doing Dr. Symonds's work as nearly as possible in Dr. Symonds's way, only not as well, in all probability, as the absent healer would himself have done it.

XXXI

It was late when Mark reached his hotel. There was not a horse to be had in the vicinity of the Lake View, and he had to walk some distance before taking the cable. The cars were full, and stopped all along the line with a continuous bump and jar extremely trying to nerves made sensitive by such an experience as his had recently undergone. He was tired and out of sorts when he reached his room. A bright light shone through the keyhole. "I must have left the electrics turned on," he said to himself; "but what ails this infernal lock?"

"Hold on; I'm coming!" called a cheerful voice within. The bolt slid back, and Joe Norton appeared, his blond locks standing on end and his eyes hazy with sleep.

"Where in thunder did you drop from?" growled Mark, not altogether pleased with the nature of the surprise.

"From New York, of course," replied Joey, unabashed. "I'm never anywhere else, except here. I didn't have time to write, and I wanted to see you about the exchange."

"What exchange?" asked Mark, stretching himself on the couch where Joey had been.

"Exchange of positions; you know, of course you do—you said you'd change with me and be glad to, until Uncle Eli is better."

"You're asleep, Joey," rejoined his host. "Pass the matches. And ring for some ice-water while you're about it. You may as well make yourself useful as long as you are here."

Joey did as he was bid, describing at length and with minuteness the time, place, and circumstances of the agreement between himself and his friend, concluding triumphantly, "Now, do you remember?"

"H-m, ye-es, something of the sort," returned Mark with indifference.

"And the Firm want you to go right on," pursued Norton.

"Hang the Firm!"

"They said you could tell me whatever I ought to know to-night, and go on early to-morrow."

"Sha'n't do anything of the sort. The idea of expecting a man to start up without warning and post off for an indefinite stay. Sha'n't do anything of the sort. I have several things to attend to," and Mark thumped his pillows and settled himself among them, prepared to defend himself against any arguments which might be brought forward.

"Can't I attend to them for you?" asked Joey, meekly.

"No, you can't."

"Try me and see." Joey smoothed his hair with his fingers and tried to look reliable.

"What do you know of my personal affairs?" asked Mark, irritably.

"Mighty little, that's a fact," agreed Joey. "But I could explain your being called away, and that you will return soon."

"I could write that."

"You can write it too, but you know there's nothing like a personal interview."

Mark deliberated. To tell the truth, his business affairs were where they could be left with a few instructions, and as to personal matters, he could break his appointment with Uncle Oliver Ross by letter, and charge Joey with a verbal message to others whom he had promised to meet, but—what would Eloise Gordon think of him if he deserted her now? He had promised her, while they waited in the hall for Carl, to return the next day and see how Miss Larrabee was getting on.

"You see the Firm are so sure of you," urged Joey, cunningly, "they're forever holding you up to me as a model of promptness. And you needn't stay there, only till I get Uncle Eli started on the right road."

"I'll see," said Mark, "but go to bed, now, for Heaven's sake! I'm dead tired."

"I know you are, poor old chap, you show it!" exclaimed Joey, compassionately. "Things will look differently in the morning."

They did.   After a hearty sleep, the experience at the Lake View grew unreal; the responsibility he had laid upon himself seemed unnecessary, after all.   He let Joey pack his trunk while he wrote half a dozen letters, leaving them to be mailed or delivered as he directed.   The letter to Eloise he wrote last, and held it in his hand meditatively.

"How do you want that one to go?" asked Joey, coming to the table.

"I haven't decided," replied Mark, slowly. "I've tried to be very explicit, and it's as clear as mud."

"Let me explain!" cried Joey, dramatically. "I can dwell on your anguish as you never could. 'Miss Eloise Gordon, Lake View Hotel.'   I know her, she's Dering's cousin ; nice girl, too, but cold as an icicle.   I'll explain.   What was it?"

"I had been doing some — business for her," prevaricated Mark, "and I promised to see her to-day.   Perhaps it would be a good plan for you to go out there.   You can tell her just how it is, and that I may be back in a week.   By the way, her aunt is sick ; you might find out how she is and let me know.   The two are alone in the world and it is rather forlorn for the girl."

Joey promised, and Mark tried to think he had arranged everything satisfactorily, but his heart misgave him as he boarded the noon express.   The power which had drawn and held him the night before drew and held him now.   If he could have found any reasonable excuse for returning he would have done so.   What was it? he asked.

Had she happened upon the trick, herself, and did she mean to pay off the old score?

No, no, her rapt look, the open brow, the fearless eyes, gave the lie to that suggestion.   But what did it all mean?

Eloise herself could not tell.   As she sat and watched Aunt Harriet's rigid limbs relax, saw her clenched hands unfold, heard her regular breathing, and through the open door traced the outline of the man who was sitting there, she felt, as on that summer night at Beau Lieu, great coiling chains of influence encircling her, impelling her towards him.   She grasped the chair in which she sat and turned her face towards the window with an appeal for help.   The sky was full of stars.   One hung, a laughing cherub, under the eaves.   "God's light is not withdrawn," it said.

She drew in her breath with a quick sense of freedom, and then Mark Heffron stood up and looked at her, questioningly.   She gave him the signal and he went away.   The whole had not occupied half a dozen seconds, yet it seemed to her that a lifetime was compressed into them. They spread over hours of reflection afterwards and then remained undefined.   It was a wonderful experience ; would it ever come again?

Aunt Harriet hardly stirred all night, taking great draughts of sleep as one quenches a long thirst.

In the morning she called for her breakfast and ate it with a relish. By noon she was asking for her healer.

"He said he would be in some time to-day, but I don't think he expected to see you," said Eloise.

"Why not?" inquired Aunt Harriet, sharply.

"He—he doesn't do this work very often," replied her niece, with some hesitation. "We were not even to tell his name."

"Of course not, to people in the house," said Aunt Harriet, promptly. "But if he knows I am following the same line of thought—you couldn't have made it clear to him where I stand, Eloise."

"Perhaps not," replied her niece, demurely.

The afternoon wore slowly on. Aunt Harriet insisted upon being prepared to receive visitors, displaying an unusual fastidiousness in the arrangement of her hair and the disposition of the bedclothes. About four o'clock a card was brought to Eloise. She read it with a puzzled frown.

"What is it?" demanded the invalid, sitting bolt upright.

"'Joseph Norton,'" repeated Eloise. "I don't know any Joseph Norton. It must be a mistake."

"Yes, you do," exclaimed her aunt. "He's Mr. Eli Norton's nephew. We met them one day at the Art Gallery, when we went with Carl. Mr. Norton has sent him out to inquire for me. Pull that chair around, that one by the window. I shall want him to sit where I can see him."

"But, auntie, do you feel able?" faltered

Eloise, who was not sure that Mr. Eli Norton's nephew had come to inquire after Miss Larrabee's health.

"It will do me good," said the invalid, positively. "You can bring him right up."

Joey was in the reception-room, composing a graceful little speech, calculated to explain and conciliate and pave the way for himself to walk into the good graces of Miss Gordon, who, as far as he could determine, was the only nice girl left in town. But Eloise came so soon, driven before Aunt Harriet's desire, and so quietly that she caught him unprepared. He did not know she was there until she said, "Mr. Norton?" and held out her hand.

He took it eagerly. She was prettier than he thought, and knew how to dress—by Jove, she was like a picture in that white gown. In his admiration and his pleasure that she remembered him (thanks to Aunt Harriet) he almost forgot why he was there. When he recalled his errand he went at it manfully, and explained so much that any one less suspicious than Eloise would have wondered what he had to conceal.

She listened to him civilly and believed not a word he said. According to her experience of Mark Heffron, that individual invariably did as he pleased. If he had chosen to remain, he would have done so; why make so many words?

She told Joey it was really of no consequence; indeed, she had not expected Mr. Heffron, knowing that he had so many interests, so many schemes; and then, because she was offended with one man, she made herself particularly delightful to another, as girls are wont to do. Joey was only too willing to be charmed.

He begged to come again to-morrow. Chicago was dull and he was lonely. Situated similarly, he with his uncle, she with her aunt, they ought to find many points of sympathy.

They could have found one, at least, when they returned to their respective charges, for both the patients were thoroughly incensed at being left so long alone. Uncle Eli suffered a collapse which rendered him limp and well-nigh speechless. When he finally found his voice, it was the ghost of a whisper.

Aunt Harriet, on the contrary, was like a steel spring released from compression. She bounced up in bed when her niece entered and told her tartly there was room in the Old Ladies' Home for people who had no friends to care for them.

"Mr. Norton came to say that the—the gentleman who was here last night has been obliged to go to New York," explained Eloise. "I am sorry you felt neglected. He says his uncle is very weak. What will you have for supper?"

"You needn't try to put me off in that way, Eloise," returned Aunt Harriet, severely. "There has been something *ve-ry strange* about this whole performance. Carl comes in to tell me about a friend of his and goes off, and the man comes and doesn't show his face. Now, Mr. Norton's nephew appears and seems to know all about it, but I, *I* am kept completely in the dark!"

She had shaken her gray hair down about her shoulders in the vehemence of her complaint, her eyes glittered and her cheeks glowed. Eloise began to be alarmed. "There, there, auntie," she murmured soothingly, "it's all right. You must not get so excited. Lie down, now, do, that's a dear, and I will go to the steward and get something good for your supper.'

Aunt Harriet suffered herself to be rearranged in bed, but she was by no means reconciled. In her heart she resented fiercely the loss of what had been the source of her consolation and strength. She demanded reparation of all who came near, the more strenuously because they did not realize the loss or accept its responsibility.

"I am really troubled about her," said Eloise to Mrs. Harwood, who came in the next morning "to inquire."

"How did she rest last night?"

"Very well."

"And ate her breakfast?"

"All of it; but she is so unlike herself, so unreasonable. I am afraid her brain is affected."

"Not a bit," declared Mrs. Harwood stoutly. "She's been pious so long that she's got torpid. This is kinder like measles or scarlatina; it 'll clear out her system. Dan'l came home from the Farm last night with a sore throat, and I had a great time sweating him."

"I hope he isn't going to be sick," said Eloise with sympathy, more for Dan'l's wife, it must be confessed, than for Dan'l.

"I hope not," said Mrs. Harwood. "Now don't you worry about Miss Larrabee. She won't die, she's got too much vim."

Vim enough she had, certainly, to wear out her delicate little frame and ingenuity, unlimited, in devising means to try to the utmost the temper of her niece. She had every one of her old maladies in succession, winding up with an attack of earache which necessitated wearing wads of cotton in her ears and close-fitting muslin nightcaps, tied under her chin. This made her quite deaf, but instead of asking "What say?" as she used to do, with pretty, old-fashioned elegance, she yelled "*Wh-at?*" like any common, ill-bred old person.

"After all," said Joey, to whom Eloise confessed her inability to understand Aunt Harriet's latest development—"after all, that sort of thing is easier to handle than complete non-resistance. If Uncle Eli would only fight, I should have some hope of him. I'm tempted to put him aboard one of the lake steamers and take him East. He'd be abominably sick—he always is—but he'd have to fight, then."

"I don't know what to do with Aunt Harriet," replied Eloise, dejectedly.

"Come along with us."

"I don't believe she would consent."

"Take things into your own hands."

Eloise shook her head. She had not placed Aunt Harriet again under absolutism, although the latter had certainly forfeited her right to autonomy. Their little kingdom was tossed and rent, but it was no longer divided against itself, as it had been when Aunt Harriet was more polite and Eloise was more patient.

"You'd better think it over," persisted Joey. "We can take the boat to Montreal, and then go down to the coast. I know a place on the South Shore. You could get some fine water-colors there."

The suggestion was a tempting one. Eloise felt that she could not hold out for many days at this rate. With the exception of an occasional walk with Joey, there was nothing to break the strain upon her nerves.

Carl had gone to Mackinac with the Rosses and the Ayers, and Mrs. Harwood was housebound with Dan'l, whose sore throat had developed into what he designated as a Touch of the Old Difficulty. Mrs. Glenn and the children were at Geneva, where Mr. Glenn spent his Sundays.

The substantial guests of the hotel were all out of town. Those who remained were noisily gay or aggressively melancholy over their financial straits and the prolongation of the strike. The very atmosphere of the place was distressing.

"I wish I could feel that it is best to go," said Eloise, after a mental review of the scenes which she had left and to which she must return.

"Of course it is best," he insisted. "Hullo! what are they doing here?" They had turned in at Jackson Park, where the site of the White City was being rapidly transformed into a park. A rude track had been laid, and upon it trundled wooden cars drawn by horses.

"What are you doing?" inquired Norton of a workman who was assisting the horses to dump their loads of dirt.

"Makin' a hill," answered the man, patting the mound affectionately with his spade. "Same as they have over to Washington Park."

"Making a hill!" replied Joey, as they walked on. "I say, Miss Gordon, let's go where they grow!" and yielding to a sudden irresistible longing to get out and away from artificialities of all sorts, "hills" included, Eloise answered,

"I will do it."

XXXII

Ir was not difficult to convince Aunt Harriet of
the advisability of a change, although she pre-
ferred to term it a change of thought rather than
a change of air and scene. She had felt the opposition of the people in the house for some time,
she said, and now they were "holding her down."
The attitude of the strikers affected her like-
wise, and so did the presence of the soldiers on
the lake front. She seemed to be completely at
the mercy of adverse elements, without a roof of
physical limitation over her head, and stripped
of the cuticle which protects more undeveloped
souls. Eloise, who had computed, before Joey
left her at the door of the hotel, the cost of the
journey and the probability of a return in pictures, was encouraged to proceed with her preparations, and telephoned Joey to that effect. He
was not less prompt. Within a week he had received his leave of absence—accompanied by a
caustic letter from Mark, inquiring if there was
anything else he wanted—and they were off.

The weather was perfect, every one remained
on deck and in the best of spirits ; Uncle Eli came
out of his lethargy without the spur of seasick-

ness, and Aunt Harriet began to be her old amiable self. At Montreal they found letters from Point Carey, where Joey had written for rooms, and went thither without delay. From beginning to end the excursion moved as smoothly as if there had been a Cooke or a Raymond to plan and control.

"And yet you don't seem satisfied," pouted Joey, on the evening after their arrival, as he walked with Eloise. "Now really, did you ever see anything finer than that?"

He had led her by a circuitous path to a bluff overlooking the sea, which shone like silver. On its margin writhed and curled the tangled seaweed, and great rocks, scaly with mussel-shells, lay half in half out of the water.

Eloise shuddered. "It is uncanny," she replied, and, turning, pulled a wild-flower by the roots. "I would rather have this one flower than miles of that," she said with feeling.

Joey started in surprise. Her tone took the heart out of his enjoyment. "I thought you'd like it," he said with disappointment. "You have seemed so happy all the way."

"I have been," she answered quickly, "and I don't know why I feel as I do now, only — I expected to get somewhere, and it's only another shore, another question, another mystery. I feel left in the lurch."

Joey drew nearer to her, but she seemed unaware of his proximity. She pushed her white yachting-cap back from her brows and gazed moodily over the waste of waters.

"I almost wish," she said, "that I could believe as Aunt Harriet and your uncle do. They may be tormented by other people, but they are never in doubt about themselves."

"Ye-es," drawled Joey — the drawl was to cover a retreat — "the world is made up of two kinds of people, those who deceive themselves and are comfortable, and those who tell themselves the truth and are uncomfortable. We want to tell ourselves the truth, still we'd like to be comfortable!"

"But how do you know they deceive themselves or that we tell the truth? How do you know anything? It is all unfathomable, mysterious, dreadful, like the sea?"

She drew the soft petals of the flower across her lips, caressingly. Joey watched her. "As to that," he said, jealously, "you don't get away from those things on shore."

"No. I suppose they'd say this flower was the Expression of an Idea," she answered. "I wish I could find something without any thought in it."

"Try Miss O'Keefe," he suggested. "She doesn't even know she's a flirt. Her coquetries are of the sticky-fly-paper order; they gum everything, unconsciously."

Eloise laughed as she was expected to do, but her face grew grave again.

The silver was vanishing from the sea. Its faint sighing had become a moan.

"Let us go," she said, turning her back upon the sound.

As they neared the Glenallan a boy came running towards them, an ungainly young setter at his heels. "I've been lookin' everywhere for you," he gasped.

"What is it? Is any one—" began Eloise.

"Both of 'em," interrupted the boy. "Doddridge's mustang fell over the cliff, cart and all, right on top of 'em." Eloise waited to hear no more.

The Glenallan was ablaze with lights, and guests were dancing on the piazza. She broke through a cotillion and darted into the house, Joey close behind her. The proprietor's wife met them in the hall.

"Getting along all right," she announced cheerily. "Mr. Norton come out splendid. The doctor's with Miss Larrabee now."

Eloise flew past her, up the stairs and into the room which she shared with Aunt Harriet. A man was bending over one of the little white beds, saying something in a low voice to the occupant and rubbing her hands. She opened her eyes and smiled at him, Aunt Harriet, who abhorred all manner of physicians and held a stranger as an enemy until he proved himself otherwise, smiled at him as one smiles into the face of a saviour.

"Hand me that cup, please—the one with the spoon in it," said the doctor, without turning his head. Eloise obeyed and stood beside him like a child, awaiting further orders. One deft hand and arm slid under the pillow and lifted the sick woman's head, the other held the cup to her lips. She did not refuse it, but drank as if he had pledged her a health.

"Is she going to die?" thought Eloise with a pang, "and so feels that it doesn't matter? Is it pity which makes his voice so sweet?" She watched the long brown hands let down their burden and arrange the pillows; they even wiped Aunt Harriet's lips and smoothed her hair, went under the bedclothes and felt of her feet, then made all trim and straight, not fussily, but with a swift, resolute touch, the touch of healing.

He turned, at length, and she saw his face, an ordinary, unromantic face with broad bulging brows, large nose, and untrained mustache.

"Give her a teaspoonful of that medicine in the cup every half-hour if she doesn't sleep," he said, and abruptly left the room.

Eloise followed him. "Doctor, is my aunt going to die?" she faltered.

"Why, no," he answered smiling, "she will be all right in a day or two."

"Doctor," cried Joey, emerging from the opposite room, "tell me, what do you think of my uncle?"

"Doing well," answered the doctor; "there's

nothing the matter with either of them except nerves. They were pretty thoroughly scared."

"But I thought—"

"Didn't the horse—" began Eloise and Joey, simultaneously.

"The boy said the cart and the horse fell on them," finished Eloise.

"The young villain," exclaimed the doctor, "I'll wring his neck! I told him not to alarm you. Good-night; if you want me, I'm at the Pavilion opposite—Dr. Dow," and before they could put another question he was gone.

"We-ll!" breathed Joey in a long sigh.

"I feel as if I had very nearly had 'something to cry for,' as the nurses say when the children cry for nothing," said Eloise.

"Is there anything I can do?" he asked.

"No, thank you. Oh, what an escape!" She held out her hand and he pressed it sympathetically. Each was conscious of being glad that the other was there.

She did not see him at breakfast, for she awoke early and "hungry as a bear," she told the waitress, whom she inveigled into serving her while there was yet no one in the dining-room. Together they prepared a tray for Aunt Harriet, and Eloise carried it up-stairs.

"Did the doctor say that I might have fish?" murmured the patient, lifting her heavy lids to scrutinize the tray.

"I didn't ask him," confessed her niece.

Aunt Harriet resolutely closed her eyes. "I shall not touch a mouthful without his permission," she said.

"Why, auntie?"

"Eloise!" and the eyes came wide open with a snap, "that man saved my life, and I shall not do one thing contrary to his wishes."

"I know he was extremely kind, but I don't see how that necessitates your fasting until he tells you to eat," replied Eloise, impatient, for the breakfast was cooling. She set it down with a thump.

"Kind!" repeated Aunt Harriet. "He pulled me out from under those dreadful hoofs"—she trembled and grew white. Eloise bent over her.

"There, auntie, don't try to talk," she said, soothingly. "Don't cry!" for two tears had oozed out from under the closed eyelids. "You may do just as you please."

"Eloise," said Aunt Harriet, with dignity, "you disturb me. I should like to be alone. I want to give myself a treatment." With a smothered ejaculation, Eloise rushed out into the hall, nearly tumbling into the arms of Joey, who had evidently been meditating a siege.

"I didn't know whether to knock or no," he said. "You've settled the question. Have you had breakfast? Don't you want to go for a walk?"

"Want to go? I'm smothering!" cried the girl. "But I don't know as I ought to leave Aunt Harriet—although she has just sent me away."

Joey shrugged his shoulders. "I'll rig her a

tocsin, as I did for Uncle Eli, a tin pan and a cane; it would wake the dead. The chambermaid has promised to keep an eye on my room; that leaves one for yours. Come on!"

Eloise paused irresolute. "Perhaps we had better wait and ask the doctor," she replied, at length.

"By the way," cried Joey, "I went over to the Pavilion and hunted up his record last night. He's a Keeleyite or the next thing to it; that is why he is so at home with nerves."

"What is a Keeleyite?" she inquired, looking puzzled.

"You know, the Gold Cure and all that sort of thing—reforms drunkards, opium-eaters, cigarette fiends. He has a lot of them at the Pavilion, in the wing of the house. It isn't generally known. I wish he would come. Shall I go after him?" Joey beat a tattoo on the rail of the balustrade against which they were leaning. Eloise herself chafed at the delay. When one is young and full of life and the wind blows over the sea, it is hard to be tied to a dull boarding-house at the beck of age and illness; and there was nothing the matter except nerves—the doctor said so.

Through the hall window they saw him coming at last, driving a lot of children before him as a collie drives a flock of sheep. He had routed them out of their clam-digging and sent them home for dry shoes and stockings. They brandished their hooks and shouted their stories at him as they went.

Others, men and women, stopped him all along the way. "He will never get here!" muttered Joey. "I'm going down to hurry him along."

They came up together, chatting amiably, but Joey looked glum. "The doctor thinks," he explained to Eloise, after the usual questions concerning the patient had been asked and answered, "that one of us had better stay here, within reach of the two rooms; so, as soon as he has seen Miss Larrabee, you'd better go. I'll have my turn later."

The doctor was already in Miss Larrabee's room, taking her pulse and her temperature as solicitously as if his life as well as hers depended upon the result. She gave him a long detailed account of the evening and the morning, including the story of the fish, and he listened as the Sultan listened to Scheherezade. "I will stop in the kitchen and order some broth," he said, in conclusion. "They know me down there and let me take all sorts of liberties." He twisted up some powders and threw them on the table, saying to Eloise, "One every hour. I'll give her one now; it's nine o'clock. You can go, but be back by ten; and tell Mr. Norton to be within call. I'll see his uncle directly."

Eloise put on her hat and left the room, feeling like a child sent out to play. She gave Joey his message and was soon pacing up and down the hard white floor of the beach.

The gloom and mystery of the previous night

had vanished; in their stead reigned gayety and good-will. The yachts were racing in the open space outside the bay, and near the shore row-boats were rocking merrily. Fishermen casting their lines, bathers splashing and sprawling, youths and maidens pitching their umbrellas on the sand made pictures everywhere against the azure and chrysoprase of mated sky and sea.

"I must unpack my brushes!" said Eloise. "I will paint that gateway of cliff for one—it leads to the end of the world; and this overturned hulk for another, with a boy diving off into the sea, where the boat can go no more; I will paint—What a face!"

Crouching among cushions, in a niche among the rocks, reclined a woman, her chin on her clenched hand and her elbow on her knee. Her profile cut the dark background of the rock with cameo-like distinctness, a picture of despair become indifference. She turned as Eloise came up, and stared at her out of great cavernous eyes, testifying like extinct volcanoes to fires which had been. The girl shuddered with vague horror of what she saw — not mere lines and furrows, scourge-marks of pain and strife; faces have borne these and carried with them the look of having met an angel in the way. This woman had met a demon.

"Good-morning," she called to Eloise. "How are your father and mother after their accident?"

"Is she crazy?" thought Eloise.

"They were lucky to get off with their lives," continued the woman. "I saw it all from my window. Another minute and the horse would have been right on top of them."

"They are not my father and mother," said Eloise, now comprehending her meaning, "but my aunt and Mr. Norton's uncle."

"They told me it was your father and mother," returned the woman, "and I haven't had a chance to speak to the doctor about it. You ought to have seen him pull them out of the way. I wanted to throw up my hat and give three cheers, but it was too far for him to hear me."

"Then he did do it !" exclaimed Eloise. "My aunt said he saved her life, but I thought she did not know just what had happened. He said nothing."

"Of course not," said the woman, proudly. "He never does say anything. He makes as light of saving a life as another man would of eating his dinner. You've got to know him—but you never will unless he has to do something for you. We were brought up side by side, but I never knew him until lately."

"I have heard that he belongs to a—a—life-saving station," said Eloise, delicately.

"That's the way to put it !" cried the woman, her eyes flashing like wet steel. "Most people speak of what he is doing as if it was something to be ashamed of. I don't care who knows that I am one of them."

Through the ruin of her faded face flushed the glow of former beauty. All the artist in Eloise awoke, and something more than the artist awoke also. "I wish you would tell me about him," she said. "May I sit down beside you?"

"Do!" exclaimed the stranger, making room among the cushions. "I'm only too glad to find some one who likes to hear about him. There's no one like him on this earth. Others do good occasionally, but he is the only one I ever saw who does it all the time for the love of it. He has a perfect passion for saving people."

"Has he always done this — this work?" inquired Eloise.

"Well, now, that's a long story," replied the stranger. "I don't know's I ought to tell you, but you seem so interested. It isn't any secret out our way, and people don't think any the less of him, but it's different here."

"I don't belong here, said Eloise, quickly.

"It was this way," began the story-teller, who was not hard to persuade. "He started in to practise in his own town, where every one knew him. Every one liked him, too. It was Dr. Jerry Dow here, there, and everywhere. His name's Gerard —Dutch, I believe. After a while he went East and got married and brought his wife home." She paused and pursed up her lips. "The less said about Mrs. Dow the better. He was awfully good to her—you might know he would be—but nothing suited. Finally, after her child was born, she went off East and that was the last of her. He wrote and wrote, and then he went after her ; but he came back alone. Then he took to drink. Folks said Dr. Jerry Dow was going downhill fast. Even then he never neglected his patients. When he hadn't any head for other things, he'd know what he was about with them. They thought so much of him they'd wait for him to get over a spree rather than go to any one else. I've seen horses and carriages tied at his door and away down the street—you'd think it was a country meeting-house or a funeral—waiting for him to sober off. All at once he turned square around and reformed. No one knew how. He experimented on himself, I suppose. Then he experimented on those who came to see how he did it."

"How does he do it ?" interrupted Eloise.

"I don't know. He doesn't give much medicine, but you feel the minute he takes hold of you that you're all right. Other doctors stand off and tell you what to do. He wades right in after you, up to his neck, and pulls you out in spite of yourself —I can't tell you !"

"You have told me a great deal," said Eloise, rising. "I cannot thank you enough. I shall hold it sacred."

"And you don't think any the less of him?" inquired the woman, anxiously.

"No, I don't think any the less of him," repeat-ed Eloise. She stood looking out over the restless waves, with a strange hushed feeling new to her.

"May I come and talk with you again?" she asked, gently, offering her hand in farewell.

"I wish you would!" exclaimed the woman, eagerly. "I'm alone a good deal, and I don't enjoy thinking as much as some folks do. I have too much to think about." She laughed, an hysterical laugh without any mirth in it.

XXXIII

As Dr. Dow had prophesied, Aunt Harriet and Uncle Eli recovered rapidly.   After a day or two of seclusion they reappeared on the beach, sitting in their steamer-chairs, with their umbrellas spread.

They were objects of interest to their fellow-boarders, who wove endless romances about the grave elderly man and the vivacious elderly woman who seemed never to tire of each other's society.

"Look at him now, as he leans forward to speak to her; he thinks she's too sweet for anything," said Mrs. O'Keefe.

"And look at her, how she listens to him; she thinks he knows it all," said Mrs. Tyler.

"I wish we were near enough to hear what they say," exclaimed Mrs. O'Keefe.

She would have been sadly disappointed. Uncle Eli had declared, "This is the first time in weeks that I've been able to get rid of a belief in headache;" and Aunt Harriet's glance was one of congratulation, nothing more.

"Have you said anything to Dr. Dow about The Science?" she inquired.

"Not very much," replied the old man, guardedly.

"I have," said the impulsive little woman beside him. "I told him it was all he needed."

"What did he say?"

"He said he didn't doubt it had done me good."
Again they exchanged sympathetic glances.

"Just look at them," said Mrs. O'Keefe to her
companion. "They're ready to eat one another up."

"Joey says the doctor has some kind of a hospital or sanitarium for nervous troubles," remarked Uncle Eli.

"So Eloise told me."

"Just think how The Science would help him
in that!" and she clasped her hands with a devout
look up into the sky.

"She's got it bad," said Mrs. O'Keefe.

"I was afraid Eloise would take a prejudice
against him," sighed Aunt Harriet. "His English is rather queer, and Eloise is so fastidious.
The first summer we were both at a Summer
School she was *frantic* over the speech and the
manner of the people we met. But she has really
gone out of her way to be kind to him. There
she is now, talking to him, down there by the
water."

"I wonder where Joey is," mused Uncle Eli.
So did Mrs. O'Keefe. "This isn't the first time
the girl has given Norton the slip and gone off
with the doctor," she declared. And for once Mrs.
O'Keefe was right.

Several days elapsed before Aunt Harriet noticed anything unusual; but, after her attention had been called to what was going on, she became suspicious, the accused was already convicted and awaiting execution. With a look of solemn determination on her face, such as it had not worn since she burned her medicines, she mounted the stairs to the attic room which Eloise had adapted to her work.

"Come in!" called the ringing voice of her niece in response to an energetic knock. "Oh, it's you, is it, auntie! Sit down. I'll be where I can talk to you in a minute."

Aunt Harriet placed herself on the edge of a chair containing a jar of goldenrod and waited, putting up her eye-glass to scrutinize the room. It was under the bare ridge-pole of the Glenallan, and there were no draperies save those the spiders had wrought, but the light was good and the artist was happy.

She laid down her brush at last and turned to her visitor. "Did you have something in particular to say to me?" she asked, for Aunt Harriet had never been in the attic room before.

"Yes, I have something very particular," replied the little woman, nestling back against the goldenrod and nestling forward again when it tickled her neck. There were only two chairs in the room. "Eloise, I have been talking with Mrs. O'Keefe, and I am much disturbed."

"I should think you would be," returned her

22

niece. "I was in hopes you'd let that sort of people alone here."

"Eloise!" exclaimed Aunt Harriet, with severity, "the woman came to me out of the goodness of her heart, because she thought I ought to know how imprudent you are."

"I, imprudent?" inquired the girl, with surprise.

"Yes, imprudent, taking long walks every day with a stranger," cried her aunt.

"That man saved my life, and I shall not eat a piece of boiled cod without his permission," mimicked Eloise.

Aunt Harriet looked disconcerted, but she had a mission to the fatherless and motherless girl before her, and she nerved herself to perform it. "I have nothing against Dr. Dow," she said, with dignity. "He is well enough in his proper place."

"Dragging women from under the heels of runaway horses, for instance," returned Eloise.

Aunt Harriet flushed. "I think I am as grateful to Dr. Dow as you are," she said, quickly; "but one is not obliged to marry every man one is grateful to."

Eloise laughed outright.

Aunt Harriet looked grave. "This is a serious matter, Eloise. I did not mean to tell you. I do not believe in discussing such subjects with young girls, but you drive me to it. *Dr. Dow is—is a married man, and has a partial divorce from his wife and child.*"

"It is a complete divorce, auntie; the wife and child are dead."

Aunt Harriet did not know what to say. She had played her last card and Eloise had taken it. There was nothing to do but to throw herself on the generosity of the young woman whom she was trying to influence. "Eloise," she cried, tearfully, "it will break my heart if you do not marry well. People never forgive you for that sort of thing; they will forgive everything else, but they always feel, if you marry badly, that you brought it on yourself."

"Who talks of marrying?" demanded Eloise, with a frown. "Can I not find help and strength in the companionship of a noble soul without this everlasting question of marrying being brought in? Oh, Aunt Harriet!" she sprang from her chair and confronted the little figure with its background of goldenrod, "can't you see? Why did you go to those people who helped you? Why did you mourn so when you had to give them up? Because life was too much for you. It is too much for me. I must have help, counsel, strength. This man gives them to me. I can't have your blind faith, but through the charity which he has taught me I get something to take the place of faith, something we have been told 'never faileth,' and faith does fail, you know it does."

In her imperious defiance she towered above the small, slight woman, who shrank beneath the words as if they had been blows, and slid out from under them as soon as she could.

"Of course, if you say there's nothing between you, I believe it, Eloise," she said. "But after you had refused such fine-looking men—and, say what you please, you do want some one you can introduce to your friends and be proud of." She moved towards the door and looked back as she reached it. "You're all I have," she faltered, and her lip began to quiver.

Eloise went to her. "Don't worry, dear," she said, and took the little creature in her arms. "You are all I have, too." She kissed the quivering lips into composure. "Don't worry, dear," she repeated.

"I won't again," Aunt Harriet answered, and went down the stairs with a lighter heart than she had carried for many a day. It was such a relief not to feel obliged to take care of Eloise, and so pleasant to feel that Eloise took care of her.

Once more alone, the artist returned to her easel. The tolerant tenderness, which had survived irritation and amusement in the recent interview, lingered and filled her with its glow.

"I am getting to be willing to let even Aunt Harriet be herself," she mused. "Perhaps I shall gain the true artist feeling after a while, with its insight into the nature of things and patience with what it finds there."

Dreamily she touched up the picture before her

with deliberate, delicate strokes, wondering when she had felt so secure and strong before.

A sound of voices from the yard below broke in upon her reverie.

"Hullo! where did you drop from?" in Joey's unmistakable drawl.

"From New York. 'I'm never anywhere else,' as you said once upon a time." That was Mark Heffron. "You are to go on to New York to-night," he continued. "*I'm* doing the relief act now."

Then they mounted the steps of the piazza and all the listener heard was "never getting over a thing," from Joey, and "a scaly trick," from Mark; but this was enough to convince her Joey had told the truth about Mark's leaving Chicago against his will. What of that? Mark Heffron was nothing to her.

Yet she dressed carefully before she went down to luncheon, as a girl sometimes will for a man who is nothing to her.

Mark and Joey were waiting in the lower hall, when she came down the stairs with Aunt Harriet leaning on her arm.

"Uncle Eli has gone in," said Joey, after greetings had been exchanged. "I've arranged for this chap to take the corner seat until after dinner; then I suppose he'll have my place."

"Hear the hospitable ring in his voice!" exclaimed Mark, whose spirits seemed to rise as Joey's fell.

"Of course he dislikes to leave his uncle," returned Eloise.

Joey acknowledged her championship with a grateful glance.

"I'll look out for Uncle Eli," promised Mark, and began at once to take the old man under his genial patronage.

"What are you going to do this afternoon?" asked Joey in low tones of Eloise, while Uncle Eli and his new cicerone entertained each other.

"By the way, Joey, your train goes at four," called out Mark from the corner seat.

"I'm not going on that train," replied Joey, defiantly, "I can't get ready."

"Oh, yes, you can. I'll pack for you," cried Mark. "One good turn deserves another."

"And I have some other things to attend to," said Joey, scowling.

"I'll attend to them," responded Mark, cordially. "Mail your letters, deliver your messages—everything. You'll really have to go, Joey. I promised the Firm you'd be there, and ' they have such faith in us both.' Uncle Eli will get along all right with me."

"Yes, yes," urged the old man. "Don't stay on my account. Mark will take care of me."

Joey sulkily submitted, and uttered his farewells at the door of the dining-room.

"But I shall see you again in Chicago this winter?" asked Eloise, with more than her usual friendliness, because of Mark's teasing.

"I hope so," he answered, dejectedly, and followed Mark upstairs.

"Sit down and write your letters while I pack your trunk," urged the exasperating fellow. "I'll deliver them. You know 'there's nothing like a personal interview.'"

"Come, that's enough," growled Joey. "There's no use in running a joke into the ground."

"Who said anything about a joke?" inquired Mark. "I'm in dead earnest—and I half believe you are."

Joey made no reply, but proceeded with his packing, refusing all offers of assistance.

There was no time to spare. By the time the trunks and bags were ready and the expressman had been summoned, the suburban train for Boston was nearly due. They struck off across the fields to the station, Uncle Eli and Aunt Harriet waving them good-bye from the piazza. Eloise had gone for a walk.

"There she is now," said Joey, pointing to the high bluff by the shore, where a slender, graceful figure stood outlined against the sky. Another figure accompanied it.

"Who is that man?" inquired Mark, sharply.

"That is Miss Gordon's dearest friend," replied Joey, with malicious satisfaction. "You've been barking up the wrong tree, Mark. He's the one."

XXXIV

WHAT Mark saw of Eloise Gordon and Dr. Dow went to confirm Joey's statement. Hardly a day passed without finding them together, and so open was their preference, so frank their good-fellowship, that they ceased to be considered by the People in the House. The doctor's patients also were privileged to make demands upon Miss Gordon's time and sympathy. Mark met them coming and going to and from the studio, pale, hollow-eyed women and a dilapidated man or two. He asked her if she was painting a Last Judgment and if these were the "goats." She did not frown, as he anticipated, but replied, good-humoredly, that they were friends of hers.

"Then you do have friends who come to the studio?"

"Why, yes; do you want to come?" she returned. "You may, of course. Wait, I am finishing something I should like you to see; wait four days."

He waited impatiently. The days were long and dull. There was little to do for Mr. Norton except to talk of the Science; when this became a bore, Mark dodged. Then the old man went back to Miss Larrabee, the steamer-chairs, and the umbrellas.

The rest of Point Carey resolved itself into a nursery during the day, when the men had gone to town, and into a ballroom at night, when they returned.

The patrons of the place were chiefly well-to-do, commonplace, young married people who enjoyed themselves, each other, and their children, to the utter disregard of unsympathetic bystanders. Mark moped about the piazza with a novel and a cigar, took long, solitary walks, and decided that he had not bettered his material condition by stepping into Joe Norton's shoes.

Evenings were devoted to Miss Larrabee and Mr. Norton, who believed a rubber of whist was good to take at night. They always played together, and Mark played with Eloise. The silent alliance, offensive and defensive, the pertinent language of eye and hand, afforded opportunities of a kind. He studied her face, the clear hazel eyes, with their border of black lashes, the fine arch of the brow, the delicate nose and firm, sweet mouth. Once or twice he realized that she was studying him. He had meant, when he came, to explain his abrupt departure from Chicago, but somehow the occasion seemed lacking.

The four days lengthened into eight, and still he did not receive his summons to the studio.

"I believe that picture is a myth," he said, one night, as she gathered up the cards and prepared to follow Miss Larrabee, "or else you do not mean me to see it."

"It is not a myth," she answered, quickly, "and I do want you to see it. Every day I have thought I could send for you, and then I became dissatisfied with my work and went back to it." She paused and sighed. "Inspiration is so brief, yet the following it out takes so long." She moved towards the door. There was no one in the parlor but themselves.

"Why are you in such a hurry?" he asked. "Sit down and talk to me."

She shook her head. "I must be at work early ; the light is best then. Perhaps I can send for you some time during the morning."

"I shall go back to Chicago if you don't," he threatened.

He lingered about the piazza all the following forenoon, and went to luncheon resolved to pack the trunks and the steamer-chair and to start with Uncle Eli without delay. Miss Gordon did not appear. "I carried a glass of milk to the studio," said Miss Larrabee ; "that was all she wanted."

Mark took his book and retired to a shady corner of the piazza. The Glenallan was very quiet. The children and their mammas were taking afternoon naps. There was no sound save the tinkling bell of the baker's cart and the far-off rumble of the sea.

"Mr. Heffron," called an eager voice, "if you will come now !" and Eloise herself stood before him, still in her brown Holland apron, and with her fair hair in confusion about her heated cheeks. She led him up the stairs to the attic room where bars of yellow afternoon sunlight lay along the floor.

"I couldn't stop until I finished it," she said.

Upon the easel lay a large canvas, familiar and yet new, the scene of the wreck she had tried to paint in Chicago. He looked at it long and earnestly, and then he looked at her.

"I meant it this time," she said, softly. "I have clung to the masts until my fingers were stiff; I have thrown that rope until my arm ached; I have fought those waves and feared and dreaded them; and I have shouted myself hoarse over every man who came ashore."

The tears were rolling down her cheeks; she wiped them away with the dingy apron.

"I suppose I'm all paint and everything," she exclaimed between a sob and a laugh, "but I don't care. 'He that saveth his life shall lose it' in Art; I've found that out." She took off the apron and tossed it into a corner. "This is the nearest approach I can make to a toilet," she said, smoothing the folds of her light summer gown.

"You seem to have found out a great many things all at once," Mark returned, "methods and material, yourself, and your fellow - beings. I have fancied you were finding me out of late."

"I do understand you better than I did," she

confessed, with a friendly glance. "I used to think you laughed because you didn't care; now I know it is because you do, only—"

"What is it? Go on," he urged.

"Oh, it is a shame!" she cried. "So few of us can see any order, any solution of the problems, and you *do* see; but you won't assume the responsibility of it, or—or the burden of your influence." She had folded her hands in her lap and was regarding him earnestly.

"In other words, I am a coward and a shirk," he said, with a look that pierced like a lance.

"You don't go far enough for that," she cried, determined not to retreat. "You have no convictions to be untrue to."

"Thank God for that!" he exclaimed. "There is nothing that limits like a conviction."

She did not reply, save by that direct, serious gaze, yet all at once his manner changed.

"Eloise," he said, gravely, "it is myself that I do not believe in. I need some one to believe in me to make me believe in myself."

Still she made no answer, but sat and looked at him until she saw nothing else, and he seemed far away, his voice sounded indistinctly in her ears; but as he started to come towards her she aroused.

"No, no," she cried; "it is too late!"

"Why is it too late?" he demanded. "Do you think because you have felt *this*," pointing to the picture, "that there is nothing more? You have lived in only a part of yourself. You needn't go into a convent because you have realized the bond of brotherhood."

"I have no idea of going into a convent," she answered, sore at his misinterpretation.

"Then it is that fanatic doctor," he exclaimed, "with his deep-sea dredge, grubbing after refuse and dragging it back into a world well rid of it. Who is he, anyway, to play at being Providence and interfere with the laws of nature ?"

"He is the first *reality* I have met," she answered, on the defensive at once. "You and Mr. Norton say fine things, but he does them. He has helped me as much as he ever did the 'refuse.' You yourself did not care for me until he taught me self-reliance and—and charity. Whatever I am I owe to him." She stood up, defying him, and he brought all the batteries of his fierce desire to bear upon her in vain; another man stood between them, a small, insignificant man, with haunting, helpful hands, and a voice with a note of loneliness in its music.

"You are mistaken," he said, more gently. "You had it in you; circumstances would have developed it. And I have cared all along. Why else did I compare every one I met with you and feel so uncomfortable when you were displeased, and dump out poor Joey, neck and heels, that I might have his place?" He was relaxing his gravity; at sight of this her own increased.

"I am a special dispensation to keep you from

Philistinism," he said, lightly. "You will bring up in the Bible Society, doing borders for Sunday-school books, if I don't save you."

"The responsibility is not yours now," she answered, coldly. "It is mine."

"I believe you are right," he returned; "it is yours for both of us. You say I ought to be different, to live up to my possibilities. Make me what you choose." He was smiling at her as only Mark could smile, and speaking pleadingly. His very winsomeness told against him with her.

"Oh, that plausible tongue of yours!" she cried. "It makes me distrust everything you say. I am not the Eloise Gordon who believed in you. I have got over that."

He turned to the picture with a sneer. "Those things are so much easier to do with paint and canvas," he said, mockingly. "In real life we look out for ourselves and avoid disturbing emotions."

He turned to go, then, looking back, saw something in her face which made him pause.

"You have not got over it; you do care!" he exclaimed, coming to her side.

"Did any one who once cared for you ever get over it?" she returned, passionately; then her will, like a sword stroke, severed them. "I choose not to care!" she said, proudly.

He bowed with silent dignity and left the room. She heard his footsteps on the stairs and on the gravel walk, and she saw him hurrying towards the shore, as if driven by the Spirit into the wilderness.

The shadows were lengthening on the floor, and the coolness of the breeze which came in at the window told that night was near. Still the picture on the easel stood out with insistent brightness, whenever she looked that way. The reaction of her joy in it had come upon her, hastened by the storm in her breast, cheapening and distorting its painted parody.

How much went into how little, after all! The experiences which were to make her a great artist, the facing of facts, the telling herself truths about them, the courage, the patience, were they not for the sake of art, but just a mere matter of living? Was art to show what life is, not what it may become? Then what is life's revenge, in terms of art, upon a woman who kills her love because of her pride, because of her fear, because of her selfish protection of what may be valueless?

The shadows had lengthened and deepened until they filled the room. The velvety darkness smothered her. She covered herself with a cloak, and swift and silent as a shadow slid down the servants' stairway and out of doors.

The night was gay with stars and there was a brave young moon ; by their light she found her way to the shore and hid herself among the rocks. The sea came up almost to her feet, the unfathomable sea which she dreaded, the cold, remote, unfriendly sea which she hated; but she listened to it now.

"If I yield, then he will not care," she said to it. "My power over him is in my resistance to his power over me. How can I give without giving, how can he have and not hold."

And the gray old sea told her the secret of Circe and Calypso, who gave without giving, whom men had but could not hold?"

"That is not what I mean," she replied. "There must be another way, or Life is cruel. What is Life's answer to the puzzle she offers?" But the sea went on with its purring and said no more, for the sea is a pagan.

Helpless and empty and desolate, she looked up into the sky, as human beings are wont to do, when everything has failed below. A long cloud lay like a roof above the horizon and under its eaves hung a star.

At once everything changed; she was in the little room at the Lake View, with Aunt Harriet breathing softly in the bed, and Mark Heffron starting up to question her with his brilliant dark eyes.

She was stronger than he, and he knew it. She dared to be stronger, for her power was the power of the universe. This, then, was the heart of the mystery plucked out and held up before her; the mystery which men sought when they hollowed their temples and crept into them, when they worshipped the seed, the earth that produces and sustains ; the mystery which puts the apple of temptation into the hand of Eve, and the babe of redemption into the arms of Mary, and holds the woman accountable for more than her own weakness and lack of wisdom.

Hark, there were footsteps coming ! She heard them above the rustling sound which told the wind had found the few leaves on the shore ; and she stood up, waiting. Slowly and heavily he came on, not noticing her, for his head was down. Suddenly he looked up. Her cloak fell off like a calyx, and she blossomed before him, a lily, slender, straight, and fair.

With a low, glad cry he sprang towards her, then stopped and flung out both hands in eager protestation. "Before God, I did not bring you here !" he exclaimed. "This is not my doing."

"I know it," she answered; "I choose to be here."

There was no mistaking the meaning of her words. A sudden sense of his own unworthiness smote him.

"Eloise," he said, humbly, "there are other things. If that coat doesn't fit, there are others which stick like the shirt of Nessus."

"I know," she said, gently.

"But you don't know," he returned, with a laugh which was more grave than a sigh would have been from him. "I have a devil, Eloise."

"Most people have," she answered, softly, "and an angel, too."

He drew nearer, and touched with remote reverence a straying tress of her hair.

"Oh, you *woman!*" he whispered. Even then the image of another stood between them, the image of him who had taught her what it was to be a woman and how to win a man's love. She shivered as one does when Fates and Destinies stand out for the moment's recognition.

He lifted her heavy cloak and folded it around her. "Come," he said, drawing her back into the seat the rocks had shaped for them centuries ago; and the throbbing of their hearts, the rhythm of the sea, and the silent march of the stars were all one harmony.

"If this could be the end!" she murmured.

"There is no end," he answered, and laughed again, daring whatever might come. "There are no finalities, as there are no beginnings. I have loved you always, even when I did not know it."

But she, nearer in her ignorance than he in his wisdom to the unrevealed secret, only repeated, "If this could be the end!"

FINIS

THE WORKS OF
WILLIAM DEAN HOWELLS

MY LITERARY PASSIONS. 12mo, Cloth, $1 50.

STOPS OF VARIOUS QUILLS. Poems. Illustrated by HOWARD PYLE. 4to, Cloth, Ornamental, Uncut Edges and Gilt Top, $2 50.

THE DAY OF THEIR WEDDING. A Story. Illustrated by T. DE THULSTRUP. 12mo, Cloth. (*In Press.*)

A TRAVELER FROM ALTRURIA. A Romance. 12mo, Cloth, $1 50; Paper, 50 cents.

THE COAST OF BOHEMIA. A Novel. Illustrated. 12mo, Cloth, $1 50.

THE WORLD OF CHANCE. A Novel. 12mo, Cloth, $1 50; Paper, 60 cents.

THE QUALITY OF MERCY. A Novel. 12mo, Cloth, $1 50; Paper, 75 cents.

AN IMPERATIVE DUTY. A Novel. 12mo, Cloth, $1 00; Paper, 50 cents.

A HAZARD OF NEW FORTUNES. A Novel. Two Volumes. 12mo, Cloth, $2 00; Illustrated, 12mo, Paper, $1 00.

THE SHADOW OF A DREAM. A Story. 12mo, Cloth, $1 00; Paper, 50 cents.

ANNIE KILBURN. A Novel. 12mo, Cloth, $1 50; Paper, 75 cents.

APRIL HOPES. A Novel. 12mo, Cloth, $1 50; Paper, 75 cents.

CHRISTMAS EVERY DAY, AND OTHER STORIES. Illustrated. Post 8vo, Cloth, $1 25.

A BOY'S TOWN. Described for HARPER'S YOUNG PEOPLE. Illustrated. Post 8vo, Cloth, $1 25.

CRITICISM AND FICTION. With Portrait. 16mo, Cloth, $1 00. (In the Series "Harper's American Essayists.")

MODERN ITALIAN POETS. Essays and Versions. With Portraits. 12mo, Cloth, $2 00.

THE MOUSE-TRAP, AND OTHER FARCES. Illustrated. 12mo, Cloth, $1 00.

FARCES: A LIKELY STORY—THE MOUSE-TRAP—FIVE O'CLOCK TEA—EVENING DRESS—THE UNEXPECTED GUESTS—A LETTER OF INTRODUCTION—THE ALBANY DEPOT—THE GARROTERS. In Uniform Style; Illustrated. 32mo, Cloth, 50 cents each. ("Harper's Black and White Series.")

A LITTLE SWISS SOJOURN. Illustrated. 32mo, Cloth, 50 cents. ("Harper's Black and White Series.")

MY YEAR IN A LOG CABIN. Illustrated. 32mo, Cloth, 50 cents. ("Harper's Black and White Series.")

By GEORGE DU MAURIER

TRILBY. A Novel. Illustrated by the Author. Post 8vo, Cloth, Ornamental, $1 75; Three-quarter Calf, $3 50; Three-quarter Crushed Levant, $4 50.

Certainly, if it were not for its predecessor, we should assign to "Trilby" a place in fiction absolutely companionless. . . . It is one of the most unconventional and charming of novels.—*Saturday Review*, London.

It is a charming story told with exquisite grace and tenderness.—*N. Y. Tribune.*

Mr. Du Maurier has written his tale with such originality, unconventionality, and eloquence, such rollicking humor and tender pathos, and delightful play of every lively fancy, all running so briskly in exquisite English and with such vivid dramatic picturing, that it is only comparable . . . to the freshness and beauty of a spring morning at the end of a dragging winter. . . . It is a thoroughly unique story.—*N. Y. Sun.*

PETER IBBETSON. With an Introduction by his Cousin, Lady * * * * * ("Madge Plunket"). Edited and Illustrated by GEORGE DU MAURIER. Post 8vo, Cloth, Ornamental, $1 50.

That it is one of the most remarkable books that have appeared for a long time is, however, indisputable.—*N. Y. Tribune.*

There are no suggestions of mediocrity. The pathos is true, the irony delicate, the satire severe when its subject is unworthy, the comedy sparkling, and the tragedy, as we have said, inevitable. One or two more such books, and the fame of the artist would be dim beside that of the novelist.—*N. Y. Evening Post.*

MARK TWAIN'S JOAN OF ARC

PERSONAL RECOLLECTIONS OF JOAN OF ARC.
By the Sieur LOUIS DE CONTE (her page and secretary).
Freely translated out of the Ancient French into Modern
English from the Original Unpublished Manuscript in
the National Archives of France, by JEAN FRANÇOIS
ALDEN. Illustrated from Original Drawings by F. V.
DU MOND, and from Reproductions of Old Paintings
and Statues. Crown 8vo, Cloth, Ornamental, $2 50.

A wonderful story of the most wonderful woman in history.
It could not be told in the bare historical record. The author
has wisely chosen the form of fiction, and has thus, while pre-
serving every thread of the historical fabric, woven into its text-
ure those lost threads which restore the native charm of the
story as it was lived. The tale is told in the guise of a narra-
tive as it might have been written by the playmate and page of
Joan of Arc. It is characterized by the simplicity and quaint
humor which have given the author his pre-eminent distinction.
Mr. Du Mond visited the scenes intimately associated with the
action of the story, and in his illustrations we see the results of
his careful studies of the manners and customs of the time, the
quaint architecture, and have flavor of the home-life of the
period in all its rugged picturesqueness. The pictures most
fittingly supplement the text.

BY THE SAME AUTHOR:

New Library Editions from New Electrotype Plates. Crown 8vo,
Cloth, Ornamental:

THE ADVENTURES OF HUCKLEBERRY FINN. Illustrated.
(*Ready.*)

A CONNECTICUT YANKEE IN KING ARTHUR'S COURT.
Illustrated. (*In Press.*)

THE PRINCE AND THE PAUPER. Illustrated. (*In Press.*)
Other volumes will follow.

PUBLISHED BY HARPER & BROTHERS, NEW YORK

*☛ For sale by all booksellers, or will be mailed by the publishers,
postage prepaid, on receipt of the price.*